# Key West Camouflage

## Hide In Plain Sight

## Wayne Gales

ISBN-13:  978-1484157404

ISBN-10:  1484157400

Dedicated to my father, Frank Gales
"Write what you know about"

# Acknowledgements

I guess I can only blame myself. If I had killed everyone off in the first book, I wouldn't have been so compelled to bring them back for a sequel. *Treasure Key* was a compilation of short stories, some written a decade ago, reformatted and rewritten to create a story line. A lot of *Treasure Key* is quasi-autobiographical. I pulled the first book out of my head and from my heart. Key West Camouflage, I pulled out of the blue sky (or my ass). It's much different, a little more action, a little more sex, a lot more mystery. I was still able to pull from some past experiences, including my many trips to Baja California as part of several race teams in events like the Baja 1000. The character Trip O'Donnell, whom you will meet shortly, is a combination of several people that I knew during my racing days, all rich casino owners with expensive hobbies. Suffice to say that the racing description, locations and cubic money spent on that crazy hobby are accurate.

My trip to England and mainland Europe reflect real places and near-real people. I had to make the underwater sequence technically accurate to keep my real son Matt (portrayed as Brodie) from busting me if I was incorrect about how to do a deep water technical dive.

The definition of fiction is that you are writing – and reading something that *could* happen. I guess these books fit that definition.

Our hero is a busy boy this time.

Special thanks to Lisa Owens, the editor that fixed all my lousy grammar, and also to Corryn Young, who designed a killer book cover.

I hope you enjoy.
Wayne Gales
July 2013

# Table of Contents

# Prologue – From "Treasure Key"

Former Navy Seal, professional treasure diver and rock and roll bass player, Russell Bricklin, "Bric" Wahl was a penniless, nearly homeless, single father, living hand to mouth in Key West, working on a salvage boat. He discovered an ancient Spanish shipwreck full of silver coins and bullion while working for his employer, Harry Sykas. Although the sunken ship's manifest said the wreck should also contain a large cache of gold bars, they discovered none. At the same time, Bric also found three large Civil War era gold bars, unrelated to the wreck that he decided to keep to himself. Bric thought he was fabulously rich, only to find the bars were just gold plated lead. He did get a large bonus for finding the treasure and bought the houseboat he was living in.

Things looked up for only a short time when his boss threw him a curve, and asked him to move to the corporate offices in Tarpon Springs. Having no transportation and no place to live, he landed on a crazy plan to "drive" his house, a four-unit apartment built on a barge – to Tarpon Springs. Bric and his family, along with one of his tenants, Kevin "Scarlet" Montclaire, a six foot five inch tall, three hundred pound cross-dressing drag queen successfully completed the voyage, only to see the boat sink in Tarpon Springs Harbor. His former landlord, treasure hunting legend Bo Morgan showed up, and retrieved the "worthless" lead bars, showing him that they were actually filled with millions in pure gold. Bric returned to Key West with his family and re-kindled his relationship with an old girlfriend, Karen Murphy. One day, pouring over documents and photos of the wreck, Bric realized that he had a very clear clue where the missing Spanish gold might be. Located in a natural preserve, he would have to figure out a way to get the treasure, but for now, with money in the bank, Bric and Karen planned an around-the-world vacation. They ended up in Puerto Rico, where they hatched a plan to create a clothing line and open a store back in Key West. Karen headed to the island to get started, and Bric took a vacation to Las Vegas and Baja. Suddenly, he wasn't able to reach Karen. Suspicious of foul play, he returned to Key West in disguise.

His suspicions turned out to be well founded.

# One Year Later.....

Once I had a name, it only took a few days of subtle inquiries to find out who Julie was and that she worked at Fat Tuesdays. I parked myself across the street at The Bull, nursing beers, hiding behind my Costas and wearing different types of clothing every night. I hadn't been in town for nearly a year, and even though everyone knew me, nobody was looking for me, especially in a week-old beard, pink flowered aloha shirt, baggy shorts, flip flops and a green digger hat. Throw in a German or Spanish accent and the disguise was complete.

The second night I sat upstairs at The Whistle, entering via the back staircase that leads to the clothing-optional Garden of Eden, located on the roof of the bar. This time I had on my normal Key West camouflage, long sleeved fisherman's shirt, long bill cap, cargo shorts and topsiders. Only the Costas stayed on, and I was still able to remain invisible by lack of association. I drank my beers and watched Julie from a distance. Despite what appeared to be an indisputable fact, I just couldn't believe this was Karen's new lesbian lover. For one thing, this lady was not your typical vision of a lesbian, if there was such a vision. Tallish, about five-eight, straight brown hair, tight body and a nice tan. She was cordial but not flirty with customers and worked the night with professional if somewhat distant efficiency.

Night three. I arrived late and just hung around the area. I had converted myself into a street bum. A trip to the Salvation Army store gave me the perfect outfit for four dollars – worn out canvas army boots, long dirty coat, camo trousers, and a big floppy hat that hid my face nicely. A little brown shoe polish on my face and hands completed the transition, and the juice from a can of oil-packed tuna poured down the back of the coat kept the tourists at a distance. A half-empty bottle of Four Roses wine in my hand, with the wine poured on my shoes and the bottle re-filled with Welch's Grape juice finished off the masquerade, both in vision and odor. At two a.m. Julie left work and walked south down Duval. I followed on the other side of the street. She was moving pretty quick, and I had to break out of my wino persona to keep up, but I managed to keep track of her. She hung a left up Truman and then right on Simonton. Half a block later, she ducked into a little alley, and I just managed to make it to the driveway to see a light go on in a cottage at the back. My work done, I headed back to my current home, an old Chevy van, and drove to Stock Island where I parked on a quiet street, crawled in back and went to sleep.

Night four. Showtime. I cruised down Duval and slowed enough to make sure Julie was still at work at midnight. I parked the van at the city parking lot, put my wino outfit back on, without the makeup and wandered up Simonton Street. The first time I walked by her driveway, there was a couple walking down the street, so I stumbled and staggered by, stopping to piss on a fire hydrant to complete the image. They turned away in disgust and any chance of facial recognition went away. My second pass down Simonton was quiet and clear, and I ducked down the alley to her cottage. On the off chance she was a trusting soul, I tried the front door, but it was locked. The back door was also locked, but the window next to it was slightly open. I popped the screen, slid one of the Jalousie windows out of its frame, and reached the doorknob. The advantage of being a non-smoker meant that my nose could confirm she didn't have some big dog as a pet. No food and water dish in the laundry room and no petrified puppy presents in the back yard were other hints. I could snoop in peace. The house was old, probably built in the 1880's and every step made the old cypress floors creak and groan. I pulled out a little LED flashlight and started looking around. Nothing special. Clean, neat, dining table, couch and chair. Living room, bedroom, kitchen and bath. It was probably servant quarters when the big house was built, or a guest house.

Feeling a little embarrassed, I started pulling drawers in the

9

dresser and poking around. Shorts, tops, undies. Ah, a nine millimeter Glock handgun, loaded, with one in the chamber. I popped the mag out, jacked the round out of the chamber slid the bullets into my pocket, snapped the clip back in and put it back in the drawer. Then the closet. A few hanging outfits and boxes. Then I found a shoebox on the top shelf, and I pulled it down. Bingo. Phone bills and bank statements that showed a private account opened by Karen. I squeezed back a few tears that blurred the print - huge deposits over the past few months, and equally large bank transfers. With just some quick and dirty math, it was likely this was most of my money. I don't have any idea in the world why she would take good clean unencumbered cash and create a paper trail, but there was about three hundred thousand of our retirement fund sitting there on paper. I'll need to get out to Boca Grande pretty soon and dig up that gold or my van will become permanent housing.

I slipped the statement and some other suitable incriminating evidence in my pocket, checked the fridge and found a cold Heineken. There was a bottle of Ouzo, that fiery licorice-flavored Greek liqueur sitting on the countertop and I poured some in a tumbler, and then settled down on the La-Z-Boy in a dark corner. I idly dripped a few drops of sweat from the Heineken bottle into the tumbler and watched the clear liquid turn milky white. The beer took the edge off, and the Ouzo put it back on.

It wouldn't be long now.

I heard feet crunch up the gravel driveway, the sound of keys in the door and in walked Julie. Her top was off before the door was closed, and the bra hit the floor a second later. She reached for the fridge for a beer, and I was suddenly grateful that she had not taken inventory earlier before leaving. She stood in the light of the open refrigerator taking her first sip, and I admired the package. Not a tan line to be seen, some neat tribal body art on her lower back and silver dog-bones through each pierced nipple. I would guess a "c" cup but not a millimeter of sag. They looked real and amazing.

Well, I always said I was a lesbian trapped in a man's body.

10

As she took a second pull on her beer, she reached down and unhooked the first two buttons of her shorts. Appropriateness stepped in front of voyeurism, and I decided to make myself known.

"Ah, you might want to stop there," I ventured.

Julie jumped about a foot in the air, dropped her beer and turned toward me.

"Now that's alcohol abuse."

"Who the fuck are you?" Julie responded. I admired that she made no effort to cover herself. This was a girl comfortable in her own skin. The combination of the backlight from the refrigerator and the mottled light shining through the front Jalousie window louvers on her body was about to make it difficult for me to walk. I still couldn't see a single tan line.

"I'm not here to hurt you," I answered. "Just need a little info."

"Oh, you're him."

"Yes. I'm 'him'. It appears we share a common acquaintance."

"She wasn't 'sharing', you jerk. Karen loved me!"

I let out a tired sigh. "Julie, I don't really care anymore. I just need to find her, figure out where you fit in this puzzle, and vanish into the sunset. Care to tell me the story?"

She seemed to relax a tiny bit. Even a little smile. "Look, I've just spent nine hours having drunk assholes like you paw all over me. Can I take a quick shower and then I'll tell you what I know."

I motioned toward the bathroom with my beer. "Keep the door open," I said. "Just to keep all the cards face up."

Julie walked toward the hallway, letting her shorts drop to the floor as she walked by. I don't recall that many lesbian exhibitionists, but I saw no reason to give issue. She didn't have a follicle of hair on her body below her neck. The shower went on, and I enjoyed my Greek boilermaker while catching the occasional glance of tanned body through the door. "Give me a second and I'll throw something on!" she called as she turned toward her bedroom.  She stepped back out in the living room a moment later, nude, dripping wet holding the Glock in both hands, cop style. "This will be easy.  A bum breaks into my house while I'm in the shower.  I hear him, get my gun, and I shoot him when he threatens me.  I thought you were smarter than this."

"Oh my.  I didn't know girls had guns.  Well, guess you have the drop on me.  Might be difficult to explain to the cops how that nine millimeter slug passed through your attacking bum, this easy chair and the back wall, and I don't feel much like getting up and making it easier."  I took another pull on the Heineken. "Checkmate."

She hesitated for a moment and made a decision.  Pointing at my chest she pulled the trigger to a rather feeble "click."  Like a crook shooting at Superman, she used the gun as her last bullet and threw it at my head.  It sailed high and right and blew through two window panels and the screen with a satisfying crash, landing on the gravel in the driveway while I held the beer and Ouzo up so they wouldn't gather any glass fragments.  I sat the drinks back down and reached in my shirt pocket, digging a couple of the rounds out.  "Looking for these?  Too bad you threw your gun away.  Now, let's set some ground rules.  Nobody knows I'm here.  Nobody even knows I'm in the Keys right now.  I'm perfectly capable and, at this point, more than happy to snap your pretty little dyke neck, slide a knife through your ribs and into your heart, or choose any of a half dozen other ways to punch your ticket.  I win, you lose. We talk now.  Truce?"

All the fight went out of her.  Still dripping wet and nude, she pulled a dining chair into the middle of the living room floor spun it around backwards, got another beer from the fridge, and sat down.

"I've got a lot of questions, but the first one is obvious. Where's Karen?"  Julie took another sip, brushed her damp hair back, and looked straight at me.

"She's dead."

# One Month Earlier......

After bouncing around the planet for a year, filling in the bucket list and enjoying everything from fresh grilled *Langostino* (either giant shrimp or baby lobster, depending on how you look at it) at a country club in Guadalajara, squid cooked in its own ink in Venice, vodka poured down an ice luge in a hotel made entirely out of blocks of ice in - you guessed it - Iceland, baked salmon at a native American cookout in Palmer, Alaska, a meal to die for at the Seafood Market restaurant in Bangkok and a Dungeness crab feast from Pike Place Market in Seattle, we decided to hole up for a while in Puerto Rico. It was a chance to recharge our batteries, surviving on sensational Saturday pork roast pig-outs at a local *Lechonera*. I worked on my lousy golf game and Karen started developing clothing designs and a business plan for our line of apparel in Key West. Since long ago I had called the clothes we locals wear – namely fishing shorts, topsiders or flip flops, Columbia Outfitters fishing shirts for men – similar outfits or light, thin airy shifts for women – Key West Camouflage. You could tell tourists by their garb – aside from their Minnesota snow white complexion, the tendency to wear pure white Nike sneakers, calf-length athletic socks, aloha shirts and Bermuda shorts, not to mention panty hose and heels on the ladies, made it simple to cut them out of the pack. The desire for many tourists not to be singled out by the locals prompted us to come up with a line of clothes that made you look local – hence the name, Key West Camouflage.

While Karen was planning her first trip back to Key West, I had one more item on my agenda. One of my top ten bucket list things was to race in, or at least be a part of, the Baja 1000 off road race. I've watched it on ESPN a number of times, and the wide open, no-holds-barred, "run what you brung" racing, driving mega-horse powered trucks through brutal cactus covered desert truly appealed to me. Don't get me wrong, I like NASCAR, but the sport has been governed to the point of silliness, so budget teams don't get lapped every five minutes by the mega multi-team organizations. It's become a motorized version of WWC wrestling. I noticed that some of the top drivers, including three time champion Jimmy Johnson had a Baja racing background. That intrigued me even more how two such un-similar sports could have a common champion level driver.

As much as I wanted to do this race, I knew my chances were slim. It would be like calling a NASCAR driver and offering to help change tires at the Daytona 500. Well, not exactly, but nearly so. Race teams are lean and mean and no place for a wannabe George Plimpton. Then, one Sunday afternoon, while I was playing couch potato at the Dorado with Karen, they showed last year's Baja 1000 on ESPN. They focused on the "Trophy Trucks", those unlimited horsepower-gorged vehicles that impress me the most. Competing at the front was a Las Vegas casino sponsored Chevy, with a very familiar name at the wheel – Charles "Trip" O'Donnell III. I was in the Navy with a Trip O'Donnell, and his dad owned a small casino in Vegas. Then they did a spotlight on Trip, and it was unquestionably my buddy. His dad had grown his business from one small gas station and casino near Stateline Nevada to a string of five mega hotel casino resorts all over the country, utilizing Native American land for many of them. Leaning on his Irish heritage, they were called the "Pot O Gold" and were hugely successful. The elder Charles O'Donnell II was more or less retired, and his son was now in charge of this huge company, and apparently spending his Sundays and his family inheritance riding the edge of death in an eight-hundred horsepower Trophy Truck.

If there was ever a ticket to Baja, this was one staring me right in the face. I had no doubt Trip would remember me.

14

I had saved his life.

It was during the Grenada thing. This unmitigated clusterfuck of a "military" exercise was a disaster from the beginning, and we had to evac the team in a hurry while we were supposedly "winning", and we caught a lot of small-arms fire in the process: I got creased across the ass, and Trip took a glancing blow off his ribcage. A shard of rib apparently nicked his lung, and it started to bubble, then collapse. Another buddy and me got him into the water and picked up with the squad. I never saw him after that and actually I never knew it was Trip I helped save until later. At the time, it was dark and we were all decked up in camo makeup. Lots of guys were hurt, some were missing, and some were KIA. It was weeks later that I got a note from him thanking me for keeping him away from the pearly gates.

Now, a few dozen years later, he's trying to kill himself in the desert. Lucky guy.

So, I figured what the heck? Might as well see if I can call in that marker. I placed a call to the Pot O Gold corporate offices and started working my way through the layers. Trip was now President and CEO and a very important person. But I know the system.

"O'Donnell Enterprises, how may I direct your call?"

"Charles R. O'Donnell, please."

"One moment," (music on hold)

"Exccutive offices, how may I direct your call?"

"Charles R. O'Donnell, please."

"One moment," (More music on hold. Long on hold, could have heard Free Bird twice)

"Mr. O'Donnell's office."

"Good morning, Bric Wahl calling for Trip." (Thought I would just eliminate the 20 questions).

No joy. "I'm sorry, Mr. Brickwall, Mr. O'Donnell is not available. May I ask the nature of your call?"

So much for tact. "Sweetie, that's my real name, and Trip will know it. I *Promise* he will take this call, and if you blow me off right now, you will probably be selling keno tickets in Biloxi

Mississippi by Thursday, so give us both a break and just slip my name in front of His Highness. That's B.R.I.C W.A.H.L."

Silence on the phone for a moment. She probably spent all day long running interference, but likely not with this level of pressure. And she also may have spent a month in Biloxi one night. "Hold please," was the rather curt answer. It nearly snowed thru the phone.

Two more "Free Birds" and the long version of "Light My Fire" later the line came back to life.

"Bric, you old son of a bitch! Where the Hell are you? In town? I'll send a car for you!"

"Nope, actually I'm in Puerto Rico, but I just watched an hour of your ugly face playing banzai through the desert in the Mexico. And congratulations for that win, by the way."

"Yeah, thanks. We got a check for $3,500 for winning, which just about paid for the free tee shirts we had to bribe the Federales with on the way home. This sport ain't for thrifty people. So what occasion honors me with your call? Man I haven't seen you since I was blowing pink bubbles through a bullet hole in my side."

I told him about my interest in off road racing, that I had a little time on my hands, and a few bucks in the bank, and was wondering if I might be able to tag along as a helper, watcher, windshield cleaner. Whatever....

"You wanna come to Baja?" Trip roared over the phone. "DEAL! We're heading down this weekend to pre-run. I'll be back in town next Wednesday. You get yourself here, and I'll handle the rest. Just call Betty back with your flight info and she will have one of my mules meet you at the airport. I'll give you the details after that. Leave your money at home, this week's on me!"

He gave me his secretary's direct line before hanging up and then passed me back to her for some more info. She was a little more than pissed at me for roughing her up, but I talked through a smile and threw all the southern charm I could at her. It had absolutely no effect, but she knew she was stuck with me, so it was at least civil, if not cordial.

16

escalator, and a commuter train t
to the bottom of the drill about as g
knew the drill about as g
connection time, fiftee
Air Traffic Contro
to clear our ga
Hertz com
plane
Ve

Five days later I
Atlanta. Karen drove m
She was heading back t                                     ↵ get a
storefront secured and stai                          ..ces and permits.
With my so-called "crim                          in Monroe County, we
decided to put the business      ...i name.  I had also called Bo and
gave him instructions on how much cash to give her out of the
stash in his floor safe.

San Juan to Atlanta, and non-stop Atlanta to Vegas.  You gain
four hours, so you leave at nine in the morning and get there at
three in the afternoon.  Did I mention that I hate flying?  The only
thing I hate worse than flying is flying and changing planes in
Atlanta.  The damn airport is just too friggin big so that every time
you have to include this hub in your itinerary you are subjected to
either four hours of boredom or fifteen minutes of adrenalin filled
terror.  It goes something like this, or at least I think it must -
every evening before the following day's flights, a team sits
around, and checks to see how many passengers from the Delta
flight out of Chicago are transferring to flights that go to Las
Vegas, Boston and Miami.  Then they plot the farthest distance
that the most people have to travel from the Chicago flight to all
those connections.  The distance between those flights is
determined to be the farthest possible and still be located in the
state of Georgia.  Combine that with concourses that you could
comfortably land a 747 *inside of,* a trip down a four hundred foot

...at always departs just as you get ... you're starting to get the picture. I ...od as anyone. I had a thirty five minute ...h of which had been eaten up by San Juan ...r and another five or so waiting for another flight ...e. It looked like I was gonna be OJ Simpson in a ...mercial between flights again. I blasted out of the ...ith my carry-on bag, looked at the screen for my flight to ...as. We landed at terminal "E", and the Vegas plane was at the ..."T" gates. That's as far as you can go. I bounded down the escalator and jammed myself into the shuttle train with an inch to spare. After what seemed like a week later, we stopped at the "T" exit, and I bee-lined up the escalator, three steps at a time, hit the top and down the concourse at a dead run. I'm in damn decent shape but no spring chicken. I made the flight with about fifteen seconds to spare and nearly had to be carried into the plane.

At least I was too tired to be scared. I gunned down three vodka/cranberries before we hit cruising altitude and was snoring in fifteen minutes.

When you step off a commercial flight in Las Vegas you are instantly confronted with the town's unwritten but very public policy. LEAVE ALL YOUR MONEY HERE BEFORE YOU GO HOME. The second you walk down the jetway you are assaulted with the ding ding ding, whistles, music, lights and glitter of slot machines, all giving the hint if not promise of delivering you uncounted riches at the very next pull of the handle. After you go to your hotel you are subjected to more of the same. Heck, there are slot machines in grocery stores, laundromats, Seven-Elevens, gas stations, funeral homes, child care, you name it. It appears the churches have not looked at this form of donation yet, but it's just a matter of time. I have more money in my pocket than I've ever had in my life now, but had no temptation to help balance the Nevada budget with it. I whisked past the gauntlet and walked through baggage claim to the exit. It was late October, so God had turned the pizza oven that is officially called the Vegas Valley down to only about two hundred fifty degrees. Yeah but it's dry heat. I felt my Conch skin start to dry into chronic psoriasis in ten seconds. I looked around and saw a rather attractive young lady holding up a sign that said "Brick Wall." Undoubtedly a translation error over the phone, or Betty's idea of fucking with me. I raised my hand, and she walked over, holding hers out to shake.

"I'm Meghan, Mr. Wahl and I'm here to take you to Mr. O'Donnell. Please come this way."

Following her was a treat. I would guess about 21 years old, tanned and not a toothpick, with a pair of tight blue shorts under a long sleeve white shirt, unbuttoned and tied at the waist to reveal a blue tank top under it. Quite the sharp getup. I expected to be escorted to a Hummer stretch limo or something but was stunned to be ushered into one of those little "bingo cars", two seats and enough luggage space to fit a toothbrush. I shoehorned myself into the passenger seat and held my bag in my lap.

"Mr. O'Donnell wants you to meet him out at the Mesquite Pot O Gold Resort. It's about an hour north of Las Vegas."

"Okay, I was, ah, expecting something a little different than this for transportation. All the Ford Fiesta's in use today?"

Meghan laughed "Mr. Wahl, we won't be taking this to Mesquite. I'm just taking you over to the other side of the airport." With that, we zipped out of the terminal, under a tunnel, and around to the south end of the Las Vegas Strip. The Hughes Executive Terminal, which was the original airport terminal in the sixties, is host to some rather exotic private aircraft, and a few old 737's that ferry personnel every day out to Groom Lake, the so-called Area 51 where secrets abound and aliens supposedly live. I kept my eyes out for a glance of E.T. while Meghan hit a button on the visor and a gate opened up. We drove to a hangar that had a large "O'Donnell Enterprises" painted on the front. The hangar door rolled up and unveiled a true adult toy store. A Grumman G-4 Jet, two King-Airs, Cessna 210, De-Havilland Otter complete with floats, a couple of crashed race trucks that appeared to be mementos, four jet-skis on trailers, a Spectra ski boat, and an assortment of Japanese crotch rocket motorcycles. "This is one of two buildings," Meghan said. The other is next door and dedicated to the race team. It's pretty empty right now because almost everything is either in Mexico getting ready for the race, or up in Mesquite for testing. They are going to do one more shakedown run in the morning and then send the race truck to Ensenada, Baja California, Mexico." She pulled inside the hangar and stopped.

"Excuse me if I sound ignorant, but are you a 'mule'?" I asked.

Meghan laughed again. "Mr. O'Donnell has a lot of staff, like Girl Friday's I guess, although about half of us are male. He has an extremely demanding work schedule and also a lot of hobbies, as you can see. His leisure time is limited, so he uses his staff to have things in the right places at the right time. He has a fishing boat in Cabo, a cabin in the Rockies, a pontoon houseboat on Lake Mead, and other things. He calls all of us "mules" but it's not meant to be offensive. Mr. O'Donnell is the best boss I've ever had."

I took all that in, and then stepped out of the mini car. The door to what appeared to be a large Condo on the hangar floor opened and a young man, wearing a male version of Meghan's outfit waved me inside. "Welcome, Mr. Wahl, my name is Brad, and I'm taking you to Mesquite." He walked down the hallway, past the kitchen and dining room, sat down in an oversized easy chair, stuck a key in the mantel, turned on the ignition and we drove off. "There's a wet bar amidships," Brad called out over his shoulder. "Help yourself, or crawl in back and take a nap. We will be there in an hour."

I went back and selected a cold Coke and offered one to Brad, which he accepted and dropped into the right seat to enjoy the panorama while we got up to speed on I-15, past the Las Vegas NASCAR Speedway, and out into the desert. This segment, from the springs that gave Las Vegas its name to the Virgin River in Mesquite, was one of the driest and most treacherous part of Old Mormon Trail. Early trappers and adventurers called it the "Jornada Del Muerto" or Journey of Death. Apparently their motorhomes weren't as nice as this one. I had never been outside of town before, and it was a treat. Brad kept a running dialogue of the history and geography of the area, pointing out the old Mint 400 desert race course along the way, and telling me about a renegade Mojave Paiute Indian named Mouse that was preying on the locals even after the beginning of the twentieth century. They couldn't figure out how he could survive in this arid land without water. It wasn't until they captured him that they found his secret, a cool natural cistern that caught the rare thunderstorm. It's still called the "Mouse Tank" and is located in the Valley of Fire State Park.

We got to Mesquite about dark, and Brad dropped me off in front of the Pot O Gold Hotel/Casino. "Just give the front desk your name, Mr. Wahl and they will take it from there" and with that, the motorized condo drove away.

Yes, they knew what to do with me. The staff fell over themselves to get me checked in and ushered into the elevator, and up to the top floor, which didn't have a number, just the letter "P" which usually means Penthouse. I know it took the room key to give us permission to go there. The elevator opened up to what had to be five thousand square feet of suite. The view at sunset over the Virgin Valley was spectacular. Trip wasn't there, so I wandered into the bar, filled a tumbler with ice, and poured a glass full of Glenfiddich single malt scotch. A half hour later, I heard the elevator and got up. Trip walked in, wearing a dusty driving suit and an enormous smile. "Bric you old dog! Look at you. Looks like you could still straight-arm an anvil with one hand and bitch-slap a bear with the other!" Trip shook my hand and gave me a rather dusty man-hug, completely ignoring the dirt he was tracking into the Berber carpet. "Hey, let me get a shower, and then we can visit. Steak sound appetizing, or have you turned into a Key West vegetarian tree-hugger yet?"

"I'm still a meat-o-saurus. Good with a steak."

Trip picked up the phone and ordered enough food for an army. "Your digs are over that way he pointed. Shower if you want. Don't get lost on the way back," he laughed.

I followed his point and ended up in a separate apartment, complete with kitchen, two bedrooms, a walk in closet with an assortment of both men's and women's sizes and a master bath that was about the size of my whole houseboat apartment. I showered and found a pair of faded blue jeans that fit, and a "Pot O Gold" logo sport shirt. Trip was just emerging from his side, and at the same time the elevator went ding, and the feast arrived. It could have been the biggest steak I have ever seen, and unquestionably the best tasting. Baked potato, asparagus, and a few dozen servers to make sure we were fed, drunk and happy.

It was just us, and we caught up on the past few decades. After the injury, Trip was given an honorable discharge, and he came back to Vegas to help his dad with the business, which at that time was pretty frugal. Dad caught the wave at the right time, found some legitimate investors, (as legit as you can find in Nevada) and started to grow the business. He made substantial investments, some wise decisions and took the company public in 1988 to the tune of a half billion dollars. Trip was a devoted son and as shrewd a business man as his father, branching the company out to build Indian Casinos in Mississippi, Florida, Connecticut, Arizona and Missouri. "We're humongous Bric. You didn't tie the name to me? I'm surprised."

"I honestly don't pay much attention to the casino business, and for the past several years, I've spent more time underwater than on dry land. You get kind of detached down in Key West."

"So tell me about your life," Trip said.

I gave him the Readers Digest version, and sort of downplayed my years where I didn't have a pot to piss in or a window to throw it out of, and fed him some of the details about my wife dying, the kids, the houseboat and my gold bricks. I ended with being in Puerto Rico and Karen's efforts to get our store open in Key West.

"Key West Camouflage. That's a terrific name and concept. Tell you what. Get that Key West store open and your apparel line all in order, and I'll open franchises in every one of my casinos. I think the idea is a hit."

We clinked glasses to cement the deal. Details would be worked out later, but if I played it right, I would be the next Vera Wang of tacky tropical clothing.

22

Now back to Baja. "Here's the plan", Trip started. "We have the race truck out west of town. I want to do a couple of solid runs in it tomorrow just to shake it down. Better now than wait till you are in Mexico to find out somebody didn't tighten something somewhere. Then the crew gives it a bath, throws it in the semi and hauls ass for Ensenada Mexico. We will fly down next Wednesday morning. The race starts Friday. After the race, we can go down to Cabo and do a little Marlin fishing. Then I gotta get back to work, but you're welcome to hang around for a week or a year," Trip went on. "You know I never even got the chance to thank you for Grenada. I was a dead man, and you saved my tail big-time."

"I didn't do it for reward, Trip. You would have done it for me."

"Yeah, I got that, but it doesn't mean I can't show you a good time."

"Thanks. So what will I do during the race? Just hate to hang around with my hands in my pockets", I said.

"Oh, that won't be a problem. You will have plenty to do. You still in as good of shape as you appear to be?" Trip asked.

"Good. I'd say better than average for my age. Why, you want me to change tires or something?"

"Well, a little more exciting than that. I'm gonna put you in the right seat for the last three hundred miles."

Wow. Friggin beyond my wildest dreams. Passenger in the race truck. "Trip, I don't want to jeopardize the race. Don't you need trained mechanics for that job?"

"Not really, I know the truck as good as anyone else, and mostly the only thing you need to do is change an occasional tire if I get sloppy and hit a rock. Rarely do these things have little problems. When you stop it's either a terminal mechanical failure or you've wadded it up. Either way, the co-driver isn't much help. What do you say buddy? Ready to rock and roll?"

I took a long drink of scotch and stuck out my hand, "let's do it!"

"Great! Trip said. That's all settled. Actually I wasn't going to let you say no, but you're enough of a man to know fun when it slaps him in the face."

"This is quite a place you have here. You should rent the other half out to, say a Pakistani family of fifty or something."

Trip laughed, "This isn't my house. It's the casino penthouse. We use it for very high rollers, VIP's, big parties, but mostly gamblers that don't want a lot of publicity. If they fly to Vegas then the paparazzi gets a sniff, and they are all over the papers. Here, they can fly directly into Mesquite, get zoomed to the hotel, up the elevator to the private entrance, and nobody knows. We get movie stars, politicians, some extremely high level government officials, both from the US and others, just to mention a few. We can, and do, convert this living room into a full-fledged casino with slots, tables, and girls in slinky dresses. It's also been turned into a giant kiddie playground, a western saloon, and even an adult dungeon, complete with chains, whips, torture tables, the full Monty as they say," Trip went on. "I live just west of the airport in Vegas. Pretty mundane place actually, except that I have a big garage for toys and a nice trail behind the house that I can ride a dirt bike all over Nevada from."

"So, I don't see a Mrs. Trip around anywhere. Don't tell me nobody has managed to lasso a catch like you."

"Twice," Trip said, carefully examining the ice cubes in his scotch glass. "Once just after the Navy when I was young and stupid. Thankfully, it ended in divorce before I got a permanent reminder of a temporary feeling. The second time was just a few years ago. Great lady, just two people going the same direction on different roads. We parted amicably. She has more money than I do if you can believe that so we just walked away clean. She still lives in town, and we have dinner occasionally." Then he smiled. "I absolutely have someone in my life. You will meet her in Mexico in a few days." And that's all he said.

We sat around the suite for the rest of the evening, getting outside of some terribly expensive liquor, talking about the old days and just catching up. I couldn't help notice the rifle sitting over the fireplace mantle, and casually walked over to examine it.

I don't think I had ever seen a gun with a bore this big that you weren't pointing in the air trying to shoot a squadron of Migs down with.

"Like it? I had it custom made, just for shits and grins. It's an AR-15 Bushmaster. Shoots a four-fifty Bushmaster cartridge. You can drop a big animal a third of a mile away, should you have the inclination. But I don't kill things anymore." He pulled it off the wall and handed it to me. Balance wasn't great, but you could feel the muscle. I drew down the sniper scope and looked out the window. I was comfortable I could pop a reflector off a semi on Interstate 15 four hundred yards away. "That's quite a piece," I remarked, handing it back.

"Hey that reminds me," I remembered. "I need to replace my sidearm. I lost it when the houseboat sank. It must have fallen out the door when the boat tipped. I've got a concealed weapons permit, and with the amount of treasure that I mess with, I always like to carry."

"Hell Bric, lots of guns to buy in Vegas. What do you want? .357? 44Mag? We'll pick something out when we get back to town. You can get it when we get back from Mexico."

"Well, that's just it," I said. "The gun I lost was a Ruger Blackhawk .357 with interchangeable cylinders to .38 or 9 millimeter, but I would like something a little different. Okay, a lot different. I'm open to suggestions, but just don't want normal."

"Okay," Trip said, obviously in thought. "Let me make a call. We might be able to handle this tomorrow morning when we are testing the truck." Trip picked up his cell and dialed a number from his contacts. He chatted quietly on the phone for a minute, gave some directions, and hung up with a chuckle.

The following morning we ate breakfast in the casino, climbed in a red Chevy Dually, and drove to the desert area where the race truck testing was being conducted. It was quite a setup, two large semis, one with a large canvas cover extended over the Trophy Truck. There were also two pre-runner chase trucks, a few ATV's and either the same motor home as the one I was brought here in, or a duplicate. Completely out of place was a true relic. I would guess a 1967 Jeep "Jeepster" faded white, with a canvas top. For its age, it looked pretty straight. Leaning against the hood was a guy sipping coffee from a paper cup. About my age, a little less hair on top and a lot more mustache in front, and a look about him that made me feel a tiny bit uneasy. Like he always knows something that you don't.

Trip climbed out of the Chevy and walked over to the Jeepster. "Bric, I want you to meet a real close friend. Shake hands with the Caretaker."

I stuck out my hand and was delivered a real knuckle crusher. I responded the best I could and maybe barely got the best of it. This guy had some grip. "So I hear you're looking for something interesting in a piece." That was his form of a greeting.

"Caretaker is a licensed firearms dealer," Trip offered. "He specializes in exotic stuff. Strictly legal, but sometimes extremely rare. He keeps my security people in good hardware, and I occasionally shoot him off to Europe or Asia for a buying foray. It's a mutually beneficial friendship. So my friend, what selection did you bring?"

"No selection," Caretaker growled. "Just one, and if he don't like it, he's not really serious about buying big boy toys." He reached into the front seat of the Jeepster and pulled out a small leather bag, unzipped it and pulled out a very recognizable piece. I carried one almost exactly like it when I was in the Navy and not doing water-drops.

"Trip says you're ex-Seal so this will fit your hand just fine. It's a Springfield Armory 1911-A1, Colt clone with a seven-round mag. It's a re-make of the pistol carried by Army officers from 1911 until 1985. It's full of hand loads. Go ahead."

Trip nodded, and I looked around for something to shoot at. Being the Nevada desert, which was settled, explored and overrun by miners for a hundred years, there's always a tin can in the neighborhood. I spotted one about thirty yards away, hefted the .45 and squeezed one off. The dirt exploded about a foot above and to the right of my target.

"Sweet!" was the only thing I could say. I squeezed off the

26

second round.  This time the rusty can and about thirty inches of the surrounding desert seemed to cease existence.  I handed it back to the Caretaker with a big silly grin. "Wrap it up. What do I owe you?"

Caretaker almost cracked a smile. "That's the right order from someone that can probably afford it.  The piece, the carrying bag, holster and fifty hand loads.  I'll let you have it for half a grand."

"Sounds good to me," I said, about a half octave higher than my normal voice. "I'll have to do a bank withdrawal for the cash. Trip, I'm sure you can assist."

"I can do better than that Bric."  He pulled his cell phone out and spoke quietly for a few moments, then pulled a business card from his wallet, jotted a few words and handed it to the Caretaker. "Friend, just drop by the casino cage at Mesquite.  The cash will be there in your name,"  he turned to me. "The least I can do for a friend.  Call it an early birthday present."

I didn't know what to say, but knew arguing would be fruitless. "Thanks," was all I said and shook his hand.

He grabbed my hand and slapped me on the back. "Okay, done with boy toys, time to play with a man's machine!  Step into that there little motorhome and check the closet.  I'm guessing you can dig around and find a driving suit that will fit.  Hop to it!"

The "little" motorhome was a match to the one I got here in. Slightly smaller than a railroad boxcar, it had two segments that popped out when parked; the master bedroom and the dining area. I walked in and turned left, thinking about dropping bread crumbs along the way so I could find the door again.  The third door I opened rewarded me with about a dozen identical three quilted layer, Nomex fire suits, all emblazoned with the "Pot O Gold" logo and leprechaun insignia.  I rummaged through and found one that looked roughly the right size and pulled it on.  It was a little loose and too long, but livable.  I pulled my tennies back on and ambled outside.  Trip was already dressed when I got out there, and he handed me a full face helmet with an air-hose attachment on the side. "Try that on for size. I think it will fit."  It was snug, but I think that's a good thing.  I pulled the helmet back off and went to check out the truck.

Listed as a Chevy Silverado 3500, you could tell even from a distance this wasn't exactly what you would find on the neighborhood showroom floor. In this case, most of the "skin" - the fiberglass body parts that make it look like a showroom stock truck – were off the frame, so its "bones" were showing. The cab was intact and looked pretty much like a truck, but the front and rear fenders and the hood had been removed. It looked like something you would use to go rock climbing in Finland. Trip wandered over and gave me the quick tour. "Shocks cost a thousand bucks each, and there's three on every corner. Tires are thirty seven inches high and cost four hundred each. Engines a hand built Chevy racing V-8. I have a guy in California that builds them for me. He also does dragsters and street machines. Eight-hundred horses and about forty grand a pop. Chrome moly tube frame chassis, hand made by my crew. Huge cooling system and a super nav system. I know where I am every second, and so does the team. Fuel cell in the back that holds fifty gallons of racing fuel that costs six bucks a gallon. Just a touch under four miles per gallon. This ain't a sport for the faint of heart." He climbed into the driver's seat and motioned me to get in. "She'll do one-sixty on a dry lake bed and soak up a four foot hole like it's not there. If it holds together we're in the hunt for the win every time, but keeping it together for a thousand miles, well, that's the trick."

I pulled myself through the window, and a crewman leaned in to get me strapped in. "Tighten the lap belt as tight as you can. Leave a tiny bit of room in the shoulder straps. This is just a little test run, so we don't need to hook up the clean air system. Nobody in front of us today to make dust."

I squeezed the helmet on, and Trip started flipping switches. Fuel pump, fans, radio, and then mashed a red button and the motor roared to life. This unquestionably isn't your grandpa's pickup. He let it warm for a few minutes, slipped it into gear, and we idled off. The gauges all flicked to life, and we were up to temp. Trip eased the throttle down and slid through the gears. Strangely you wouldn't think these things would use automatic transmissions, but they do. The fulltime four-wheel-drive kept the wheels pulling, and the long leg suspension kept them hooked up. I looked over, and the only sizeable dial on the dash was a tachometer. No need for speedometers, no speed limits. You just go as fast as you can.

The sensation was phenomenal. You saw massive jumps, bumps, hills, ruts, ditches, and you would brace yourself, only to feel the truck pass over them with hardly a bobble. Trip jerked the truck around some tight corners like it was on rails. We dropped onto a dirt road, and he let it out for about a mile or two, then up a steep side hill, did a tight turn at the top and back down again. We went back and forth on that road two or three times and then hit a series of really big moguls, called "whoop-de-doos" in the desert. Trip later told me that they are a by-product of all this long-travel suspension. Back in the old days, a desert course would stay fairly smooth for a whole race since the little VW dune buggies had less wheel travel than a modern day mountain bike, and the wheels would spin instead of dig. Then off road buggies and later trucks started growing longer legs, and traction got a lot better, which then resulted in bigger and bigger ruts. This happened on motocross courses too, but big desert races seriously started seeing this change. So now, we were on an old desert race course, and the ruts were humongous. With the space-age suspension, the ride was smoother than I could imagine, but I was still getting whacked around quite a bit. After a half hour or so, we returned to the camp. Trip shut the truck down and climbed out. I had another big silly grin on my face for the second time in the morning. "That was a hoot!" I exclaimed. "So why did you just spend a half hour trying to kill this thing of beauty?"

"Glad you liked it," replied Trip. "Next week I'll be doing that, only a lot more seriously, for about seventeen hours. The big gotchas, like a grenaded motor, tranny, drivetrain stuff, can break anytime, but that tiny little wire that connects the left handed woodruff key to the flux capacitor that maybe wasn't put on right in the shop is what we're trying to detect," Trip said with a grin. "This shakedown run will find that kind of thing. All the guys have to do now is wash her down, do a quick go-over and throw it in the Semi.  Ready to ride along?"

"You bet," I answered. "The whole thousand clicks. Where do I sign?"

"Hold on, buckaroo. I'm just gonna put you in for about 300 miles to give my 'regular' co-driver a little break.   Right now, I want the gang to show you the tricks to changing a tire.  That will likely be the only thing you will have to do."

I spent the next hour getting familiar with the tire changing system.  Slick little deal. Two beefy  air-powered jacks, one on each side, a compressor and air tank, and a regular plastic Pelican waterproof (or in this case, dust proof) box bolted on the back with a pneumatic wrench and twenty feet of air hose.   Get a flat and you jump out while the driver stays strapped in.  He fires the jack from the driver's seat while you pull the spare out of the back rack.  Grab the wrench, unbolt the flat, and throw the spare on. Just like NASCAR, the lug nuts are glued to the new wheel, so you just jam it on, hit the lugs with the air wrench and you're done. Wrench and hose back in the box while the driver pulls the jack back up, jump in and away you go.  You strap yourself back in at speed and hope to Hell you don't hit a big bump before you're safely hooked up.  Total elapsed time, about a minute.  The tire and wheel weigh about eighty pounds, so you need a little inspiration to get the job done.  If you are in the thick of the chase, you just leave that dead spare and the three hundred fifty dollar wheel where it lay.  Likely it got hurt when you got the flat anyway.

We headed back to the casino to clean up, and then over to the airport where one of the King-Airs was waiting.  Trip is a pilot, but he had one of his pilots in the left seat.  It was a smooth fifteen minute flight back to McCarran.   Another mule was there to take us to the Pot O Gold, this time in something a little more substantial, a bright green Suburban with hotel logos all over it.

"I've got you a room here," Trip said.  Not quite as elegant as the one in Mesquite but I don't think you will complain.  You're cleared for 'RFB' which means Room, Food and Beverage. Everyone will think you are a serious gambler so no need to spend a penny. There's also a $5000 draw in your name at the cage, so you can hit the tables and give it all back to me, keep it or win a million and we'll both be happy." Trip grinned with that *"You buy the lunch, I'll buy the Cadillac"* smile.

Trip sent me to the front desk while he excused himself to do work things. He was true to his word, and my mere name caused a bow wave of uniformed humanity to surround me like dancers in an Elvis movie. I was checked in, given my VIP card and whisked to my room in a few minutes. All I had was my little carryon bag. (The hand-cannon was being held in safe keeping until I knew where I wanted it sent. (I don't know if my concealed permit was valid in Puerto Rico, but I doubted it), but it still took three bellmen, the Front Office Manager and the assistant Casino Manager to check me into my suite. It wasn't quite the K-Mart size that the suite in Mesquite was, but it was still a palace. They showed me two telephones. One should I wish to call anyone in the world, and the other phone, no buttons – just pick it up and it rings - to satisfy my every whim. Food, drink, transportation, company (yes, that kind of company). JAFI. (Just Ask For It). I reached in my pocket for a couple of twenties, and the whole staff backed off. No no, Mr. Wahl, not necessary. This level of the hotel is cashless, and everything is taken care of. And suddenly I was left alone.

It felt like half the air in the room left with them. After sitting inside an eight-hundred horsepower monster for thirty minutcs my ears were still ringing, and the silence felt eerie. I wandered through the room and found the shower, hosing off a few pounds of desert. I pulled on a pair of shorts and reached for the outside phone. I hadn't talked to Karen for over a week. We aren't clingy, and didn't have that need to know where each other was every second of the day. She had a phone and knew I would reach out to her if there was need. I dialed her number and hit her voicemail. I gave her my direct line to the suite and hung up. She would call back in due time.

Other than a satisfying steak dinner, a feature show with a magician, and a moderate dent in their beer inventory, I didn't take too much advantage of Trip's hospitality. I did rent a car and took a drive to visit that Mouse Tank that Trip's driver told me about. Far from the neon and asphalt experience that defines Las Vegas, the Valley of Fire State Park is forty minutes, and a world away from the strip. So called because of the spectacular colors in the bare sandstone outcroppings, the scenery was breathtaking. Following the signs, I parked in the lot and started a walk up the sand wash. The rocks were covered on both sides by petroglyphs, carved in the sandstone thousands of years ago by the mysterious Anasazi Indians, a tribe of Native Americans about which few things are known. Some of the images were obviously people; some hung like John Henry the Steel Driving Man. Antelope, wolves, birds, fish and others less recognizable, along with designs, spirals, and other images. Fascinating to watch as I trudged up the wash. I'm in pretty decent shape for my age, but this sand was like walking in oatmeal. By the time I had made the few hundred feet to the Mouse Tank, I had popped a sweat in the late October air. It was a "go-wee." You get there, look down at a little pool of water and go, "wheeee!"

Then you turn around and go back. Actually pretty neat and if you ever go to Vegas, it's worth the trip.

# Flash Back

That night I was cruising through the Las Vegas Review-Journal newspaper and opened the entertainment section. What comprises an eighth of a page on a Thursday in your local daily paper can be as big as a New York phone book in Las Vegas. This town IS entertainment. I casually cruised the columns, which started with the "A's" and ALL NUDE SEX SHOW to the "Z's" ZERO CLOTHING SEX SHOW. In between, there were a few more mundane items. Then I ran over an ad that I literally couldn't believe. JOE AND DON CANDY WITH THE CANDY ASS COUNTRY BAND. How about that! My old band from like a million years ago, back when I played rhythm guitar and sang like I was a frog with a throat condition. They played during high season in Key West for about eight years. The last year they were there, Joe, the bass player, contracted a nasty case of hepatitis "B", exacerbated by some kind of Hong Kong drippy dick venereal thing that he picked up by hanging around the back door of the Key West Scrub Club and practicing unprotected nookie on the local talent. I walked up on stage one night, and Don handed me Joe's bass and gave me a ten second instruction class. "Key of A!" and off we went. I fumbled and fiddled around and by the second weekend was holding my own. Playing bass and singing at the same time is kind of like rubbing your tummy and patting your head – doable but tough. Anyway, that was my introduction to bass playing, and I've never looked back. Right after that I went into the military, and they drifted off. I never thought of them until they just showed up on the paper in front of my face.

They were playing a lounge show at the MGM, so I caught a cab and cruised over that night. I crawled into a booth in the back and watched them play. They had a decent show, played with the crowd and did old and new country tunes. The waitress came over for my order, and I asked for two beers a little paper umbrella and two straws. She gave me a look but walked away and delivered the goods as ordered. I dropped a ten dollar bill on her tray, put the straws and umbrella in one of the beers and asked her to deliver it to the band. I took my beer, slouched in my seat and pulled the hat down around my eyes to watch the reaction. They literally kranged to a stop in the middle of "Rocky Top", one of their old standbys. Don took the beer and asked the waitress where it came from. She pointed my way, and they peered through the house lights to see if it was whom they thought it was. Joe just decided to take a leap of faith, and responded with the ultimate gotcha and pointed at me while he walked up to the mic.

"Ladies and gentlemen, we have a surprise for you tonight! Live and direct from an exclusive engagement on the island of Key West, we welcome Bric Wahl, who will sing his original song, a number one hit for two weeks in 1974 in Bozeman Montana, 'Part-Time Love.' Everyone, give it up for Bric!"

The lounge crowd applauded, and somebody threw a spotlight on me. There I was in a fishing shirt, Hook and Tackle shorts, Reef sandals and my signature "Old Guys Rule" hat. Not exactly appropriate garb for a stage show, even a lounge show, in Las Vegas. Well, what the Hell, I got up, weakly waved to the crowd and jumped up on the stage. One song won't hurt me. The guys all gave me a big man-hug and back slaps. We promised to sit and chat later. Joe jumped off the stage and made a bee-line for my waitress, petite, shapely blonde with a full-sleeve tattoo on her right arm. I gave the band the cords and changes and one, two, three, we were off and playing my signature song. I couldn't help notice Joe in full rut, and the waitress couldn't help notice that Joe was handsome, rugged, apparently single, with the urge to merge. If I had tried that kind of move I would still be spitting out teeth, but Joe always had a way, and before my song was over, the waitress had vanished with the regular bass player. Don turned to me after the song ended and said with a sly smile, "looks like you're in the barrel for a few more." I shrugged and resigned myself to staying on stage. There aren't many country songs I don't know, and I can fake about anything else, so it didn't take a lot of effort. Actually a better way to pass an evening than sitting

34

in my room watching a dirty movie.

Two songs turned to three, and then four, and after an hour and a half, when the band took a break, I was beginning to wonder if I was going to have to do a change of address. Don just smiled and asked if I could help an old friend out while another old friend scratched an itch. I asked how long they played till. "Only till two, and I'm sure Joe will be back before then. Least I hope so. He's got the car keys." I got back up and did three more sets, and after last call, and announcing our last tune, there strolled in Joe, hair un-combed, shirt rumpled and a shit-eatin grin on his face. I hadn't played for several months, and my fingers and hand were cramping something dreadful by the time we were done. With my right hand curled into a fist anyway, I was half tempted to sock him in the nose, but I didn't and I knew he knew I wouldn't. "Well, was she worth the effort?" I asked. "Oh yeah!" Joe answered. "I've wanted to tap that since we started. Just never could figure out how to be on point when she got off work. Your timing, my friend, was impeccable."

We shared beers and talked old times till sunrise. I promised to drop by on my way back through town after the race. "No stand-ins this time buddy," I said. "Or I'll tell her about your night with three hookers, a German shepherd puppy and a Shetland pony."

A few days later I got a voicemail on the room phone from Trip. I was picked up at the front of the resort at six a.m. for a ride to the airport and flight to Ensenada. What I had not received was a call from Karen. I tried one more time, left a message about where I was going and that I would touch base when I got back. Her phone went directly to voicemail which meant the phone was turned off. I was a little curious, but not worried yet. For all I knew, she had hooked up with some friends and went camping for a week on Saint Somewhere. Or Alaska. No biggie.

# Baja –
## The only sport where the competitors pay to be there and the spectators get in free

Trip was in the hangar at McCarran. He was multi-tasking, talking on a Sat-phone and texting on his Droid. He smiled and nodded toward the King-Air, and I climbed inside. There were a few other people there, and I introduced myself around. One was female and striking. Short blonde hair haloed around a honey-tanned face and a smile that could melt your heart. She was wearing ultra-short khaki cutoffs and a thin strapped black tank top, and just about nothing else from what I could tell. Sitting down, I would guess her to be five ten or eleven standing up, and built like the proverbial brick shit house. This gal worked out a lot. She shook my hand, firmly, like a man's handshake and introduced herself. "Suzanne, I'm Trip's girlfriend."

I always knew Trip had excellent taste in women. She smiled that smile again, and I just smiled at her stupidly. A few minutes later, Trip bounded up the stairs, and the pilot fired up the big twin Beechcraft. Normally the drive from Las Vegas to Ensenada would take a good eight to nine hours, partially because there is no direct road there, and you had to either go through most of Los Angeles to get there, or drive little roads through the desert to San Diego. In the King Air, we were about one hour forty minutes wheels up to wheels down, and the coffee was superb.

I could get used to this.

I knew I was a guest, and not a functional team member. This was a day to keep out of the way and not ask a lot of questions. I would be given direction when the time came. One of the green, hotel-branded Suburban's met us at the airport and drove us into downtown Ensenada. Trip told me if we got separated, I had a room at the Estero Beach Resort. Just take a cab and we would get back together tonight. Tech inspection day for the Baja 1000 is probably the biggest day of the year for this town. Ensenada has grown in the past twenty five years or so, with a cruise port, more year round tourism and a developing infrastructure, but the "Baja Mil" is still the big event. Locals love the race cars and love the economy boost. Tech inspection was right down Main Street, and crowds of locals, race teams, and children packed the main drag. Street vendors were selling everything from blankets to silver bracelet souvenirs, and rolling carts tempted your palate, (and potentially your digestion) with *"carnitas"* fish tacos, snacks and beverages. I found a little sidewalk taco-stand and settled down to people watch. Coronas were a buck, and you could get two "tacos" - seasoned, grilled and chopped steak on a homemade corn tortilla – for another couple of bucks. It might be Mexico, but Yankee dollars were happily accepted. For condiments, there was a large tray of bowls, containing various sauces, cilantro and crumbly Mexican "Queso Fresco" cheese. A scoop of this and a scoop of that, fold it in two and take a bite  I've likely had better meals in my life, but at that moment I couldn't put my finger on when and where.

Knowing I was going to be riding in a motorized Cuisinart much of tomorrow, I neither over-drank nor over-spiced my meal. I paid the tab, and wandered off to find the race truck. There were literally hundreds of racecars, thousands of crew members, and tens of thousands of spectators and locals. I quickly realized there wasn't a decent chance, or for that matter, a good reason, to find the truck and the team. I walked down a side street, hailed a cab and ordered Estero Beach Hotel Resort as a destination. After weaving through traffic, we cleared downtown and headed south for a few miles, then down a rather non-descript side street, emerging a few minutes later at a rather dated hotel, stuck in the sixties, right on a wide expanse of muddy tidal flat. A room was waiting for me, and, as promised, all paid for. It had been a busy morning. A nap sounded good.

I dozed off to a frightening dream. Bad guys were digging up my gold, I couldn't find my girlfriend, and all I could do was hide from people that were trying to kill me. Then someone discovered where I was and pointed a humongous gun with a huge barrel at me....

BANG BANG BANG! I jerked up from the bed in a cold sweat, not remembering where I was for a moment. Then heard the bang bang again as someone was knocking on my door. I opened the door, and there stood Suzanne. No longer in 'corporate' attire, she was taking advantage of that amazing body. A white, nearly sheer sleeveless blouse was unbuttoned and tied at the waist, revealing a lot of tanned midriff, serious cleavage, and a reasonable portion of both breasts. Her navel was pierced with - if it was real – about a four carat ruby on a gold ring, and it was apparent through that thin blouse that similar jewelry adorned both nipples. Her torn cutoffs were short enough to nearly eliminate imagination, and did nothing to hide two supremely ripped and tanned legs. She was sexy, and she knew it. "You're late for dinner!" she announced. "You," I answered, "look like what started the riot." Was my snappy response, "but I wasn't aware it was possible to be late for anything in this country," I yawned. "Where do I go?"

"We're eating at *'El Cuevo De Los Tigres'*. Throw on a shirt and I'll drive you."

The "Tiger's Cave" was near the resort. Again, down a dirt road side street through a slum neighborhood, right to the Pacific Ocean where the restaurant was perched on a bluff at the beach. Expecting a Spartan dining opportunity, I was surprised, first at a very pleasant ambiance when you walk in and second a large glass case full of Mexican, American and international dining awards. This place specializes in local seafood, and I jumped at the rare chance to enjoy abalone. A large shellfish, abalone meat is tough as a boot when raw. You take a big meat hammer and pound the crap out of it for a half hour, dust it flour, and sauté in butter for about twenty seconds. The abalone, along with an octopus cocktail appetizer and a few fried shrimp almost made me forget that taco stand lunch.

Dinner over, we shared a tequila toast and a group prayer and then Trip went over some last minute details. I would start the race and ride about 250 miles from Ensenada to San Felipe, on the gulf side, then get out and let the regular co-driver in, take a rest then climb in the Cessna to the West Coast of Baja and climb back in the truck and race to the finish line, about another couple of hundred miles. Everyone was chatty and relaxed, but you could feel the tension on this night before the race. A question occurred to me. "Who is your regular co-driver? I don't think I've met him."

Trip smiled his sly smile again. "Oh you have met my co-driver. She gave you a ride to dinner."

Suzanne smiled at me and then tossed her tequila shot.

"Well, knock me over with a feather! Whoulda thunk?"

"What, you don't think a frail little girl can ride in a racecar?"

"No, not that at all. I'm seriously pro-feminist, but those tires and wheels weigh about 80 pounds each. Changing one in the middle of the dessert after riding in a Cuisinart for six hours just don't seem right for a damsel in distress."

Suzanne dropped her elbow down on the table and held up her hand. "Care to arm wrestle for a hundred bucks?" she asked.

"Sucker bet, Bric," Trip called out from the other end of the table through a mouthful of flan without looking over at me.     "I guarantee you will lose. She uses that trick to keep her in beer money."

I tipped my cap in respect and declined the offer. I had no doubt she could pin me in three seconds. Hand to hand combat, well that might be a different story unless she was the role model for GI Jane.

We all headed back to the resort and turned in for the evening. It was gonna be one long twenty hour session tomorrow.

# Sit Down, Shut Up and Hang On

For a race of one thousand kilometers, about 650 miles, you would think the start would be O-dark thirty. Well, it is for the bikes and four wheelers, who start right at sunrise a few hours before the trucks and buggies. The promoters fondly give all the scooters a little head start before launching an eight-hundred horsepower fire breathing trophy truck down the course every minute. Those guys on the bikes are FAST. At least the top riders are. The slow ones can be found at the end of the race smeared on the bumper of a truck. It's unbelievable more people don't die in this sport. Usually you get a smattering of broken bones, a few concussions, and maybe one fatality every other year. Spectators get hurt more than competitors, mostly because the racers are in full pads, helmets, boots and fire suits. Spectators are in blue jeans, baseball caps and huaraches, and stand on the outside of the nastiest corner on the course, and then often build some sort of booby trap to see if they can cause a wreck. Rollovers happen, cars crash, spectators die.

Trip suggested that four roadside fish tacos slathered in green hot sauce and washed down with a six pack of Pacifico Sun beers would not be a healthy breakfast. I opted for a carb load and made a huge bowl of cinnamon brown sugar instant oatmeal. Gatorade was the beverage of choice; it doesn't go through you like water does and replaces electrolytes. I tried to pee, but not a drop. Rookie nerves I guess. Trophy trucks were the first four wheeled vehicles off the line at ten a.m., and we were number fourteen. After tech inspection the day before, the vehicles are impounded, so we caught a ride from Estero Beach into town, and claimed the race truck. Trip was in a great mood, anxious to get started, noisy, slapping backs and shaking everyone's hand, whether he knew them or not. All the chase crews had either left this morning or last night, and there was only one king-cab pickup with a few tools to see us off. With as much prep that goes into the truck, it shouldn't need any help leaving the line. At nine, we climbed in and got cinched up. *NOW* I knew I could pee. Oh well, at this point you just have to wet your diaper. Couldn't hold it for another five hours. The crew attached the air hose to the helmet, flipped on the fan motor, and I got the first taste of dry, musty, rubber flavored, filtered air. It didn't smell that good right now, but in a zero-visibility cloud of Mexican talcum powder, it will taste like a tropical breeze blown past a cocoa butter covered Playboy model. I flipped up the visor for the time being, slipped on my Costa Del Mar Corbina blue mirror sunglasses and got ready for battle. I laughed out loud when I looked at the dash. The dash in front of Trip had a dozen gauges, lights, switches and meters. My side merely had a hand-made sign taped on the dash. Three lines;

**Sit Down**

**Shut Up**

**Hang On**

Well, I like simple directions.

The crew jacked up the rear end and Trip fired the motor. He put it in gear and let it idle with the drive train working. That lets the parts and gear grease get a little warmed up before dropping the hammer and launching off the start line and going from zero to one-twenty in ten seconds with a rear-end full of cold grease. The jack was removed, and after a few handshakes, thumbs up and high fives, we headed for the staging area. Some bridge troll with a clipboard named Bill looked at us and pointed to our spot in line. I recognized many names from watching the races on ESPN. Baldwin, MacCachren, the Herbst brothers, Brian Collins, and NASCAR driver Robby Gordon, to name a few. We were lined up right in front of Robby and Trip told me he would let him by early. Robby doesn't have a lot of second place finishes in the desert. He rolls it up in the winner's circle, tows it back on a strap or wads it up in a ditch. Trip is fast and as much of a favorite as anyone. He's a talented driver and has very well-funded

41

equipment. With a little luck, he can win.

Of course, in this race, there is only one kind of luck, and it's never the good kind.

We inched up toward the start line, one car length every minute. The crowd was thirty deep, and close enough to touch. The locals love this race, both for the noise and the excitement and for the huge revenue injection into the economy. Everyone cheered their favorite, and the bright green Chevy with the leprechaun painted on the hood was always a crowd pleaser. At the start line, the race promoter shook Trip's hand, wished him luck and a safe race. Trip buttoned up the side curtain safety net, dropped his visor and gave me a wink. I knew we had less than a minute, but it seemed like an hour on that start line. Suddenly a flag waved, and Trip dropped the hammer. I got that "shot out of a cannon" feeling again, but this time it was not a test run. The difference was subtle but genuine. We roared down the street, hit the brakes, and made a left turn on the pavement, tires squalling, then up to speed as the truck dropped into the sand wash. I would guess we were doing about a buck-thirty when we flew over a huge man-made jump then immediately under a bridge.

I didn't have to pee anymore.

I couldn't imagine Trip was leaving much room under the gas pedal and was laid out pretty wide open down the wash when I felt a jarring bump from behind. Trip ignored and we got hit again, this time a little harder. Trip eased a fraction of an inch to the right, and I caught a glimpse of the number seven as Robby Gordon squeezed by on the left. It didn't occur to me what that much horsepower would do in a rocky sand wash, but as he cleared us and pulled back on the track, I was suddenly being sandblasted by dirt, sticks and one rock about the side of my fist that just missed sending me to the tooth fairy. This part of the track is a little wet so no dust, but Trip still backed down for a few seconds to let Robby get away from us, thereby avoiding large dental bills or unexpected cranial surgery. Ten minutes later we were clearing downtown Ensenada and pulled out of the sand wash and up a dirt road. We were instantly surrounded in blinding dust, and that stale air began to taste a lot better. Trip backed way off the gas now as we felt our way up the road.

For the next half hour, which seemed like half a day, we drove in this huge beige cocoon. The only way you could tell you were moving at all was the engine noise, but I couldn't tell if we were going thirty or three hundred. Then we topped a rise, the terrain changed, and we could see again. Off in the distance you could see a dozen little puffs of dust, the field of trucks that started before us. With the dust a little less brutal we could all start racing. Trip had told me the early part of the course was rough, rocky and rugged. After that, he said, it got worse as you drove off the "summit", down to sea level on the Gulf of California side. It's early in the race, and the tortoise can beat the hare. Trying to be too aggressive in this terrain and you will tear a corner off your car. Go too slow and your back bumper gets more dents.

Two hours after the start was our first pit. I had a radio in the helmet, and was told to call off checkpoints when we went by. Trip was also calling landmarks as we passed them. I had read about desert races all my life, and exotic Baja locales like the "Pepsi Stand," The "Tire Store," and "Three Poles," were hardly recognizable spots. The Pepsi Stand was a board shack that used to have a large Pepsi Bottle Cap sign nailed to it. Tire Store was just a road crossing now. It once had a giant tractor tire half buried to note the location. Three Poles or *Tres Posos* in Spanish was an intersection between the road from Ensenada and the highway from the US down to San Felipe. All wonderful names, but just blips on the road to regular people. At Ojos Negros, a small village was the first pit stop. I had practiced and witnessed pit stops, and knew what to expect. We rolled in to our semi, took on gas, four tires, got a quick drink of Gatorade, and we were gone.

Any kind of racing has three parts. You start and sort out the running order. Then there's the middle part where you set a pace and survive. Then you actually start racing during the last third. Baja isn't much different. The first pit was the end of the "start." Now the next six hundred miles or so was the "middle." Take care of your car, race the course, and stay out of trouble. I only had one more leg to San Felipe, about another 100 miles, but it was rough, dusty, rocky and rutted. Good shape or not, this was starting to wear me out a bit, but it was beyond exhilarating. Trip is an excellent driver, and you could tell how much he was pacing the truck, babying it through big holes and short shifting the automatic transmission to keep the revs down. It was like a ballet.

We pulled into our pit stop by the San Felipe Airport just before noon. This was a longer stop. We changed four tires, took a load of gas and changed co-riders. I'm not a big guy, and Suzanne ain't that dainty. I dropped the side curtain, popped the seat belt, and she jerked me through the window like a bag of dirty laundry. By the time I turned to help buckle her in she was buttoned up and focused. They dropped the jacks, Trip hit the gas, and off they went in a cloud of dust. We were cruising in the top ten overall, and that's all that mattered for now. We would race later if we had too. I found an empty camp chair, and someone handed me a cold Gatorade. It tasted like the finest wine, the coldest beer and the freshest spring water in the world, all rolled into one. My number-one goal for the moment was to get the world to stop rolling up and down and left to right. The middle ear is not designed for this kind of abuse. I didn't have a job for the next nine hours, so I relaxed and listened to the "Weatherman", a guy that has volunteered for years to be a single source of relayed info, on the radio while he coordinated safety crews, answered dumb questions and argued with the locals in pidgin Spanish. I don't know why Mexican citizens living in the middle of the desert have a need of UHF radios, but I suspect it's not to search for stray cows. Either way we were undoubtedly disrupting their chatter, and it was obvious these locals were not impressed with the revenue the gringos were bringing to the neighborhood.

We didn't rely on the race organization for radio support. We had two planes, a King Air and a Cessna 210 and kept one in the air all day long, relaying information, split-times and other details. Private aircraft are not permitted to operate south of the border after dark, so we positioned the King Air so it would spend the night in Ensenada. The 210 would ferry me over to the west coast just before dark, fuel up on a dirt road and then file a flight plan for San Diego California. It would get in the air while it was legal and then sort of drag its feet over the race course until it went bingo on fuel, then make a beeline for the border. That gave us about three hours additional aerial coverage and only have to bend the rules a little bit.

Throughout the afternoon and into the evening Trip was holding his own. Gordon was leading, which was expected and other usual suspects were in front, but we were hanging in the top five and in the hunt. About ten p.m., The Weatherman radio station reported that Gordon was out with a blown transmission, and now it was anybody's race. Trip started to push a little, and by the time the race car got back to our pit stop, we were in third and eating second-place dust. Just like the last time, only in reverse, Suzanne had her belts off and the side curtain down before the truck stop. She unfolded herself out of the passenger seat like a leopard. I tried to look as fluid, but didn't have the moves. Anyway, I was in, buckled up and ready before they got four tires and gas. I looked at Trip for a hearty "Hi-Ho Silver" but he was unresponsive, grim, determined. That was a definite race-face. He could smell a Baja 1000 win and nothing would get in his way.

Racing at night was a whole new experience. Despite enough high-intensity lights on the truck to cast a shadow on the moon, at over 100 miles per hour you could outrun those beams darned easily. Your mind played tricks. You imagined every bush was a cow. Every dust cloud a wall, or fence or hill. Trip had done this before and had pre-run the course several times. He knew there were only a half dozen real danger points between here and the finish and the rest of the time he relied on faith and a very expensive suspension package to keep him shinny side up.

Another hundred and twenty miles, fuel up one last time and then a dash to the finish. We were locked in a three-way struggle for the overall win. Equipment and skill levels were about the same, and it was going to be luck that determine who would win.

# Like I Said Before,
# There's Only One Kind Of Luck In This Sport

Despite being nearly equal, we were gaining on second place, and were close to leading overall on time. With a hundred miles to go, Trip was willing to take a chance and get up in his dust to try and make a pass. Poor visibility in the daytime spelled impossible visibility in the dark. We knew we were getting close, but visibility was less than zero. If second place drove off a cliff, so would we. Suddenly I caught a glimpse of a red taillight in front of us, right when Trip did. He caught a gear and buried the gas pedal. We gave him a good taste of the "Chrome Bumper." All the drivers are friendly competitors, but this was for the Baja win, and he wasn't moving over. NASCAR driver Jeff Gordon once said he would run over his mother to win a race. Carl Edwards overheard the conversation and agreed. He solemnly said that he too, would run over Jeff's mother.

Apparently the other truck had to slow for something in front of him, a bike or a bump and Trip hammered him hard the second time, lifting the yellow Chevy's rear end completely off the ground. Trip still didn't give in and we kept giving pressure. Suddenly Trip caught a glimpse of a fork in the road to the left and he cranked the wheel over. Instantly we were dust free and alongside him. It was a gamble. This fork could end, turn away from the course. Or be a parking lot for fifty spectators. This time we were lucky, and it paralleled the course for over a mile. It was a drag race. But we slowly pulled ahead. Half a car length, three quarters. "Clear!" I shouted into the mic, and Trip crashed through the brush to put the other car in our dust. My heart was pounding out of my chest, and I realized I had been holding my breath for the last two minutes.

I radioed to the chase crew that we were physically in second. The physical leader had started well in front of us, and we didn't need to beat him to win. There was just a little dust hanging around the course to mark his being in front of us. If there was such a thing as cruising to the win, we could do it. Just keep the rubber parts down the shiny side up, run a clean pace with no mistakes and Trip could get his win.

Trip had been behind the wheel without a break for a long time. Exhaustion, pitch darkness and the tiniest lapse of memory was all it took. We were going up the side of a mountain on a narrow dirt road, and the left front caught a little rut. The truck pitched left, Trip counter-steered to the right, and suddenly we were an airplane. I heard the engine roar past redline as the wheels tried to get traction on thin air. Trip keyed the mic for one quick "HANG ON!" and then we hit the first time. Hard. The truck went back in the air and slowly barrel-rolled to the left in the darkness. Second hit. Harder and we started a forward tumble. Finally, we started making more contact with ground than atmosphere and the truck bounced end over end, then rolling on its side down the mountain. I had no idea if we were going to fall thirty feet, three hundred or three thousand, but we crashed for a what seemed like hours but was more like five or six seconds. I was thrown against the five point harness a dozen times and thanked heaven for chrome moly tubing, Simpson harnesses and a very good Bell helmet. That being said, I finally caught one wrong and banged my head silly on the roll bar once too many times.

Way too hard.

I was in boot camp during Seal training. They put you in this cockpit looking thing, strap you in, and then run you down a ramp into a pool at an ungodly speed. You hit the water, and it goes upside down. You have to keep your wits, find your harness, unbuckle and swim to the surface. It's disorienting, confusing and scary, but you kind of know what to expect. I almost choked to death the first time and the rescue team had to drag me out. I did it three more times after that and got better every time. Today it probably saved my life. I woke up in the dark, ears ringing, upside down and disoriented with not a clue where I was. Slowly I started to remember. *Race. Truck. Crash.* It was deathly silent, except for a steady hiss of something wet hitting something hot. Could be water, could be fuel, but it was time to starting thinking about getting out. I pulled the visor up and reached to my left. "Trip!" I called out. No answer. I reached over and felt him hanging from his five-point, limp and lifeless. You literally couldn't see your hand before your face. Holding part of the doorframe cage with one hand, I unhooked my belts and rather un-gracefully fell to the roof of the truck. Finding the latch to the side curtain, I got it open and crawled out onto the mountainside. Distantly above you could hear a truck go by. You could tell we had fallen a long ways down that mountain, and likely nobody would find us before daylight. I stood and checked all body parts. I was sore as Hell and my head was killing me, but nothing seemed broken. I still couldn't see my hands in front of my face, but my eyes were starting to adjust, and the starlight eventually made things appear. Time to see what I could do for Trip. The other side of the truck was on the downhill side, and you couldn't get into that window, so I crawled back into the cab from the passenger side and tried to get a read on my friend. He was unconscious, and I couldn't even tell if he was breathing. There was no way to tell if or what was injured, and I couldn't leave him hanging anyway, so I worked myself under him and got his harness loose. I was able to cushion the fall and keep him from breaking his neck if it wasn't broken already. Suddenly the mystery of what was dripping was no longer a mystery. With a "Whoof!" the front of the truck caught fire. High-test racing fuel burns with enthusiasm and there was fire around us in a few seconds. No time for ceremony, I backed out of the cab in a hurry, dragging Trip's body behind me. Out of the cab, I stood up and dragged him another thirty feet in a hurry. By then the whole truck was a merry blaze. Contrary to all the TV shows you watch, cars rarely explode. They just burn to the ground. This one didn't disappoint. The only notable sounds were the four tires and the spare, which popped with loud bangs right toward the end of the blaze, and the compressed air tank, which blew its safety valve with a pop and a scream. Despite the loss of the truck, it was at least likely that half million dollar signal fire would bring help sooner than later.

Sitting in the dark, I wished I had the sense to put a little pocket flashlight in my driving suit, along with a Sat-phone, some aspirin and a couple of ice cold longnecks. Assuming the damage, whatever it was, had already been done, I unstrapped Trip's helmet and gingerly pulled it over his head. Feeling the carotid, there was a pulse, not strong, but steady. That's a good thing. Standing up made me dizzy and my head hurt worse than ever. I sat down, cradled his head in my lap and waited for help. There was no physical way to scramble back up that mountain in the pitch dark and try to flag down a racecar on the outside of a blind corner.

It seemed like forever, but slowly the sky started to lighten in the east. I could still hear race cars on the course above me, and started to think about climbing out and looking for help when I heard the sound of a chopper and the green and white colors of the casino's Bell Long-Ranger came into sight. The carcass of the truck was still smoking, and they came right to us. Just because I've always seen it on TV, I tried to get up and waved my arms, even though it was obvious they could see me, but dizziness and nausea plopped me right back down. There was a road a few hundred feet below the wreck, and the helicopter sat down in a huge cloud of talc dust. Suzanne was first out and worked her way toward us. "Trip's unconscious!" I yelled before she got to us. "We need to get him to a hospital!" Suzanne the Amazon turned into Doctor Suzanne and kneeled down next to Trip. "Pulse sixty, breathing shallow, left eye dilated. Concussion I think. By then two of the crew had made it up to us with a backboard, "C" collar and thankfully a bottle of cold water. They strapped Trip on the board and headed for the chopper. I was able to wobble down on my own power, and with a little help got in and seated.

We lifted off and made a beeline for San Diego, about a hundred miles north.

My Baja experience was over, just like that. We took Trip directly to Scripps Mercy Hospital and the ER team took him out of the chopper. Suzanne kissed me on the cheek and closed the door of the chopper behind her. We lifted off, headed to Lindberg Field where I got in one of the King-Airs from the helicopter. A brief clearing of customs, and it was wheels up. We were back in Vegas in fifty minutes. A mule met the plane, took me back to the hotel where I got out of my filthy driver's suit, showered and found more clothes in the closet. There was a knock on the door and the hotel physician announced he had been asked to give me a look-over. "Maybe a mild concussion, but nothing that a few aspirin won't fix," he advised. I'd heard you were not supposed to sleep with a concussion, but I doubt anyone could have stopped me. I fell on top of the covers and fell into a deep and dreamless sleep.

Sometime later that night the phone woke me up. It was Suzanne. "Trip had a bad concussion but had regained consciousness, and he hasn't stopped yelling at anyone in earshot to give him a phone so he could call you." She handed the phone to him.

"Bric!" How the fuck are you? What happened?"

"Big old bad mountain came up and slapped your ass," I answered. "Sky-ground-sky-ground-sky-ground, as I recall. I think I lost count after that, and it was dark anyway. You were taking a nap, so I dragged your lazy carcass out of the truck before you became a crispy critter."

"I heard," he answered, more quietly now. "Looks like you're my hero another time. You gotta stop this life saving shit or I'll owe you my whole company."

"I'll just settle for your girlfriend," I answered. "Just kidding, well maybe not, but hey, you need to marry that one. She's a keeper."

"Yeah, well you can't clap with one hand. I've asked her a hundred times. She'd rather live in sin. So, they're gonna keep me

50

here for a few more days. Hang around and we can swap lies when I get back to town."

"I'd love to," I answered, "but I need to get to Key West quick. I'm getting seriously concerned that I haven't been able to reach Karen. I think I better go look for her. I'll stay tonight and then see if I can get a flight out in the morning."

"Ten-four, I understand," replied Trip. "Okay, get it sorted out then come back for a week or ten. We got our fun cut short and need some more play time. Don't worry about a flight. I'll get the G-4 thawed out and have you run right to Key West. Suzanne will set it all up. That will make it easier for you to carry your new toy home too."

Sometimes it's nice to have friends in high places.

# Curiouser and Curiouser

The following morning a mule picked me up at the hotel to take me back to the Hughes Executive Terminal. I had been here for - how many days? – And hadn't put my hand in my pocket to buy hardly anything. I stopped at the ATM in the hotel lobby to get some pocket money. I swiped the card, punched in my PIN and asked for a hundred bucks. UNABLE TO PROCESS THIS TRANSACTION was the response. Okay. There should be like twenty grand in that account. I tried the Check Balance inquiry. It showed a whopping six dollars and thirty cents.

Whoa.

On the way to the airport, I tried Karen again, and this time it came up with a "The number you have dialed has been disconnected – Please check the number and try again." Concern turned to a twinge of panic. I decided to call Bo Morgan. He had to know what was going on since Karen had come by to pick up some cash. Bo answered the phone. I hardly got out with "Hey Bo, it's…." when he cut me off. "Hey, Jimmy! I've been waiting for your call." I was about to correct him when I remembered one of the few electronic gadgets he ever embraced was caller ID. He knew who was calling and didn't want someone else to know. "Jimmy, I'm about to run out the door, but I wanted to let you know you're all set for that fishing trip. Tack will take you out. When are you going to be here?"

"Tomorrow or Tuesday," I answered slowly, sort of disguising my voice.

"Make it Wednesday," Bo answered. "We won't pick you up

at your old place, but meet me on the steps of my old back porch, say oh-dark-thirty?"

My mind was spinning, but I knew better than to blow the cover. I just answered "Got it." And hung up. Bo's a smart old pirate and knows something is going on. He must think his house is bugged, and he doesn't want anyone to know he's talked to me. He also doesn't want me to show up at "my old place" which is the houseboat I still own right next door. The steps of his old back porch? He doesn't have a back porch. His houseboat just opens to water and the bay. Then it came to me. The dive platform on the back of the Captain Morgan. We used to call it the porch. So, he wanted me to come to the house in the dark by water, sometime very early Wednesday morning.

Got it.

Curiouser and Curiouser

The limo was waived through the gate at the executive terminal and pulled up to Trip's Grumman G-4. The G-4 is a real jet. Eighty eight feet long, costs about thirty five mil, has a range that will get you from Miami to Paris with plenty to spare and can cruise at 40,000 feet. This one was configured to seat nine people and had a wet bar and delightful little bedroom in the back. Today it was just me, a pilot and co-pilot, who also served as a steward should I need anything. I might have enjoyed the ride except I didn't know what mess I was flying into. We taxied down to the end of Runway Zero-Seven and zipped into the sky effortlessly with only one passenger and a tiny duffle bag with one large gun for luggage. I found a Coke in the fridge and settled in with my thoughts. The phone on the table in front of me rang. I shrugged and answered. It was Trip.

"Hey Bric, got everything you need? That clunker ought to get you home no problema."

I filled him in on current events. "Wow, sounds like you have a mess and a mystery on your hands. What can I do to help?"

"Well, if one of your crew has a spare hundred, I could use a quick loan. I don't even have cab fare."

Trip laughed. "I can do a lot better than that. Did you look in your gun bag? I put a few bucks in there for a deposit on our little clothing store concept. That's yours to keep."

I unzipped the duffel to find a bundle of hundreds – a ten-thousand dollar 'deposit'.

"Wow, Trip, that's quite a commitment. I'll make sure it comes back with interest."

"Forget it," he answered. "Just find out what's going on and keep me posted. Don't worry about the money. It's one thing I have to burn. Anything else I can do for you?"

"Now that you mention it, this cash changes my options. Can you have the crew change their flight plan? I need to land in Miami. I don't think it's a smart idea to make a grand entrance."

Best I get to Key West quietly.

The change in destination to Opa Locka Municipal Airport was performed with barely a nudge to the left. Landing a little past six, I thanked the crew, and they fueled, buttoned up and turned back around for the trip home to Vegas. I walked out front of the terminal and inquired, in Spanish, where the nearest used car lot is. *"Si Señor. Esta allya. Cinco minutos maximo."*

Years in the sun had darkened my skin to the point I could pass for Latino. That being said, lots of the *Cubanos* in this neck of the woods had blue eyes, fair complexion and light colored hair. My Spanish was passable, at least good enough to find a beer or a bathroom, but I didn't think I had enough skill to buy a car. I tried to pass for a local in the cab so the driver would never recall a *Gringo* taking a cab from the airport to a used car dealership. The driver pulled up to a lot. All the signs were in Spanish, and the name – *Dos Hermanos* – Two Brothers Auto Sales, ensured they were experienced in selling cars to people that might not be legal citizens, or have a driver's license, for that matter. I was looking for something specific, and I asked the driver to wait for a moment. A glance to the back of the lot was sufficient. I paid the cabbie and walked onto the lot. I wanted a van, old, rusty, non-descript, anonymous. There were several that filled the bill. I made a fairly quick deal with the salesman, only worked him a little on the price and drove out fifteen minutes later in an old

54

white Chevy van, paying an extra few dollars for a screwdriver. Motor sounded decent, but it only had to get me a hundred fifty miles or so. I didn't plan on keeping it, or driving it away from Key West for that matter.

Finding a local Cuban restaurant, I had a plate of *Lechon Asada*, rice, black beans and fried plantain. Beer sounded good, but I had a long night ahead of me, and a long day tomorrow. I drove through the neighborhood until I found what I was looking for, an abandoned car in a vacant lot. Quietly in the dark, I slipped around behind the car and pulled the license plate off, then went back to cruising for my next step. After an hour, I finally found my next objective, parked, shut off the lights and waited. By midnight, the neighborhood had quieted down, and I stepped out of the van and walked over to its near-match. A tired, white Chevy van of about the same vintage. Relieving it of its plate, I replaced it with the one from the derelict. I drove off to a Wal-Mart parking lot and put the plate on my van. Now if someone ran the plate it would match what I was driving, and it could be weeks before the unsuspecting *Piasan* discovered the swap.

# Back on the Rock

Tuesday morning before working my way down the Keys, I went in the Wal-Mart for a few creature comforts and then a dive shop for some real gear; re-breather, mask, snorkel, fins, weights and a few other necessaries. I was glad I had ten grand as I was burning through it rather handily. Then it was down the road, US-1 to Homestead, Card Sound Road to Alabama Jack's for a dolphin sandwich, and then over the bridge where I almost left that lead brick full of gold. It seemed so long ago, but it was only a little over a year.

A lot of water had passed under the bow since then.

Observing the speed limit and all the traffic signs, I got to Key West late in the afternoon. I pulled into the Sears Town parking lot and crawled in back for a nap, setting my new dive watch to wake me up in the middle of the night.

Midnight on a November Tuesday in Key West. It doesn't get much quieter than this. I started the Chevy and drove quietly down the street to the parking lot behind the Elks lodge, parked next to the water and killed the engine. I sat another thirty minutes to make sure nobody was watching, gathered up my gear, pulled on a black long-sleeved Under Armor shirt and a pair of black sweats, locked the van and hid the keys inside the back bumper. Sliding into the water, I pulled on the re-breather, mask and fins and quietly snorkeled out and around the point. It was a few hundred yards to Bo Morgan's place, and I could see his houseboat in the distance. I stopped half-way and waited under a dock for another hour, making sure my eyes were adjusted, and trying to see if there was any activity in the neighborhood. Satisfied it was clear, I checked the re-breather, pulled the mask back on and slid back underwater. Re-breather units are cool stealth units, letting you dive quietly without making lots of bubbles. Handy if you are around spooky fish and handier if you don't want to announce your presence. That part of the bay is skinny water, but I was still a decent six to eight feet under most of the time as I approached the compound and the back of the *Captain Morgan*. I took one little peek to make sure I had the correct heading and then eased up to the back of the boat as quietly as possible. I brought my head up and nearly had a heart attack when I was greeted with a sloppy Doberman kiss from Lucky. Bo was sitting cross legged on the back step of the Morgan. "You're getting sloppy, Bric. Lucky got me up a half hour ago to tell me you were in the neighborhood."

"I'm not sloppy," I whispered. "That friggin dog has ESP. Always has," I pulled the mask off and hoisted myself up beside Bo, my feet dangling in the clear water. A few little grunts and snappers cruised around my flippers, barely visible in the darkness, looking for a snack. Suddenly a narrow shape darted out from under the boat, and a baby barracuda flashed by, catching one of the unsuspecting grunts right out from under the flipper. Ah, the circle of life. Sitting at the end of the dock, facing away from the houseboat and Hilton Haven Drive, it was highly unlikely that anyone could hear, or see us. We sat there for a few minutes in the silence. I knew Bo would start talking shortly.

"Karen showed up almost two weeks ago, and I gave her the cash as we discussed. Seemed like the normal Karen. She told me she had a lease on a storefront on Duval, and was meeting with several designers over the next week. A few days later somebody rings the bell at the gate, and there are three shady characters standing there in front of a windowless mini-van asking in a bad accent if I knew where she was. I told them I only knew her as one of my ex-tenant's girlfriends and that she hadn't been around for more than a year."

Bo looked up at me. "I don't think they bought it. I'm guessing that someone is either watching the compound or at least checking up on me. I think someone is listening to my phone conversations too. Nothing concrete but just an uneasy feeling that I was being watched. You know that feeling."

I sighed. "Bo, I wish I'd never figured out where the gold

might be, and wish even more I hadn't tried to do the honorable thing and tell Harry. It's caused me nothing but grief. I came into town quietly because I felt something was fishy. Couldn't reach Karen for several days to start with. She's the only person other than me that knows where that treasure is. I was starting to think maybe she's pulled something, but now I'm sure Harry is up to no good. Now I'm worried that you are getting caught up in this too. Where's it gonna stop?"

"Well," Bo answered. "For me and Tack, it stops here. I'm your friend, but too old to get in the middle of this, whatever it is. I've got some cash if you need it. I can go in the house right now and get you a few grand, but I need you to stay away, not call and keep me out of it until it all blows over."

"I've got some money, but thanks," I answered. "Not to worry, I'll keep you clear of the crossfire. I think for a few days at least, I'm going to go native so I can snoop around without drawing attention. Any suggestions on where to start?"

"You might not believe me," he answered, "but Tack told me he heard she was shacking up with a broad."

"You mean renting a room?" I asked.

"Ah, not exactly. A lesbian named Julie. Works as a bartender on Duval. That's really all I know."

My head was spinning. I honestly didn't know what to say or think. I just sat there with my head in my hands.

Then Lucky, who had been dozing on the dock next to the Captain Morgan, picked up her head and gave a low "woof." Bo stood up and said. "Hate to be rude, but you need to ride off into the sunset, or in this case, sunrise. Take care of yourself and good luck. When this thing blows over, I'll welcome you back in my home, anytime. So long." And he casually strolled back up his dock without waiting for an answer. I slipped back into the water and made my way back to the van. I had enough information to get started, and it only took a few days to find her, confront her and listen to her story. That's how I ended up in her living room that late fall night.

# Hide in Plain Sight

All the feelings of hurt, anger and betrayal were instantly replaced by a huge pit in my stomach. I slumped in Julie's chair and looked at the ceiling for a moment.

"Are you positive she's dead? I haven't heard a word about this," I said.

"Let's say ninety nine percent sure," she answered. I know bad people were looking for her, mostly because they couldn't find you. I told her there was a contract out, and I tried to help her, but I think they found her, and these people aren't big with leaving witnesses."

" 'These' people? And who might 'they' be?"

"My full name is Panyoda Julia Coutremanos," Julie said. "I was born in Tarpon Springs, and I'm related to about everyone in that town."

Ah, the light came on. She continued. "About two months ago, an associate of your ex-boss paid a visit. Told me they were looking for you because you made off with something that belonged to them. They knew Karen Murphy was in your company. I told them I vaguely knew who you were but had not seen or heard anything of you being in town for nearly a year. They told me to keep an eye out. Family thing, you know."

Julie finally seemed to notice that she was displaying a lot of flesh, got off the chair and pulled on a long tee shirt that was draped on the dining table. It just barely covered the top of her thighs, but that seemed sufficient. She re-assumed her position after grabbing another Heineken, even offering me a refill, which I accepted. I thanked her for the bottle and couldn't help noticing just how pretty she was when she brushed by my chair.

Her story continued.

"It was only a few days later, late in the evening that a pretty, blue eyed brunette, came to the bar and ordered a Rumrunner on the rocks with a whooee. It was quiet, and I thought she was really hot. Just the prettiest blue eyes. (don't I know it?) She told me she had lived here for years and had been on an extended vacation with her S.O. She was here looking for a building to open a store and move back. She finished her drink and left. She came in a few nights later, and we talked more. I honestly got the feeling she was there to see me, and I started to flirt."

She stopped the conversation and looked straight at me. "Don't get me wrong, I don't pass the trash or chase every little piece of tail that walks in. I thought we were connecting. Anyway, the third time she came in, I asked if she wanted to go someplace else after work for a drink. She said 'why not'. I got off a little early and met her at 801, and we drank a lot of beers. After an hour or two it started to come to me that she was THE Karen. I was torn, but had to ask her if her 'S.O.' was named Bric. She said yes.

"I didn't know what to do, contact my family or warn her. I finally decided to tell her she was in danger. I didn't tell her how I knew or who it was. She seemed surprised, but not terribly so. Then I asked her where she was staying, and she said the Doubletree, so I invited her to move in for a while. I figured the best way to keep her out of trouble was under my roof."

"And you guys were lovers, sleeping together, making love? I almost can't believe it," I said.

"This might come as a surprise, but I honestly don't give a rat's ass what you think. And I have no intention of giving you some sort of pleasure out of hearing intimate details." She pointed at the bedroom. "You obviously went in there and violated my privacy. You can see there's only one bed."

I mulled that over for a few minutes. Karen never indicated, acted or hinted that she was anything but one hundred percent straight. Oh, she would grab the occasional tit or ass, and she kissed as many girls as she did boys, but that doesn't make someone gay or bi – it just makes them friendly. Heck, I even hinted once that I would be game for a three-way, and she didn't talk to me for a week. Oh well, you learn something every day.

"So, I haven't heard anything about her being killed. That

would be big news in this town. What makes you think she's dead?"

Julie got up and walked over to the desk, picked up a copy of the Citizen and handed it to me. It was dated nearly three weeks ago. The headline was all in caps.

BOMB DESTROYS CARS IN CITY LOT

"Did you read about this?" she asked.

"I heard something. Big explosion on the top deck of the city parking lot on Caroline. Blew up one car and damaged several others. Top of the lot is still closed down I think," I replied.

"The car that blew up was a Dodge minivan," Julie continued. "ATF estimated as much as a half-pound of C-4 plastic explosives were behind the driver's seat, and several full plastic gas cans. There were one or two people in that van that weren't identifiable. Nothing to trace. No dental records, no body, no clothes. Completely obliterated. DNA has not come up with a match."

"And you think this was Karen?" I asked. "Why?"

"The van was traced as being stolen from a motel in Tarpon Springs two days earlier – where all my family lives. I think they found Karen, killed her, brought the van here and used it for a coffin. No evidence, no way to trace. I'm just assuming she's never given a DNA sample."

"Probably not, but there's still no reason to assume it was her is there?" I was grasping at straws.

"Read this page." She handed me a page from the Key West Citizen three days later. The hair on the back of my neck stood up.

*"The only identifiable item recovered from the wreck was a small golden octopus that had apparently held a gem or pearl."*

"Karen said you gave her that necklace that you had made for her. She never took it off. You know what it was holding," Julie said.

Yes, I did. It was a four carat emerald from the Atocha. A blast like that would have turned a non-gem emerald like that to dust.

Karen was gone.

# Beware of Greeks Bearing Gifts…. of C4

A few days later I was still in street person attire, wobbling east down Caroline street past Simonton, slowly working my way to my van that was currently parked in the city parking garage, top floor, right on top of a very fresh patch of concrete. It was as close as I would ever get to Karen again, I knew. I was planning on sleeping in it tonight on Stock Island, instead of my usual spot in the Memorial Garden by Mallory Square. I was in a real quandary. I needed information, contact with the "real" world, but in my current role as a street bum, that was nearly impossible. My need to stay invisible was really in conflict with a need to figure out what was going on. My lifetime 'go-to' guy, Bo Morgan was not going to be an option this time. He knew everything and everyone in town, but I was seriously concerned for his safety, and he politely, but firmly told me that, as much as he wanted to help, I was *persona non grata* around the compound for now. It was very possible his house was under surveillance by some or all of the bad guys, not to mention the cops. The second I showed up at his back door we would likely draw a bigger crowd than we would want. I needed someone that I could trust that was not part of my frequent inner circle, knew the town and how to snoop without it looking like snooping. I glanced over toward the Fishwagon and my savior was delivered to me.

Mick Murphy.

Mick and I aren't actually friends, but we have a nodding acquaintance, and have occasionally shared a table at Schooners or at Buzzards. I even helped him out of a little jam once when he was tangled up with some Mexican mob guys, providing a little street muscle to discourage bad guys from doing bad things. Micks as Boston and Irish as you can get. Short enough to pass for a leprechaun, he sports a full red beard, usually has a cigar sticking out of his mouth, and dresses in classic Key West attire, fishing shirt, shorts, beach sandals and, in his case, a tattered Boston Red Sox baseball cap. I hear he makes a living as a writer, making enough money to get by, and never enough to get out of the hole. Mick likes young pretty girls, old Irish Whisky, expensive cigars and sailboats. He has a healthy respect for the law and total disregard for authority. He's my kind of guy. Right now he was sitting on one of the street side stools at the Fishwagon and was working on a dolphin sandwich and nursing a longneck Budweiser, that being the only form of alcoholic libation that Buddy sells. Seizing the opportunity, I wandered over to the north sidewalk and ambled up by him.

"You gonna eat all of that?" I asked, trying to stay in character for the moment.

Mick stopped at half bite and glanced up at me. His very readable eyes flashed a moment of disgust, then instantly softened as his Irish charitable angel kicked him in the left ear. He put the sandwich down and pushed the plate toward me. "Go ahead, but you better move on. Buddy won't let you hang around."

I was hungry and didn't mind sharing the best fish sandwich in Key West. I nodded thanks and took a big bite. "How bout that longneck?" I ventured.

"Hey friend, my charity goes just so far. Beat it!" Mick answered.

"Man, for good Irish Southie boy you don't have much of a sense of humor." I smiled past the sandwich and knew that would give him a clue that I wasn't what I looked like. I couldn't bear to let my teeth look rotten. I just made sure didn't smile much when I was in character. Mick squinted and looked at me hard. I set the sandwich down and slid just enough of the right sleeve up on my Army surplus jacket to show my eagle and trident Navy Seal tattoo.

"Bric! Jesus man, don't you know the whole world is looking for you?"

"No," I answered dryly. "I love to not shower for three weeks at a time, eat cold tuna out of a can and sleep on bricks with a day-old Citizen for a pillow. Meet me in the fifth floor of the parking garage in fifteen minutes. I need a friend."

"Bric, you're a cool guy, but I hear you're a hot product with people on both sides of the badge. I've spent so much time at the Monroe County Sheriff's office over the last year I'm starting to get my mail there. I don't know if I can help you. I'm a realist. Why should I get involved?"

"Because," I answered, "I'll give you an exclusive story that could get you the Pulitzer. The only deal is, you can't tell it till I'm off the hot plate and all the subjects are either behind bars or on a slab."

Then I just shut up.

Mick is many things, but his curiosity was either his biggest downfall or his best talent. He loves a good mystery, and the rumors on the streets had probably filtered well through the Coconut Telegraph.

"What kind of story?" he finally ventured.

"Murder most foul, Spanish gold, Greek hit men, and at least one or two missing or dead persons. And that's just in the last few weeks. Interested?"

He only hesitated a moment. "What's on top of the parking garage?" he asked.

"Proof."

"Let's take that walk," Mick finally answered.

I strolled ahead and took the elevator to the top of the parking deck. The van was in full sunlight, so I opted for the available shade in the corner by the elevator. Ten minutes later I heard the elevator mumble and Mick Murphy emerged, cautiously. He looked around to see if we were alone.

"Let's stand in the stairwell," he said. "I really don't want to be seen with you."

"Mick, it's a friggin Tuesday in November. Nobody is going to come up here looking for criminals. That stairwell is hotter than a pizza oven. If we hear a car, we can duck for cover."

He didn't look happy but nodded. "Okay Bric, this better be good. Talk to me."

"I've got some things over in my van that I can show you, but I'll tell you the story first. After that, you can decide if it's worthy of your efforts. In exchange, I need a little sleuthing done. Something that you're pretty good at, as I recall."

"Okay, shoot," he said.

I told him about the doorstops, the gold, the lead and the gold, the clues about the Spanish gold treasure, leaving out the location, and about Karen and me taking a year to travel. I touched on my trip to Baja while she came here to set up a business, her disappearing, my meeting with Julie and the revelation that she was apparently the unidentified person in the car that blew up right where my van was currently parked. Murphy soaked it all up for about three minutes, and then emitted a low whistle.

"Okay, I confess, that's a helluva story," Murphy said. "Why haven't you gone to the cops with all of this?"

"I am, from what I've picked up, a 'person of interest' regarding the whereabouts of Karen. She came into town over a month ago, filed for a business license, opened a bank account and dropped out of sight. They apparently haven't put two and two together regarding the body in the blast, and they want to talk to me. And my story to the cops would be that Karen and I know where ten million bucks in gold is, the Greek mob wants it, and she's missing? They would toss me in jail and throw away the key."

Mick smiled. "Good point. So if I get the exclusive on this cockamamie story, what do I have to give in return?"

"I just need you to scout around a bit, figure out whom and how many are looking for me, names, where they might be found and so on. I just have to stay a step ahead of them, or they are gonna try and make me dead."

"I suppose I can do a little checking around," Mick said, a little apprehensively. "Where will I find you?"

"Buy a grouper sandwich at The Fishwagon on Wednesday afternoon. I'll drop by and help you eat it again."

Then I remembered something I always wanted to ask him. "Hey Mick. You and Karen have the same last name. Are you related?" he laughed. "Boston has a full page of Murphys. In Dublin the Murphys have their own phone book. We might be related, but it could be from a thousand years ago."

"Ok. Just curious. Anyway, looks like the coast is clear. Let's go over to the van, and I'll show you some proof for your story."

We had only taken about three steps in that direction when the van exploded in a huge ball of flame. The blast blew a hole into the level below, and knocked Mick and I up against the elevator door. Thirty feet closer and we might not have survived. As it was, I was nearly deaf for the moment, and Mick was bleeding from his nose and one ear. As soon as I came to my senses, I helped him to his feet. "Need any more proof? I think we need to get the fuck out of here now," I said. He was disoriented, and I led him to the stairwell and down the steps to street level. I had no doubt the elevator was dead from the blast. We walked across the street to Finnegan's Wake, which had emptied after the blast and had all of its north-facing windows blown out, and into the men's room to clean up a bit. I helped Mick wash his face, and gather his composure. "Let's get out of the area," I said. "Gonna be a lot of company in the neighborhood soon."

"I have a better idea," Mick said, still a little disoriented. He pointed south. "You go this way, and I'll go that way. Hanging around you is way too dangerous." And he wobbled off to the north, past the fire trucks toward Caroline Street and around the corner out of sight. As he suggested, and wisely so, I headed south, away from the melee, going back into my 'street bum' mode. I was for sure in no hurry. Now I was truly homeless. My ID, the gun, the rest of my cash, passport, cell phone – all turned to confetti, scattered over the town in a giant mushroom cloud. I guess it answered my question about anyone knowing I was in town, but posed a lot of other questions, like; How? And Who? I thought I had been doing a respectable job of keeping a low profile. Somebody had figured something out. Maybe my decision to park over Karen's bomb blast sight wasn't too smart. I headed south, past the Old Town Bakery, past the cemetery, and eventually ended up at Higgs Beach. I really didn't know where to go, and didn't know if they actually knew who and where I was, or just figured out what I was driving. For all I knew, they were putting the hit on every street bum on the rock, maybe beneficial for tourism, but very poor odds at getting the right person. I needed to find a better hiding place I guess.

I wandered up the beach and ended up across the street from the salt ponds, the unofficial hobo village of Key West. Buggy, muggy, wet and exposed, it was pretty well the last resort, and that's where I was at the minute. I found an abandoned camp; three pieces of cardboard under a plastic sheet strung over a bush, and laid down to sleep. Dozing in the humid air, I subliminally heard footsteps crunching the seashells on the path. It was very dark, and I kept quiet, hoping they would pass by me. The footsteps stopped in front of me. I opened my eyes and was looking down the barrel of my .45 All I could see in the dark behind the gun barrel was someone smiling. I heard a click then - BOOM! The rolling thunder sat me straight up in a cold sweat. Nobody was around. Another dream. Then I heard the rain start a short distance away, and seconds later it was pouring. No shelter, no place to go.

# Rio Rio

I was getting close to bottom, and I couldn't see any way back up. I sat there in the mud until daylight, soaking wet, tired and hungry. I still had a little cash, so I walked up to Dion's Quickmart and traded a few soggy dollar bills for a large coffee and a box of sugar donuts, then back down to Higgs Beach. The major downside to playing a street bum is that you couldn't stay very clean. I had no house, used public toilets, and showers were a luxury I had a rare opportunity to enjoy. The beach was my solace. I could drop the disguise and take a swim on South Beach, no different than the average tourist. Almost nobody that lives in Key West actually goes to South Beach, so the chance that someone might see me out of my disguise is unlikely. I hung my soaking wet army coat on a tree branch, slipped out of my baggy pants and strolled out to the water in trunks, a floppy hat and Blu-blockers. I waded back out to the nearly deserted beach, plopped myself down and had breakfast. I glanced to the person to my left. Attractive, slender woman in a Jamie Lee Curtis sort of way, short grey-streaked hair, short like it was growing back from chemo kind of hair. She was hunched over, smoking a cigarette and pondering life through sunglasses, peering at distant shrimp boats as they cruised the edge of the reef. She was only wearing a tattered pair of shorts, decorated with more air than denim. Beaches here are illegal to go topless, so I admired her bravery. Key West's finest could cruise by at any moment and offer a ticket or an arrest. I could tell by her attitude she genuinely didn't care what they, or for that matter, anyone else cared.

I munched donuts and glanced at her out of the corner of my eye. She got up off the sand, dropped her cigarette, and walked toward the water. My eyebrows rose as I couldn't see any hint of tits. Now I wasn't sure. Boy, girl, none of the above? It's Key West and genders often blur. He/she/it slipped into the water and swam out into the calm ocean. I finished my nutrition and wanted to get back in the water too, but it was awkward. I just sat there, and watched, wondering.

Eventually, the mystery person came back out of the water and walked straight toward me. I appeared to not pay attention, but my curiosity was killing me. Glancing out of the corner of my eye I could see the entire chest was covered with a very elaborate tattoo. The person picked up a towel and cigarettes and walked over to me. "May I?" she said with a distinctive French accent. "Free beach, cop a squat," I responded. Then it came to me. This was a woman - bilateral mastectomy, scarred chest, and a vivid and apparently fresh Tree of Life tattoo covering it. She sat on the sand in front of me, legs crossed and lit a huge joint. The crotch on the torn cutoffs was open to the breeze, exposing a tawny tuft of pubic hair. Sunglasses or not, it was obvious that I was looking at her body. Couldn't help it. "Bric," I answered and stuck out my hand. She took it and shook with a lumberjack handshake "Rio-Rio. I'm bored, and I'm lonely. My options for conversation appear to be limited this morning." Uncomfortable silence.

"Thanks for noticing me. Nice tat," I finally offered.

"Thanks. Took three weeks up in Miami to get it done. I put it on the second the scars were more or less healed. The only good thing is that my chest is totally numb. Couldn't feel a thing."

"Ah, I wasn't aware this is a topless beach," still trying to find something intelligent to say.

"The law says that women cannot expose their breasts or pubic area. I'm not exposing my breasts. I don't have any. I've already gone through that with the local *Gendarme,* and they have decided it's not worth fighting me."

"How long ago?" She knew I wasn't asking about the cops.

"Diagnosed six months ago. Lump on one side and a bad family history made the decision for me. I decided not to do reconstructive. I was married a long time ago, had two kids. Divorced in 2000. Kids are gone, and I don't know where now. My ex was on the 97th floor of the World Trade Center on nine-eleven." She sat quietly for a few moments. "Then a few months ago the playbook of practical jokes opened to my page. I had a follow-up Pet-Scan, and I lit up like a Christmas tree. Spot on a lung, spot on the liver, couple on my colon. First, second, third and fourth opinions vary on a long-term survival rate of between two years and don't buy green bananas. So I cashed in my life insurance and moved to Key West." She lit another cigarette, took a deep drag and sat silent again, staring at the ocean. I thought for a moment the conversation was over. "Okay, I told you my story, or at least part of it. Let's hear your tragedy." I mulled over how much, or how little, I could share. I decided that a topless French ex-pat wouldn't likely be a stoolie for the Greek Mafia. Still, no need to be too elaborate. "Ex-Navy, widower, two kids, grown and gone. Treasure diver, found treasure, lost treasure, found again, lost again. It's like roulette; wherever the little ball stops this time determines your fate and your fare. This time it hit the double zeros. And, I recently found out my girlfriend passed away while I was out of town." She took another long pull from her cigarette. "So now you sit on this beach feeling sorry for yourself?" she asked. (I thought to myself, well, there's the pot calling the kettle black) "I guess, sort of. Maybe just bottomed out last night when I slept on wet cardboard in a rainstorm. I'll have to pull it together, and figure out the rest of my life. Not like I don't know how to work, but you get in a rut sometimes."

"You broke?" Rio asked.

"Not that bad, but it's got to last until I can create cash-flow. I can eat, but can't afford the luxury of accommodations. My van with the rest of my worldly possessions just blew up."

"Oh, the parking garage. That's unfortunate." Rio paused again and lit a third cigarette with the butt of the second. I thought to myself, at that rate lung cancer might get her before the diagnosed one does. She seemed to be thinking something over. "I've got a place you can stay for a week or two. Nothing special, but it's a roof, and nobody to bug you. One mattress. I'll share it, but it's not an invitation. Help me buy and cook food, and I need a little help with some maintenance." She kept smoking and stopped talking. One thing for sure, she sure wouldn't yak my head off. "C'mon, let's go," she said. "I'll need that maintenance thing sooner than later." Rio flicked the butt into the sand, got up, pulled on a loose tank top and headed toward the parking lot, not even waiting to see if I followed. I jumped up, trying to pull on my pants and tee shirt while following, and grabbed the jacket as I walked by. I couldn't imagine what she had for transportation, but she stepped onto a fairly new Vespa scooter and kicked it to life. A fresh cigarette hanging from her mouth, she barely waited till I was halfway on and she twisted the throttle to the stop. Off we went like a herd of turtles, more weight than the little scooter was actually made for, but she only knew one throttle setting – wide fucking open – so we were shortly going faster than I think I have ever been on the island. First stop- Home Depot on Roosevelt and into the paint supplies. She grabbed three tubes of waterproof stop-leak caulking and a caulking gun, cashed out, handed me the bag, and it was Mister Toad's Wild Ride a half block back down Roosevelt. I was more than surprised when she slowed and turned right on Hilton Haven Drive. After Bo gave very clear instructions that I was to stay away from the compound, we were headed right for it. Rio slalomed through the trash cans and trees, past Bo's place and my old houseboat, now vacant. She pulled to a stop by a dock, stopped, parked and locked the scooter, and walked down the dock to a little inflatable Zodiac. Oh Jesus, were heading for a live-aboard boat. Well, could be worse. I've come full circle in two years. I trotted behind her with the bag of caulking and climbed on board. Her boating style was like the driving style, and she had the boat untied, and the little four and a half horsepower motor cranked and in gear before I had one foot in the boat. Full throttle and a spin-around and I rather ungracefully sat down in the front.

"Who taught you to drive?" I shouted in the wind.  "My father.  He was a French motocross star.  My life has always been some sort of race." And for the first time she smiled a bit, probably from a memory.  That smile changed her.  Look beyond the hair and the scars, and there was an exceptionally pretty but very, very sad person.

I was half-afraid that she was heading for my old derelict house out in front of Bo's place, but she bent to the left, around the small islands that bracket that end of Key West, and approached a decent sized old 'real' houseboat, the kind that were popular in the sixties.  Fiberglass body, windows on the side, ladder to the roof.
It could be worse.  Rio slowed and chopped the motor so we could drift up to the ladder at the stern; I stepped aboard and tied the bow off, then climbed up to the cabin.  Rio followed and immediately pulled the tank top back off. "Too freaking warm out here for clothes," she said.  I followed by stripping back down to my boxers, which looked close enough like swim trunks to pass muster.

"Ah, I assume, based on the items you just bought that your 'maintenance' issue is a leak?"

"That's correct.  Not too terrible but getting worse every day. I don't have any way to charge the bilge pump battery so I can't stay gone more than a few hours.  I have to go down right now and start hand pumping." "Do you have a dive mask hanging around?" I asked.  She pointed to a tired, black Voit swim mask with a half rotted strap hanging on a cup hook.  Well, I've used worse.  "Any idea where the leak is?" I asked.  She opened the hatch to the bilge.  "Let me pump it out now and you can see where it's coming from.  I think it's just a crack in the fiberglass.  I don't know if you can fix it or not, but I'd appreciate the try."  I started to pull off my boxers and then hesitated. "Rio, it's just us

72

chickens out here. I don't want to hang around in soggy boxers all afternoon. If you don't object, I'm going to take these off too."

"Suit yourself," she shrugged. "I doubt there's any equipment down there I haven't seen before. Anyway, I don't wear anything either, when I'm on the boat by myself." She looked at me, puzzled. "You have just a little too much politeness and culture for someone that has just bottomed out. I don't think I've heard all of your story." She stared at me again for a moment as I didn't answer, and then shrugged. "I guess none of my business. At least for now. I'm a pretty decent judge of character, and I don't think you're a murder or serial rapist or something like that. Maybe we talk later?"

"Maybe," I said, and then shut up. Rio stepped down into the hull and started working the little hand-crank bilge pump. There was maybe five gallons in the bottom from what I could see, not too much. I questioned, "how long since you last pumped?" She thought for a second and replied. "Maybe three hours ago," and kept turning the crank. When she got most of it out, I threw her an old towel, and she mopped the bottom of the hull. "There," she pointed, and I could see a little stream of water bubbling up just to one side of the keel. I grunted in satisfaction and went topside with the mask. I sat on the side of the houseboat and rolled backwards into the water. It was shallow, maybe only eight or nine feet under the boat. The water was normal keys crystal clear, and the usual gang of grunts, sergeant majors, small mangrove snappers and even one pretty angelfish, were using the houseboat as a shelter. Anything down here that floats almost instantly becomes a part of the food chain. Tiny fish hide under it, small fish eat the tiny fish, and medium fish eat the small fish and so on. In open seas, the food chain extends to the topline predators. The first boat to find a big piece of floating canvas, an old palette, even the lid from an ice chest out in the Florida Straits between the Keys and Cuba, and you will undoubtedly score – dolphin (dorado, mahi mahi, not Flipper), sailfish, sharks, maybe the occasional marlin will be working the food chain hanging around that junk. It's the same with a raft of seaweed, but the more solid stuff seems to concentrate the population. Here in the bay, the food chain is smaller and stops with maybe the occasional juvenile barracuda.

I took a deep breath and slid under the hull of the houseboat. I was a little out of practice, but I'm normally good for a minute underwater. The worn-out mask, along with a half week of unshaven beard meant my time under might be more limited by my face filling up than my ability to hold my breath. For that matter I could probably do without a mask, but my underwater vision is only so-so and I did need to hit a fairly small spot. It took me three return trips to the surface, twice for breath, and one to ask Rio if she had a scraper, putty knife or some such. She leaned over the side with an old flat-blade butter knife. "All I can offer," she smiled. I bent the blade into an "L" shape and returned to the bottom, scraping away the accumulated algae and old paint, to the huge delight of the little yellowtail grunts and baby mangrove snapper. The damage was evident; the victim of some shore landing long ago that encountered a sharp rock. After about ten minutes, returning to the surface for an occasional breath, I had the area pretty clean. I went back up one more time. "Cut the tip off one of those cartridges, poke something down the hole to open the gunk and load it in the calking gun," I instructed. You could tell she knew her way around tools, and accomplished the task with no further direction. "Here," and she handed the calking gun down to me. Back under the boat, gun in one hand and a butter knife in the other, and used the whole tube on the bottom of the boat, pushing in the black goop. I covered a square foot of boat bottom to help plug a leak that was maybe two inches long. Back to the surface. "Go check and tell me what you think," I shouted. She disappeared from view and came back a moment later. "I think maybe you got it!" she smiled again. When Rio smiled, a whole other person emerged, maybe the Rio before the cancer, before nine-eleven, a happier time for her.

"Throw me a bar of soap," I asked. "I've got this black shit all over my hands."

"Here," and she tossed a bottle to me. "Sailor soap. Not the greatest stuff but it's non-toxic to sea life, organic and bio-

74

degradable. That's my bathtub too sometimes." I squeezed a little onto my hands and worked up lather. Waterproof roof caulking is, (duh) designed to be waterproof, so it took a lot of scrubbing to get my hands fairly clean. I finally used an old trick and dropped to the bottom, scrubbing my hands cleaner with sand than with the soap. As clean as I thought I could get, I climbed back up the ladder into the houseboat, and she threw me a towel.

"Thank you so much. I'm not confined to short times off the boat now."

"Welcome," I replied and I dried off. "I don't know how long it will last. Maybe a while if you don't try to go anyplace, but if you got moving it would probably just peel off." She laughed. "That won't happen. The motor is dead, dead, dead. This barge was towed here by someone else and abandoned. When I found it there was three feet of water in the hull, and it was maybe two days away from sinking. Cranked my ass off for a week to get it dry. This is the last anchorage for the SS Titless." I chuckled and then put my boxers back on. I'm a closet nudist, but with just me and her on the boat, it felt more than awkward to me. Apparently it didn't to her as she never wore a shirt on the boat again. Her life on the houseboat was a lot like mine when I was on that old abandoned cabin cruiser with Brody and Grace Alice. It seemed such a long time ago, but it was only about two years. No ice, no hot food, unless you brought it with you, no toilet facilities. Actually compared to what we were living in, this was a palace. Big sundeck on the roof, lots of enclosed space with windows that closed. Not the Ritz, but survivable, and that's all I wanted to do for the moment.

Survive.

It had been a crazy few days, and this was the first time in a while that I felt at least a little secure. I flaked out on a bench and took a snooze. I briefly heard the little motor on the Zodiac fire up but didn't really pay attention. I woke up about dusk to the sound of an approaching boat motor. Rio was returning from shore in the Zodiac, I walked to the stern and caught the line when she threw it to me, and then handed me a couple of bags. "Celebration of my liberation!" she called out. "I'm not a prisoner to a leaky boat, thanks to you." One bag had a box of Kentucky Fried Chicken; the other had a small bag of ice, and a bottle of cheap vodka and a can of grapefruit juice. "They were out of Dom?" I asked. "Oh, they had plenty, but I prefer the good stuff!" and she smiled again. She wasn't on the boat for a minute before her clothes came back off. She leaned over the side with the bottle of sailors soap and sudsed up the clothes, and then rinsed them in a tub of fresh water before hanging them on a makeshift clothesline. She wrapped a towel around her waist, and we ate the chicken and threw the bones overboard, entertained by the snappers that attacked every uneaten morsel.

After dinner, Rio cracked open the vodka and poured it and the grapefruit juice into red Solo cups over ice. We toasted the day and drank silently. She sat cross-legged on the edge of the bed while I sat on a cheap plastic chair. I wasn't aroused, but it was intriguing that she had apparent complete disregard for any modesty. Maybe it was her French heritage; maybe, just maybe she was having a little fun at my expense. Regardless, she was a woman, I was a man, and we were out in the middle of the ocean drinking cheap vodka. Not like I was going to put a move on her, but I could still feel the sexual tension. Hell, I'm still human, and after a year of an intensely active love life with a very inventive woman, it had been weeks since I'd even been kissed.

I guess you don't know what you're missing till you don't have it.

Two vodka drinks later, I was mellowed out, and thankfully it was dark, so I didn't have to concentrate on not staring at her pubic hair. Conversation was inconsequential as she shared a little more about how she got here, and why she came to Key West. "This whole island," Rio reflected, "is a fucking freak show. I figured out that one more freak wouldn't make a difference either way. Problem is I'm over being social anymore. Just waiting to get sick again and die sort of takes the ambition out of you." She lit another cigarette and poured a third drink. I wasn't going anywhere and joined her. I caught a whiff of what she was smoking. She had apparently switched again to the kind that doesn't come in cellophane wrapped boxes.

"Hit?" she squeaked out, handing the joint to me.

"No thanks," I replied, a little sheepishly. "Beer and alcohol are my poisons. Don't do any kind of drugs." Rio shrugged, giggled and took a long pull on the joint, followed by a long pull on the Solo Cup. I would guess that drunk and stoned was a destination for her tonight. "So," she started back up. "You said that MAYBE you would share a little more of your story. I'm giving you a roof over your head, a couple of free beaver shots and my very best vodka. Least you can do is tell me some of your story." Her voice was starting to slur, "jus wan you to know, ain't no invitation to my body if you're getting any ideas. Thas not what this is bout."

"Not to worry, ma'am," I assured her. "I'm a gentleman and respect boundaries." I was silent for a moment, and then came to a decision. "Okay, might as well share this with someone. I don't know if I'll live out the month anyway." so I told Rio about the wreck, the bricks, the kids, the houseboat (I could almost see it from here), the trip to Tampa, Karen, traveling around the world, her coming back to the Rock, me going racing in the dessert, Karen vanishing, me coming to Key West undercover, Julie, hearing she had been killed. The attempt on my life yesterday. I left out the details about the gold. Seems like everyone that learns about it shits their brain or dies.

"Wow!" I could tell that sobered her up a bit. "And I thought my story was something. Imagine, the odds that your car blew up in the same spot that your girlfriend got killed?"

Okay, maybe she was still drunk at little.

"It wasn't a coincidence, Rio," I explained. "I parked there to be close to her. Despite all the work I did to change my identity, be underground and stay invisible, somebody figured out what I was driving and blew it up. They could have as easily killed me. I think they just wanted to scare me."

"What do they want? Why did they kill your girlfriend? Who 'da fuck did you piss off anyway?" She asked.

"Some Greeks," I replied, "they thought I stole something, but I didn't, and won't seem to take no for an answer. At this point I think it's more pride than money, but I don't honestly know."

"Why don't you go to the cops?" She queried.

"With that story?" I answered, "people I don't know want to kill me for something I don't have. Next thing I know they will be asking me about Karen's disappearance. I barely dodged a murder rap a little over a year ago based on circumstantial evidence. Don't think for a second that I wouldn't become a person of interest again in an instant." I took another drink. "Nope, I have to deal with this myself, at least for now. This morning, before I met you, I was out of ideas. At least you bought me a little time."

I heard liquid pouring over ice cubes in the darkness. "Glad ta hep," she was slurring again. We sat in silence for quite a while, both looking inwardly at our respective lives, both wondering what the next day would bring. For me, that's what it would be for now, one day at a time.

"I'm trashed," the voice in the darkness announced. "I get the left side of the bed, you get the right. Remember no funny stuff, and I sleep light."

"I'll save you the concern, Rio. It's a beautiful starlit night. Think I'll climb up on the roof and get a moon burn if it's all the same to you."

"Suit y'self," I could hear the hiss of the joint as it hit the water and then silence. I climbed up on the top deck, dropped a large beach towel on the floor and lay down. Since my Navy days, I've always been able to sleep about anywhere, as long as I'm on a boat. Sit me in a chair, prop me in a corner, hang from a hammock, sit on a beach with an air tank for a pillow, I'm good to go. I fell asleep in seconds. Dreamless, wonderful, peaceful sleep. Then it started raining. Typical Key West rainstorm. Goes from nothing to a friggin downpour in seconds. I don't mind wet, but not when I can avoid it. Well, she did invite me to share the bunk, so I climbed down the ladder, slipped out of my wet shorts and tee shirt, dried off and came to the bed.

"Rio? It's raining. Is the bed offer still good?" She

mumbled, and rolled to the left. I crawled onto the bed, lying on top of the covers, took a little slice off the right edge, and fell back asleep. It was sometime later in the evening that I felt the arm around me, and her nude body spooned up. I didn't know whether or not it was an invitation, but it felt good, and I drifted back to sleep.

I woke at dawn, and she was still sound asleep, now facing away from me on her side. I slipped over the side and took a swim in the crystal clear water, a little cooler this morning after the rain, then up on the sundeck to dry off and get some natural vitamin D. An hour later, she came up on the deck, put another towel down and lay down next to me. She didn't talk, and I didn't break the silence. Nothing was said about the night before. After a while, she spoke.

"Going to town. Want to come?"

"Maybe this afternoon," I answered. "But if I give you some money could you do me a favor?"

"Sure, what do you need?" she replied.

"A new 'me'. Cheap shorts, tee shirt, flip flops, big floppy hat, and cheap sunglasses. K-Mart should have what I need. I want to look like a tourist. The hobo thing didn't appear to fool them very well. Ah, make it a long sleeve tee shirt. This tattoo can't be visible." She traced her finger around the Eagle and Trident. "What does it signify?" she asked. "Nothing. Not a damn fucking thing anymore," I responded. "And better for you and me both that you never saw it."

She shrugged again, got up and went back down to the cabin. I gave her some of my precious cash for clothes, gave her my sizes, and added some more dollars for groceries. She got dressed and motored away. Safe or not, hiding on a boat in the bay is not my thing. I was about a third stir crazy by the time she got back in the early afternoon. She threw me a K-Mart bag with hardly a word and walked past me to the front of the houseboat. Sheesh this roomie can be moody. I changed into the new clothes, felt my week old growth of beard and decided to leave it. I needed to look like somebody else. Nothing like a little facial hair to help the disguise.

"Borrow your Zodiac?" I asked toward the front of the boat.

"Yeah, sure, whatever, but not the scooter," was the response. And then silence. I shrugged and climbed into the Zodiac. I couldn't afford to put Bo in jeopardy by walking past his Hilton Haven compound, so I motored to the right, into the entrance to Key West Bight and to the far corner by the Visitors Center, then ducked under the little bridge to the small lagoon and landed the boat in the trees. I tied the Zodiac to the bushes and headed down Virginia Street past the tennis courts and ball field toward Old Town. I walked by a news rack and dug in my pocket for fifty cents. The Citizen had a huge front page headline.

## SECOND BOMB BLAST AT CITY LOT

Lots of details. Structure was damaged so bad this time it may have to be demolished. Finnegan's Wake would be closed till further notice and Pepe's caught a complete wheel and axel assembly through the roof. Other collateral damage to various houses and businesses filled out the first four pages. On the Key West Crime Report column was one interesting report of two street bums that were allegedly picked up off the street by some people in a black SUV posing themselves as cops, questioned and released. Hmm. There truly wasn't much I could do, but the walk did me good and I didn't have to wobble around like a street bum. I didn't know how long I could get away with this change in disguise, but it probably bought me at least a few days. I figured I would walk up Duval to Front, right to the Galleon and then past the Charter Boats, and back to the Zodiac, avoiding the city parking lot and all the cops. I didn't dare actually stop anywhere and give any of the servers a good look, but it felt nice to at least get out and around a bit. I glanced toward the Key Lime Pie store, and my mouth watered at the thought of a chocolate covered key lime pie on a stick, but didn't doubt for a second that Kermit, the owner would recognize his number one customer, even if it had been more than a year since I stepped foot there.

# Fresh Old Face

I walked past Kermit's, by the old Ice House that now serves as an occasional recording studio for Jimmy Buffett, and noticed someone looking at me. I averted my vision with the cheap sunglasses, but this person was definitely checking me out. He was about as conspicuous as a nun in a whore house. In a town where socks are considered semi-formal, this jerk was wearing a frigging three piece Armani suit, white shirt with French cuffs, a red striped power tie and genuine Foster Grant Percussion Sunglasses. Beard trimmed to beyond neat. Shoes polished to a mirror. I kept walking with the intent of just blowing right by him and staying on populated streets as I beat it back to the Zodiac. As I got close, he stepped into my path and reached in his pocket. I was sure I was a dead man, right then and there, but thought maybe if I just did an all-out assault, maybe take out a knee, break his nose, maybe a spin-kick to the side of his head, I could run off and evade his friends in the melee. I decided for the nose. I feinted to the right, then came right at his face with the flat of my hand – and he wasn't there. One person in a thousand would have been able to avoid that no-look, no warning takedown, and this guy didn't even flinch. I spun to face him, feet spread, hands at ready. I wouldn't miss him a second time.

"Wanna try for two out of three?" he asked. Then smiled and took his glasses off. It had been years, decades, but that voice was unmistakable. Tim Heminger was a Navy chum that tried to make the Seals, but DOR'd (Dropped on Request) only a few weeks into the program. Said the Seals wasn't for soldiers, it was for maniacs. I only saw him once after that, when a politician's wife was in town, and he looked me up to say hi while he was helping the Secret Service check into some bad types. I guessed at the time CIA but never actually knew. Right now I was totally confused. I was pretty sure he made eye contact and stepped in front of me. Was he working for the Greeks now? All this went through my head in a flash. I couldn't think of anything smart to say, so I responded to his question.

"Good with that but the winner has to dispose of the body parts."

"Perhaps another time," he responded. "What say we go someplace for a cold beverage and a chat. Suggestions?"

"Hmm. Let's go to Smokin Tuna. Only a few blocks away and I don't think I would be recognized, especially at a corner spot at the bar. Hard to explain, but I'm kind of keeping a low profile."

"Oh, no need to explain," He responded, with a smile. "I'm well aware of your adventure. I might even be able to help you a little." He motioned with his hand, "lead on. I'll tag a few paces behind and keep an eye out for the Martians." He lifted the edge of his jacked and exposed a shoulder holster. "HK USP Tactical .40 Cal," he explained, " just to make sure everyone plays nice."

Smokin Tuna is located off Duval sort of behind the Bull. It's a cool place, and off the beaten path enough to stay under the radar. It was mid-afternoon and the place was quiet. I walked to the far end of the bar and climbed up on a stool in the darkish corner with a good view of the main entrance and the back alley. Tim took the stool next to me. After last night's vodka parade, I opted for club soda with lemon. Tim ordered a Jameson on the rocks, and we silently toasted old times. I kept quiet, figuring it was his dime to talk. Tim checked his smartphone a few times, responded to some sort of message and went back to his drink. After a few quiet minutes, which I finally decided was being used to make sure we hadn't attracted any attention, he turned to me.

"So, pretty interesting few days, from what I gather." He finally said in a low voice.

"Sure has been," and I stopped talking. I could have talked but was intrigued. How the fuck did he know how interesting my days had been, and exactly how much did he know?

Tim continued, "you seem to have run afoul of some pretty ugly characters."

"No shit."

"The government, my, ah, 'division' of the government, caught wind of some characters coming into the US illegally over the Canadian border with false documents. We didn't think they were terrorists, so we let them by and tailed them. Vancouver to LA, then by train all the way to Miami, where someone gave them the keys to a stolen mini-van. They come to Key West, and start snooping around. My people down here report that one of the two people they are asking about is one Russell Bricklin Wahl." He slapped me on my back. "Well, shut my mouth, my old didn't-drop-out Navy Seal bad-ass commando buddy. The other POI is Karen Murphy, nobody I knew till we checked her out and found out the last time she was in town, she was your main squeeze."

He motioned for another beverage. "Okay, I told you what I know, now you tell me what I don't know. Why are these guys so anxious to chat with you? Ed McMahon gives them a check to deliver and you didn't leave your forwarding address?"

I'm starting to get tired of explaining parts of this story. I thought I'd fish a little before I spilled the beans.

"Hell, Tim, you know everything else about me, my underwear size, what my farts smell like, and you don't know the gold story?"

He looked genuinely surprised. "We know you came into some cash a year ago. We know Karen opened a fairly fat bank account in Key West recently that hasn't seen any activity for weeks. So you found some treasure?" he asked.

"Well, yes, no and yes," I replied. I went on to tell him about the lead bars that were filled with gold that I was able to convert to cash. He didn't ask how, and I didn't offer. I thought for a minute and decided to tell him about the mother lode. He pulled a pad and pen out of his coat pocket.

"My ex-boss, Harry Sykas had a salvage claim on a Spanish wreck that sunk about forty five miles from here. He paid me to first find it, which I did, and then I was in charge of the salvage. We found a lot of silver, both coins and bars, but very little gold. That was sort of puzzling. You see, this ship was a salvage vessel that had taken the treasure off a Spanish ship that sunk up near Islamorada in 1733. We had the manifest on this ship and there was maybe more gold on that ship that had ever been hauled to Spain at one time. After we were done and had most of the treasure recovered, we just figured that the gold was taken by another vessel."

"But it wasn't," interrupted Tim.

"Right or at least I think so." I told him about the cannon that I found the gold plated lead ingots under that had been hauled to Harry's warehouse in Tarpon Springs. I had never seen it cleaned up until Tack Morgan showed me some pictures.

"We suspected the survivors of the salvage ship wreck dragged this eight-pound gun to shore and used it as a marker to point at where the ship had sunk so they could go back and recover the treasure after being rescued. They had even gone so far as to draw an arrow on top of the gun. What I didn't see was the arrow had a point on both ends. When I saw that photograph, I suspected whatever treasure they brought on shore with them on Boca Grande, had been buried someplace in the opposite direction of the wreck."

"And you found it?" he asked.

"Sort of, maybe." I related that I had contacted Harry and told him if he helped me with equipment, and the use of his salvage license, I would split the treasure with him sixty-forty, with me getting the sixty.

"He grudgingly agreed to the deal and spotted me some good metal detector equipment. Karen and I went to Boca Grande over a couple of days and got a huge mag hit on the detector. Then we got caught by the Fish and Wildlife for digging in a wildlife protected area, and arrested. When I got out, I told Harry the place was hot and that I was going to wait a year or so before sneaking back and digging again."

"And you never did?"

"It was in our short-term plans to recover the gold when we moved back to open our store. I guess Harry got impatient and decided to put some pressure on us, and get his hoodlum mob family involved. Harry doesn't have a clue where the gold is, only Karen and me. It appears they are putting on a full-court press at this point. Now Karen's dead and I probably will be soon, all over a treasure we don't even know for sure is there, or how much." I put my head in my hands. "I wish I had never mentioned it to Harry. I actually wish I never knew it existed."

"How much gold?"

I had to think a bit. "It's been a while since I calculated. The manifest said fifty gold bars and we found one. The weight of bars on Spanish Galleons back in those days ranged between two and three pounds, so let's say 40 bars at two and a half pounds each, ah, hundred and twenty five pounds or so. Round it off to three million face value, and say, ah, ten times that much historical value."

"Wow, his share's worth twelve million? Nothing to sneeze at," Tim looked surprised.

"Yeah, and it appears he wants my part too, and has no problem knocking off as many people as needed to get it."

Tim made more notes for a few more minutes, then closed the pad and put it and the pencil back in his coat pocket. He motioned the bartender for a third Jameson and pointed at my glass too. Then he looked up at me.

"That fills in the blanks," he reasoned. "We thought something like that was going on but not a clue what. These hoods that crossed into the U.S. have been on our scope for quite a while. Professional killers, dope dealers, guns for hire. They are here to find information, get what they are after and then hide the bodies if you get my drift." Tim took a sip from his glass, and seemed to come to a decision.

"I 'm sure we can help you. I don't want to sound cryptic, but I have a need for some of your talent, in exchange for assistance from my group. I need you to come to Miami in a few days where you can hear the proposal. If the answer is no, then we can go our separate ways, but I can tell you that you are in mortal danger right now. *Capeche?*"

I thought; what have I got to lose? "Ok, I'll play the game. I don't have enough cash to get to Miami, and no ID to get on an airplane. It's a long walk."

Tim's direction made no frigging sense at all. "Keep growing that facial hair. Trim it into a mustache and goatee, and comb a little Grecian Formula into them so there's not too much grey. Buy a one-way Greyhound ticket on the morning bus to Miami three days from today. When the bus stops at the Burger King in Islamorada, I'll meet you there." He gave me a wad of bills, paid the tab and got up. He shook my hand and turned as he started to walk out.

"In the meantime, I suggest you hide under a rock and pull the dirt in around you." And he walked out the back alley, around the corner and out of sight.

I finished the last of my club soda and walked in the same direction, toward the corner. There's a big souvenir store on the corner, and I tweaked up my tourist look with a flowered Hawaiian shirt, puka shell necklace and Panama hat. From thirty feet you might think gay, you might not and that was the plan for the disguise. Suddenly cash-flush again, I opted for a cab to take me to Dion's, where I picked up a six pack of Honey Browns, more ice, bottled water and another box of chicken. As an afterthought I picked up a carton of Marlboros. I paid the cab, walked down to the little Zodiac and motored back out to the houseboat in the dusk. Rio was sitting on the roof deck, smoking a cigarette and hardly looked up when I pulled in. I left the cigarettes on the counter and dropped five of the Honey Browns into the ice chest with the bag of ice and went up the ladder to the sundeck. She had her back to me and appeared to be rather indifferent to my arrival.

"Care for a beer?" I asked, offering the bottle toward her. Without looking, she held her hand up over her head, and I handed the beer to her. I slid back down the ladder, got a replacement and returned, sitting on the towel I had put there this morning. We sat and drank in silence for a few minutes. I finally broke the silence.

"I'm leaving in three days," I said. "Ran into an old friend that offered me a short term job."

"Tee-tee-rific," she answered. "Goody for you." She still had her back to me.

I wasn't sure what to say. "Look, if you need to be left alone, go ahead and give me a ride back to shore. I can manage," I finally suggested.

"No. Stay." She tossed her cigarette over the side and spun around, still cross legged and faced me. "I'm sorry. That was the vodka last night. I had no business touching you. It's just been so long…" and tears welled up in her eyes. "I don't know if anyone will ever want me again." And she turned back around, head in her hands.

I sat silently for a while longer. "Look, Rio, don't even say that. You are a beautiful person, inside and out. I've seen several different parts of you in the last few days. Your smile is amazing. Your will and determination through a terrible time make you a strong person. Sitting out here by yourself day after day will guarantee you will be alone. Is that what you want? Now who's feeling sorry for their self?"

I got up, and walked around in front of her and sat back down. "Go live a little. Enjoy what you can with the time you have left. Hell, I might be dead in three days. Who knows? But if I go, it won't be with a whimper." I took her by both hands. "C'mon. We have four more beers on ice, and a bucket of cluck to eat. Life could be worse." I got up, pulled her to her feet, and we went below.

"Sabine," she said after starting her first beer.

"Scuse me?"

"My real name. Sabine. I thought you should know."

"Nice to meet you, Sabine. Russell Bricklin Wahl," and I shook her hand solemnly. "It's a pleasure to make your acquaintance."

That night and the next two nights were much like the first. She drank, toked and passed out on her bed. With no rain in the sky, I opted for my rooftop retreat under the stars. I could have crawled into that bed, and might have even made love, but I wasn't comfortable taking advantage of her state of mind. I didn't ask – she didn't invite.

# Paradise Lost – And Maybe The Gold

I woke the following morning with an epiphany. "Can I get a ride to shore this morning? I'll hitch a ride back,"

"You can ride with me." she replied, "I'm heading to the beach anyway." We motored to shore and I got on the Vespa with her. "Just take me to Sears Town," I told her. Thankfully, this person of few words didn't ask many questions which was a good thing as I didn't know how quickly I could make a story up. She dropped me off in front of the Wendy's and rode off without a wave. I went in for a soda, then walked out to North Roosevelt and stuck out my thumb. Yeah, it wasn't hiding under a rock, but sometimes you got to walk on the wild side a bit. Hitchhiking in the Lower Keys can be a crapshoot. You might get picked up in five minutes and it might take five hours. This time, it took just thirty. A big black Ford Expedition pulls over with windows tinted dark as night. The passenger side back door opened a crack and I jumped in, and then realized what I was in. Holy shit. It was HARRY'S Ford Expedition. Three guys inside, darkish complexion. The guy to my left on the passenger seat looked like a fugitive from a Mad Max movie. Bald, nose bent to one side, scar that went from his forehead over his left eyebrow and down his check. About half the original number of assigned teeth. The guy behind the wheel looked like he might need a phonebook to sit on, but he also looked very mean. On the right seat was a tall, hawk-faced looking character with wire rimmed glasses. He looked like an accountant. We drove off, and I was a dead man. Then skinny turned to me, with a little smile.

"Where do you go?" he asked in a thick accent.

"Ah, about mile marker ten, señor," my mind was racing. I didn't want them to know where I was going. In my best Spanglish accent I said. "A, ah freend es picking me up at the Circle K and were supposed to go fishing on the bridge at Summerland."

"Do you live here?" Skinny asked, still smiling.

"No, señor. Opa Locka, I live en Opa Locka, near Miami." (Were these guys playing with me or did they actually not know they had the prize in hand?)

Skinny continued, "I ask because my employer is looking for a former member of his staff. He owes this person a substantial amount of money, and is anxious to get the debt paid." (Yeah, in lead, I thought) "His name is Mister Brickwall. He lives in Key West. Do you know such a person?" His smile was starting to annoy me.

"No, señor, I do not know such a person, Brickwall. Like I say, I only here to visit my friend. Do you have a phone number I can take with me? I can ask him and call you if he does."

As we pulled up to the Circle K at Geiger Key Road, the thug at my left pointed down the road and said something to the driver. They both chuckled quietly. I don't know what they said, but skinny silenced them with one word. Then he pulled a card out of his pocket and wrote on the back. "Here is my cell number. I'm happy to pay five hundred dollars if you find this person. We are anxious to go home soon." He handed me the card, still smiling. I briefly flipped it over and almost dropped it. It was Harry Sykas' salvage company card. I nodded and stepped out of the SUV. The door was barely closed when the driver spun a U-turn and headed back down A1A, spraying gravel over two cars gassing up. I walked to the steps of the Circle K and sat down. I wanted to first make sure they weren't coming back and also needed a moment to compose myself. All out hand to hand combat in the back of an SUV would have been ugly, and it would have probably ended in an off road excursion into the mangroves and me without a seatbelt on. It made me shudder.

After ten minutes, I walked across the street and down a few blocks to Emerald Drive. John "Rumpy" Rumpendorfer lived down the street. Rumpy was a long-time fishing buddy, occasional golf pal, and frequent drinking partner back in the good old days. I also loved his boat the *Wave Whacker*, and actually used it to bring home my three gold filled lead bars two years ago. I hadn't spoken to or seen him since I returned his boat motors to him from the Tarpon Springs debacle. His Toyota Forerunner was sitting in the driveway. It was still morning so I would assume he would be smoking a cigarette, drinking coffee and watching CNN. I thought about knocking on the door, but I don't think I had ever used that entrance in the twenty or so years I'd known him, so I walked around back and tapped on the screen. He looked up and didn't recognize me.

"Hello? Can I help you?"

"Yeah," I answered. Got any henways?"

He looked puzzled. "What the fuck's a henway?"

"Bout three pounds if you keep the feathers on." I took off my hat and glasses and threw a smile. Rumpy dropped his cigarette into his lap and spilled coffee as he jumped up. "Bric! Where the Hell have you been? Man the whole fuckin world is lookin for you?"

"Is that the only way anyone says 'hi' to me anymore?" I responded. I opened his sliding door and walked in to a handshake and a big man-hug.

"Whatcha been doin?" he asked. "How long you been in town? How long you stayin? You know people are looking for you. A dude knocked on my door a few weeks ago. Said he owed you money. Hell man, looks like you lost an election bet with Elton John."

I grinned. "Just a little wardrobe change so I can fly beneath
90

the radar. I've been here about a week, leaving day after tomorrow," I answered. "Look friend, it would take me more than that day and a half to tell you all the pieces, and maybe for your own health, it's best I don't fill in every blank. Someday we'll crack a good bottle of Appleton's and I'll tell you some stories, but today I need one huge favor."

"Okay, shoot. What's up?"

"Need you to run me out to Boca Grande. Make it look like a fishing trip, but I need to bring a shovel and some bags."

"Rumpy's eyes narrowed. "Rumor around town is you found some treasure, cashed it in and flew the coop with what's her name, ah Karen. You hide a little extra stash out there?"

"Something like that. These guys that spoke to you. The only thing they want to give me is a bullet in the back of the head. It appears they killed Karen but they didn't find out what they wanted to know, namely what's on Boca Grande. I'm going to go get it and see if I can make them go away. I'm in danger, Rumpy, and if they know I came here, and you helped me, then you will be in danger too. I'll understand if you say no."

Rumpy lit another cigarette, and smoked about half of it without speaking. Then he looked at me.

"Pal, I guess I need to go borrow a shovel from Gunter. I'll be right back."

We loaded the Whacker with enough fishing gear to make it look legit, and put some beverages on ice. Rumpy had a few old gear bags – enough to hold a hundred pounds of gold or so, and off we went, out of the canal. I had done this route once before by myself when he let me borrow the Whacker. Rumpy eased the twenty-six foot twin Suzuki powered *Wave Whacker* out of the canal on Big Coppitt Key and brought the boat up to plane and then aimed for a tiny cut to the right of Half Moon Key. As he got to the thinnest part, Rumpy slowed and tipped the engines up as much as possible to avoid dragging. Clear of that and still cruising at twenty-two knots over water barely knee deep, we cleared past the Harbor Keys and slid around the Ship Channel near the Pier House, then between Wisteria and Sunset Key. The heading was

due west to the south of Man and Woman Keys, toward Boca
Grande.

It was a midday morning, and other than a few private charter
boats heading out to the wall, the route had very little company,
which was just fine to me. It's a big ocean, and the chance that
Fish and Wildlife would be keeping an eye out for me near Boca
Grande after more than a year was unlikely. Regardless, if we saw
someone, we would throw some lines in the water and start
trolling. Despite medium November seas, we made pretty good
time and approached Boca Grande after about an hour. I couldn't
see another boat anywhere, and I pointed to where I wanted
Rumpy to pull in. He throttled down and expertly tilted the twin
outboards up to navigate the skinny water, chopping the motors as
we quietly brushed up on the sand.

"Wait here," I said over my shoulder as I walked away from
shore. "If someone shows up, back off and go fishing. I'll give
you a signal to bring the bags up." I suddenly realized that, after a
year, one bush might look like another and without a metal
detector I might be digging all day, but as I approached the spot,
the area looked familiar, and I was comfortable I could find the
cache. I walked a little faster to the small rise at the top of the
beach, and then stopped.

You could see the spot alright. A shallow hole and a mound
of dirt next to it. My heart fell, and I sunk to my knees in disbelief.

Somebody got there first.

You never accept a diagnosis until you get a second opinion. I
started digging into that hole and got down about three feet till I hit
something different. I got on my belly and brushed away the dirt.
Some hints of rotted wood and part of a hinge lay there, likely the
remains of a chest. I enlarged the hole and found pieces of what
looked like three different wooden containers of some sort. And
that was all. Digging any more was a waste of time. I walked
back down the beach to the Whacker. Rumpy was into his first
boat drink and listening to Bill Hoebee on Sun 99.5 when I got
there.

"I would hazard a guess you're not coming back with good

news?" he observed.

"Cleaned out," I answered, despondent. I handed him the shovel and pushed the *Wave Whacker* off. "Only one other person knew the location. Somebody must have found a way to force her to show them." I shook my head. "None of this makes any sense."

Rumpy brought the *Whacker* up on plane as we headed back toward Key West. I was deep in inner thoughts and almost forgot to have him drop me off at Rio's houseboat. Thankfully, nobody was there so I didn't have to explain being on the boat with a nude tattooed women with no breasts. I was pretty well over explaining at this point. He was polite enough to not question what I was doing there, or how I got to shore, and merely gave me a handshake and a hug as I stepped off.

"Thanks buddy," I called over. "Don't forget to forget I ever came around."

"Not a problem pal. Good luck!"

And without a wave or look back, he throttled up the *Wave Whacker* and headed up the keys.

# Gone Again

That night and the next day, I just sat on the roof of the houseboat, thinking. Nothing made sense at this point. I strongly considered blowing Tim off and not showing up, but there truly wasn't anything keeping me here anymore. A little after dark on my last day in town, I asked Rio to take me over to Garrison Bight and let me off. We had said little to each other since Rumpy dropped me off, but when she pulled up to the dock by the Visitors Center, I stood her up and gave her the best hug I could muster, and a soft kiss on the cheek. I slipped a hundred dollar bill into her shorts without her noticing, and stepped off the boat, walking purposefully toward old town. Without another word, she backed the Zodiac up, flipped it around and headed back to her boat.

I prayed my bad luck didn't follow her.

One last little sojourn before I left the rock.

I hadn't returned since I broke into Julie's house. She seemed to want to help, but after all, she was related to the enemy. Safe beats sorry any day, but I figured I could confront her one more time, and maybe she could shed a little light on what happened to the treasure. It was still early, long before she would get off work. I would make myself at home, maybe even get a good hot shower. Like the last time, I went to the back door. The house was completely dark, and the unlit porch gave excellent cover. I stood at the door and listened for a while. Total silence. I felt for the screen and was surprised to find the screen still off from my earlier intrusion, and the jalousie pane still removed. I reached in and opened the door with a squeak. I was pretty sure nobody was home, so I wasn't too worried. As I walked into the kitchen I could smell something funky. I was dying to flip a light on, but instead just stood there for a while for my eyes to get accustomed to the light. The smell was a sweet rotten smell. I finally gave in and opened the refrigerator. The light illuminated the kitchen enough to show the culprit. What used to be a bowl of fruit was covered in thick green fur, and the ants were having a field day. I saw a palmetto bug scamper across the counter too, and there were rat droppings by the sink. A loaf of bread in the fridge was green and blue too. Nobody had been here for a while. Leaving the refrigerator open for background light I walked through the kitchen to the living room. The window where she threw the gun was still broken. I checked and the front door was unlocked too. I walked into the bedroom, pulled all the shades and turned on a light. Bed was unmade, and a bath towel was lying on the floor. I suspected it was the same one she wore when I was here. Checked the closets and nothing appeared to be out of place. I pulled the drawer open and the Glock was gone. The clothes she wore that night were not laying on the living room floor either. I would guess Julie left, probably the same night I was there, and either in a hurry, or forcibly.

Seems like all I gather are more questions and few answers. Well, nothing else to be learned here, so I closed the house back up, wiped my prints off the door handle with my tee shirt and walked back out to Simonton Street. It was early evening, and I had nothing to do and no place to go before the bus left the airport the next morning. Long walk or short cab ride? Ah, better yet, I went over to Duval and hung out by the butterfly exhibit. Fifteen minutes later the shuttle van for the Doubletree pulled up, and I got in. A few minutes later they deposited me at the front of the Doubletree, and from there, it was only a fifteen minute walk to the airport. Key West Airport isn't open all night, and I didn't want to hang around in a brightly lit place anyway, so I found a quiet wall in the dark at the East Martello Fort, sat down, leaned against the wall and dozed off.

The sunrise hit my face and brought me wide awake. I didn't have a clue what time it was, but I guessed sixish. With the new facial hair, cheap sunglasses and a baseball cap pulled over my eyes, I didn't think anyone would recognize me anyway so I walked over to the airport terminal and leaned up against the building until the Greyhound office opened. A one-way ticket to Miami was forty bucks and I paid cash. The ticket agent was disheveled, disinterested and disengaged. She hardly glanced at me as she gave me my ticket without looking up. When the bus pulled in, I boarded first, walked to the back, sat next to the window, tugged my cap lower and slowly dozed off as I counted the keys, Big Coppitt, Cudjoe, Sugarloaf, Summerland......

My dreams have always been vivid, in color, real or surreal, and sometimes prophetic. The drone of the bus and the slight smell of diesel exhaust exchanged themselves for the underwater sound of a distant boat engine and the rubber tasting flavor of compressed air. I was hanging on a rope, deep down, very cold, and trying to make as few bubbles as possible as that boat motor passed back and forth. I don't scare easily, but I was scared – very scared, and I knew the people in that boat wanted to kill me. Then I heard the motor slow, slower, slower, until it stopped – they saw my bubbles.....

*"ISLAMORADA!"* The bus driver startled me awake to the real world so hard I jumped up and banged my head on the roof. The motor that stopped was the Greyhound's, and the Burger King sign signaled the end of my bus trip. The bus normally sits here about twenty minutes so passengers can pee and get a meal, and everybody steps off to stretch. My ticket was to Miami but I caught the glint of Ray-Ban Mirrors sitting behind the wheel of a 1972 red Ferrari Dino 246 convertible. That had to be my ride. I brushed my cap back and motioned with my finger as I walked around behind the drive-through. The Dino came to life with a deep-throated pipey rumble, and Tim drove behind the building, where I jumped in, more than a little surprised that the seatbelts were a five-point Simpson racing harness. Ten seconds later we were cruising the Overseas Highway at a blinding forty-six miles per hour. "So, why did I buy a ticket to Miami and get off at the Burger King," I asked. "I don't *think* anybody is following, but just safer to leave a cold trail," Tim answered. "When the bus re-boards, they will look around for a few minutes, check the shitter

96

and leave. No biggie."

"So," I continued, "You want to leave a cold trail and we drive off in the most conspicuous car on planet Earth? What's that all about?"

"Just had to dust the old girl off and take a ride," he answered, "I don't get too many chances."

"Yeah, so you pick a road that has no escape routes and a speed limit I can approach on a ten-speed." He ignored that. "I have a room booked at the Mayfair House in Coconut Grove. You can shower there. I've got clothes, luggage and documents waiting for you," he went on. "You fly out of Miami tonight on Virgin Atlantic to Heathrow. Someone will meet you there. I'll fill you in on details at the hotel."

I hate all this cloak and dagger shit, but if he can come through with his side of the deal and get these Greek mob guys off my trail, I'll keep my side, whatever it is, and, if nothing else, at least I'll get a hot shower out of it.

We motored through Tavernier and past Key Largo and Tim eased to the right as we approached the 17 mile stretch to take us through Card Sound. "Gonna stop at Alabama Jacks for some fingers and conch fritters?" I asked, hopefully. "I didn't eat breakfast."

"Nope," he replied. "Just need to clear a little carbon off the cylinders and some cobwebs out of my brain." He flipped open his phone, hit one number and said something softly, then closed it with a smile. "Coast is clear. Sherriff's are all on the stretch and my FHP buddies will politely go blind for a few minutes. Tighten your belts." The little Ferrari didn't have eye popping acceleration, but within a few seconds the phone poles started going by a lot faster. I glanced over to the speedometer and then tried to do the math to convert 225 kilometers per hour. Shit, a buck forty on this little road? Definitely more balls than brains in the left seat, except that I know he had a lot of brains. The hard 90 degree corner came up in a matter of seconds. Tim downshifted, fifth, to third with a scream, to second and then first while he pitched the little car into the left hand turn, then back through the gears to the top of the bridge, (remembering not that long ago when I stopped to change a tire and chocked the wheel with a half million dollars in gold), where I swear we caught air at the top. On the downslope of the bridge, he eased off the throttle and coasted to legal speeds as we approached the toll gate. Tim handed over two bucks with a smile and waived at the Florida Highway Patrol Officer that was parked at Alabama Jacks. He saluted the little Dino as we cruised by at thirty five.

From there, we went through Florida City and Homestead before catching US1 and back into street traffic to Coconut Grove and the Mayfair House. Built thirty years ago with Columbian Cartel drug money, the Mayfair is a design nightmare, a combination of exterior Anton Gaudi perforated sheet metal and an interior look that took elements from Frank Lloyd Wright and the bar scene from Star Wars. I stayed there a few times in the past, back before Coconut Grove was taken over by street gangs and drug dealers. Now it's not a very safe place to walk at night. It didn't matter this time – it was only a way station for my journey. Tim already had a room and there was no question that he wouldn't have to worry about his car being valeted. Rides that nice would adorn the driveway for all to see where the rich and famous, or in this case (a slightly deranged CIA spook) would be staying. It was one pm – my flight left at five.

"Your clothes are hanging in the bathroom – there's a shaving kit, toothbrush and sundries too."

"You mean I get to shave this peach fuzz off?" I asked hopefully. "Nope – leave it alone. It's part of your new you. Just shave around it." It had been several weeks since I had a real shower and I made the most of this one. Hot water, lots of soap and shampoo. I could have stayed an hour but settled for ten minutes. As promised, there was a complete wardrobe hanging on the bathroom door, down to socks and underwear. Long pants, long sleeve button down shirt, brown shoes, worn but neat, and a tweed sport coat. I'm a lot more comfortable in my Key West camouflage – Columbia fishing shirt, khaki shorts, Sperry topsiders and a long billed cap. I felt like I was putting socks on a duck, but everything was the right size and fit well. At least there wasn't a tie. There was also a pair of black rimmed glasses with a zero prescription. Again part of the disguise. I emerged from the bathroom and Tim was sitting in the chair watching CNN. I raised up my arms and did a little pirouette for approval. He applauded. "Bravo, a new man arises!" He reached in his coat pocket and flipped me a passport. "World, meet Sal T. Leibowitz." I caught the passport and opened it up, flipping through the pages. Lots of stamps, London, Frankfurt, Paris, Rome, Tel Aviv, Istanbul, Athens. I turned to the front page and there I was, thin mustache, goatee, horn rim glasses and all. Hair was a little longer, but it could pass for me.

"This guy is a made-up person?" I asked. "That's a lot of work to get all those stamps." "Nope," he answered. "Sal is a real person, works part time for us and full time for a pharmaceutical company. He's in London right now, hanging out in Kensington." He handed me an airline folder. In it were tickets from Miami to London, and on to Tel Aviv, returning in a week. "You go to London, Sal will pick up the trip from there, and then hand the ticket back when he returns from Tel Aviv."

"And he looks like this?" I asked.

"You guys could be clones," Tim answered. "All you had to do was add some facial hair and some fake glasses and your good to go. That's his bag that you will check in with. We will have another ID and clothing for you in London."

"This seems like a lot of cloak and dagger BS," I noted. "So tell me why all the hocus pocus. What will I be doing in England that's so hush-hush? And I assume I'll be doing something undercover, illegal and underwater?"

For the first time in my life, I saw Tim squirm a little and look uncomfortable. He sat there for a half a minute, staring hard at his hands that were touching fingers in a little church steeple. He smiled a weak smile and finally spoke.

"Bric, I wouldn't have come to you with this deal except I don't know anyone else that might pull it off that's not already under a Russian mob and Iraqi microscope. To say it's dangerous is an understatement. You're in a pickle and I can help. We're in a pickle, and you can help. People will die either way as a result. I'm hoping, but can't honestly promise, that you won't be one of them, but in your current predicament, you are a dead man walking right now. I know more about this than you do. They killed your girlfriend, and at least three Greek button men have a contract on your ass. They want you alive, so they can get the location of your treasure, then they will make you dead, but by the time they are done with you, dead will sound wonderful."

"Yeah, well after what they did to Karen, I can assure you that I might get tagged, but it won't be without an honor guard." I answered.

"Well," Tim responded "That's behind us at this point. The mission is to get them off your ass, and I know we can accomplish that. We can talk about that once your UK mission is complete."

"Or not if I'm dead, right?"

"That is a possibility."

"Ok, let's hear the deal. The suspense is killing me, and you're beating around the bush."

"You're going to dive on a ship from the Spanish Armada."

"Okay," I answered slowly. "That's been a secret since, ah the late fifteen hundreds. Half a hundred Spanish ships sunk off the Northern English coast after the Brit's kicked their ass. They were warships, no treasure, and by now just about nothing left to explore. I've been in that water during SEAL training. Cold, treacherous and unfriendly. The fish and chips are decent though. What's the angle?"

"A fishing trawler in the North Sea snagged something and brought up a piece of wood. Too cold and too deep for *Teredos*, ship worms. An archeological team sent down an unmanned submersible ROV and came up with this image." He handed over a five by seven glossy. The image, illuminated with lights from the sub was unmistakable; an almost totally intact fourteenth century Spanish Galleon. I couldn't help but emit a low whistle. "Darn thing looks like you could float it," I exclaimed. "She looks like she sunk last year. What do they know about her?"

"They bagged a gun off her deck and got it to the surface. They are pretty sure she's the *Nuestra Señora del Rosario*, the forty-six gun Flagship of Don Pedro de Valdés, and the squadron of Andulusia. And yes, she appears intact. Too deep for shipworms and in an apparently oxygen-free dead zone. Ships like this have been found in other places, especially the Black Sea, and the *Vasa*, sunk in Stockholm harbor and covered with mud for four hundred years, but never anything like this."

"Okay, you have a ship and you know where it is and what it is. Mystery solved. Can I go home now?"

"Well, that's just it," Tim replied. We have a problem, and now an opportunity. That's where you come in. That ROV, the only tethered vehicle capable of going that deep, got itself stuck under that galleon. That's about six million bucks sitting down there, and it needs a lifeline."

"How far down?"

"Six hundred sixty feet."

"Ah, okay," I responded. "So you've gone through the phone books and are down to the 'W' pages already and haven't found an idiot? Give me a pad and pencil. I will happily give you a list of people that have the two things you need. Hydreliox experience and a death wish."

Tim smiled his little Cheshire cat smile that I've seen a few times in the distant past. "That brings us to the opportunity part. You see, we jammed that little sub under the wreck on purpose. I needed an excuse to put a diver in the water. There's bigger fish to fry, so to speak. About a month ago, a Russian fishing trawler got caught up in one of those classic North Sea Storms. She almost rolled over, but didn't sink and her deck cargo, disguised as a life raft container, went to the bottom about a mile and a half from our armada wreck. I could care less about that little sub, but sixteen hundred pounds of weapons-grade Russian Uranium, destined for Iraq, now that's a horse of a different color."

"So I supposedly go down to rescue the sub and accidently, swim over a half mile, stick three quarters of a ton of radioactive material in my pocket, rescue the sub and go home a hero? Well, I thought this was something tough and dangerous. Where's that pad and pencil? I want to write down those names before my hand starts shaking."

"Bric let me ask you. How many divers are experienced with Hydreliox at six hundred plus feet?"

"You mean still alive?" I sighed. "Hydreliox is a mixture of helium, oxygen and hydrogen. It's used for very deep dives to prevent nitrogen narcosis and the bends. The problem is, at that depth for any period of time, you can get hydrogen narcosis. Tons of things can, and will go wrong. Very deep dives are usually conducted under precise controlled circumstances. You can't actually try to *DO* something while down that deep. You just go down and come back. Traveling a half-mile sideways? Impossible."

"You won't travel that far. You'll have a very nifty, one man, overpowered dive scooter. You hit the water, go under about fifty feet and follow a locator beacon that will be set up right next to the uranium. Over a half mile, down six hundred feet, attach the box, back about a hundred and fifty feet, park while you decompress for a few hours, pop to the surface, announce the underwater sub is hopelessly stuck, and go home. The team on the research ship don't know the real operation. The fewer that know the better chances of no leaks."

"Gee, and I thought this was going to be tough. A few questions. One. What am I attaching it to? Two, why don't you just mount an effort face up and legally and go get the shit without all this secrecy. Three. Since I'm not 'Me', who am I? Four. If I pull this off and you get what you want, what do I get? And last, and far from least, what about my kids? Understand, I'm not saying yes right yet."

Tim leaned forward on his chair, sensing he at least had a crack in the door. I could tell he anticipated these questions and was ready. "You will be hooking that box to the underside of an Ohio class boomer, the USS Alaska. We just don't have the time and equipment to fashion anything that can do that remotely. Two-The Russian Mafia won't admit they don't have the stuff, nobody will admit they are selling it or giving it to the Iraqis, and anything we try to do publicly or privately will result in an international incident beyond description. Just don't go there. Three. 'You' are an unknown, off the radar screen and Bricklin Wahl is missing in action so nobody will expect the research vessel to mount any kind of an underwater effort. The story line is thin, but from the time your existence is 'known' until you vanish into the sunset will be about 20 hours and the bad guys won't unravel the story till it's too late. Additionally, if we pull this off correctly, the baddies won't even know we got the stuff until they try to recover it, days, weeks or months from now so we'll all be in the clear." He looked up. "As for your kids, you were smart to have your daughter register at college in Washington State as Alice Russell. Not likely they can find that trail. As for your son Broderick, he's safe aboard a dive ship off the coast of Columbia for the next six months. Brody's not a target now, and this will all be blown over by the time he's back in civilization."

"Now, your part. The three goons on your tail will all be tapped out, quick, clean and publicly. Their bosses won't know where it came from, and our people, cleverly disguised as another organized crime syndicate whose names usually end in vowels, will carefully explain that the Greeks have crossed into dangerous territory, and best that any survivors scurry home. For the sake of averting a war, they will likely take heed. Your ex-boss is a wimp. He's in hot water with his family, but without their backing, Harry doesn't have a leg to stand on. Likely he won't have any legs to stand on, come to think of it. Or arms, or a head for that matter. We have friends that have done favors for that other faction so the story will check out. The gold, provided you know where it is, will be off the hot list."

"Yeah, that's a whole other story. It's missing too. If it was just that I would have handed it over and ended this mess," I replied.

"From what we hear, it wouldn't make a difference. At this point, it's personal, not business and they don't like being made a fool of. You know the dyke that Karen shacked up with? She vanished a few weeks ago. Rumor has it she was sold to a bunch of baddies in Venezuela who took turns on her for a few weeks before dousing her with kerosene and torching her on a private runway south of Caracas. Remember, she was Greek family, and they did that to their own."

That left both of us quiet for a few minutes. I know she tried to kill me, but she wasn't a bad person. That had to be the worst of all humiliations.

"Tim, I don't like that term. I even called her that once after she tried to shoot me but that was for shock value, and I regret it. Gay, lesbian, family, those are okay words. She wasn't a bad person and heaven knows I have worked with and known hundreds of gay men and women in the Keys, and even in the Navy. We made peace, and she actually tried to help me at the end. That's likely why they punched her ticket. I'll appreciate if you keep it appropriate."

"Sorry Bric, I come from and live in, a different world than you. I'll remember that."

"Tim, can't you do these things for me anyway, without me getting killed in half a thousand feet of water?"

Tim smiled, but it was a sad smile. "Gotta be a deal, my friend. We go back a long ways, but the people I work for want Quid Pro Quo. You give, you get."

I took another deep breath. "Okay. Game on."

Tim looked at his watch and stood up. "Wheels up in less than three hours. Let me get you to the Metrorail station. No sense this car drawing attention at the airport. Take the Tri-Rail to the airport and the shuttle will take you right to the Virgin counter. When you get to London take the express train from Heathrow to Paddington Station You will be met outside the station. Here's five hundred English pounds in currency. Do you know your way around The City?"

"Yeah, I've been there a few times when I was in the Navy, but you probably already know that. So I look for a sign that says Leibowitz?" I asked.

"No. that's your in-flight name. When you land let's just say they will be looking for Alf." And he smiled that Cheshire cat smile.

WTF? I hate this Boris and Natasha bullshit.

Tim dropped me off with a few last minute details, and a gift.

"Here's a dive watch with some special tricks that you will need." And he handed me a Suunto Vyper dive computer watch. "It's been modified to rate down to three hundred meters and has a built in DF that will point at that boomer, and come to life when you are within a few miles. The Alaska will be hovering over the package, and you will find a ferruled compartment under the sub by the tail with equipment and a remote plug in that will work with the com system on the dive suit so you can talk to the boat. We have supplied the dive gear you will be using. It's the best, tested and good stuff. The headgear has a com that can talk to your mother ship and a jack so you can chat with the boomer. We have a visual on the box and it's got a nice big ring welded to the top. You will have a hundred feet of good cable. Hook one end on that box and get the fuck out of there." He went on, "look Bric, we both know this depth is on the outside edge of functionality and safety. Our goal is to get you in and out of that depth in five to seven minutes."

"What's this 'we' shit Batman. This kind of work is dangerous at a hundred meters, and this is twice that deep. I will tell you right now, any tiny little hitch and I head back up. No ifs, ands or buts."

"Yeah, I got that. It's a chance we have to take."

"Here you go again with 'we'. It's ME bucky. I don't even know why I'm doing it, except to turn the heat off and get some revenge for Karen. I'm guessing the bad guys will be watching. Any chance they will interfere?"

"We don't think so. They are likely working on a salvage effort too, but such things take time and the Rusky mob doesn't have quick access to deep sea toys. They are aware of this galleon project and will watch it as closely as possible, but as long as it appears to be nothing more than it is – sunken craft recovery – it won't raise their threat level. I don't see them getting involved."

# OTP (Over the Pond)

And with that, we pulled up to the Grand Avenue Metro-Rail terminal. We shook hands silently and I stepped out of the Ferrari and headed to the escalator. Metro-Rail to Tri-Rail, one stop to Opa-locka, and then a bus to the airport. Eventually they will have the Tri-Rail terminal re-built and the transfer to the airport will be a breeze. Today it's still a delightful cluster fuck.

As I've said in the past, I hate to fly. You can cuddle me in first class in a 747 to Singapore, or park me on the floor of a Chinook with the door off in full dive gear then pitch me over the side ninety feet into black ocean in the middle of a storm and the feeling is about the same. Give me a boat, a leaky rowboat or a hundred twenty foot yacht, and I'm much happier than climbing into one of these aluminum flying-saloon-in-the-sky-coffins. Cramming my tired ass into a tiny seat between some fat slob and a screaming kid for nine hours ain't my idea of a good time. I won't say I was looking forward more to the suicide dive than this plane ride, but it wasn't that far apart. To make it worse, the ordeal was starting in my second-least favorite airport, Miami. (Atlanta is the worst). Miami International Airport is a third-world country dropped in the middle of the United States. English is a second language, and courtesy by most of the employees is not a prerequisite for employment. Virgin Atlantic departs from Concourse B, and I exited the bus, small suitcase in tow and headed to the counter. The Virgin employees are a cut above most of the international airline staff. Polite, efficient and even an occasional smile. This whole day had been such a rush I didn't really have time to consider I was traveling on someone else's ID and should I be caught, I would be cooling my heels in jail for quite a while until they figured out who I REALLY was, then I would be in prison for a lot longer. So I walked up, dropped my bag and threw my ticket and passport on the counter without much of a thought.

"Just checking one bag, Mr. Leibowitz?" the agent asked. I almost looked over my shoulder to see who she was talking too until I realized *I* was Mr. Leibowitz.

"Ah, yes, that's right."

"Mr. Leibowitz, your bag can't be checked through to Tel-Aviv as your layover is more than six hours. You may claim your luggage and go through customs in London, and then re-check it four hours before your next flight."

I forgot this guy was going on to Israel. I just nodded and smiled. She gave me my boarding pass and pointed me toward my gate. It was a pleasure to not have any carry-on. All I had to do now was run the TSA gauntlet, (which stands for Thousands Standing Around), take off my belt, shoes, wallet (which wasn't even mine, just a bunch of British pounds, a few fake photos, fake insurance cards and not much else), walk through the detector and I'm good to go. I decided to stop by the bar on the way so I could gun down some nerve medicine and then realized I didn't have a penny of American currency. Oh well, they will likely take English pounds on the plane. Besides, I wasn't drinking much lately. Playing bum for six weeks and holding onto a cheap bottle of Four Roses all day kind of kills your taste for any kind of alcohol. They called the flight and I boarded. You would think these cheapskate CIA guys would bump me up to Business Class or something but I guess they had to stay in "character" and old Sal traveled cheap, and so did I. The rigmarole for a trans-Atlantic flight is always the same, you get blankets and pillows and build a nest, the flight crew jams dinner down you the very first instant possible, then dim the lights so nobody bothers them for the next six hours. Virgin is better than most, with a good selection of movies to choose from. When the flight crew finally came by with the drink cart, I asked for four mini bottles of scotch, two tumblers of ice, a bottle of water and a headset, and offered up a fifty-pound note to cover the damages. "Eww, I'm sew sorry Sah, bot we ownlee accept credit cards in flight, you see." The attendant said in her perfect cultured British accent.

So. This is Hell.

I settled for Coke and peanuts, followed by a better than average, and worse than imaginable dinner- dry lasagna, dry bread, a tiny salad with six drops of raspberry vinaigrette, four undercooked carrots, and a cookie. I gagged down what I could, finished my Coke, and spent the rest of the night trying to read lips on some English documentary on the making of cheese. I finally dozed off, and the dream came back. Vivid, real, terrifying. I'm lying on the bottom of a very dark ocean, the droning of a boat motor overhead, passing back and forth, looking for me. If they find me, I'm a dead man. Suddenly the motors change pitch and start to slow....

**BING BING BING!**

"Ladies and gentlemen, we have begun our initial descent into London's Heathrow airport. At this time we ask you to pass all cups and glasses to the aisle so your flight attendant may pick them up. Please discontinue using all electronic devices, and move your seatbacks to their most upright and uncomfortable position, and jam your tray tables into the back of the person in front of you.............."

Or something like that.

The scenery has changed, but the routine's the same. Stumble off the plane, get in line at immigration, answer dumb questions, go get your bag, back through another line, hopefully don't have to answer more dumb questions, and then walk a few hundred miles to the Heathrow express train. Tim had given me a few base background info bytes so immigration could be navigated. The Brit's are pretty vigilant and the officer gave my passport a good once-over and looked carefully at me.

"Just passing through, Mr. Leibowitz?"

"Yes, this time," I answered. "Couldn't get a more convenient flight to Tel Aviv so I've got a pretty long layover. I think I'll catch the train into London and find a synagogue for a few hours." He thumbed through the pages, satisfied himself that I was who I was, stamped a blank page and handed it back to me. "Safe voyage sir. Just follow the signs to the trains," was his parting comment.

When Gatwick Airport opened in 1958 it was the marvel of modern transportation, offering fast train service directly into London's Victoria Station. Heathrow Airport, originally an RAF base during the war, remained rather behind the times through the decades, offering only cabs and bus connections into the city until the late eighties when the government started constructing an express train directly to Paddington Station. Heathrow is a lot closer than Gatwick and suddenly the old girl came back to life and has become the preferred way to get to the UK from OTP (Over The Pond). What could take hours now takes minutes, literally. I followed the signs and found the inbound train with only minimal confusion and some medium swearing as I had to hoist my bag over the barricades approaching the train platform. I stepped on the train, bought my ticket from the conductor onboard, and settled in for a twenty minute non-stop trip to The City.

Paddington Station is a mix of old and new. It was built in 1854 and parts have never been renovated, except for the accelerated demolition program initiated by the Luftwaffe in the 1940's that required a lot of re-building. The IRA took a few shots at it too with some selective bombs, but all in all, it still has a lot of class and style. Of course there are a half dozen souvenir shops selling – of course, Paddington Bears. I wasn't looking for bears; I was looking for a ride and the rest of my instructions. I wanted to get in, live, get out, and move on with my life, what's left of it. Nobody appeared to be glaringly obvious in the main station so I made my way out to the taxi queue. Standing off to one side was a cabbie with a sign over his head, displaying in large letters "GORDON SHUMWAY." For those of you that are not 1980's TV sitcom aficionados, that was the "real" name for Alf, the stuffed animal alien on the show. Tim had to know I would know that, but for that matter, it seemed he knew everything about me. I smiled to myself, signaled to the driver, he nodded and opened the door for me.

"Me name's Barnard, mate," he started in the thickest cockney accent this side of a 1930's English movie. "I'm your driver for the next few days. Anywhere you want to go, I'll be pleased to take you."

"Ok, where are we going right now?" I asked.

"Crowne Plaza Shoreditch, guv'nor. They've got you a right fancy room there, they have. It's in the east end, where Shakespeare first did plays, and Jack the Ripper did a little playing hisself."

Sounds like a great place to hang out. As promised Barnard pulled to the front of the Crowne Plaza. There was a weathered leather valise in the cab, and Barnard indicated my room key was in the side pocket. "Ye've got your new wallet, passport and some more money in there too," he said. "I need the bag ye came with, your passport and the wallet mate. You can keep the pounds. You'll get it all back for the trip home," he continued. "Go on now. I'll pick you up in two days, eight am sharp, unless you want a ride somewheres. Me number's in the wallet."

"So what happens in two days? Why can't I get all the instructions and plans at once?"

"Because nobody knows all the plans. Just pieces. It's safer for all, specially you."

"I'm guessing you work for MI-6?" I ventured.

"Me? Oh no, mate. I get paid by the Yanks." Then he switched to a perfect Texas drawl.

"Y'all cain't trust these limeys. We home grow our talent, we don't hire it!" And he turned to me with a big toothy grin. You could have knocked me over with a feather.

"Okay, you got me. So, again, what happens in two days?"

"Barnard slipped right back to his cockney. "I'll pick ye up and were off to Docklands airport, and you get a ticket on a commuter to Manchester on British Midlands. You take the train from Manchester to Liverpool and a cab to the boat. You'll get further directions then."

"Give me the directions now. I'm done flying for the next few days, and especially not on some puddle jumper through rainstorms. I'll leave tomorrow and take the train."

Barnard frowned, "Oh no, boss, can't do that. We must stick to the program."

"Do it my way or do it yourself. I'm not in the mood to bargain, and I'm capable, and just about ready to jerk you into the back of the cab through this twelve-inch window and take them from you," I responded.

"All right, all right bubba. Keep ya'lls shirt on." Barnard lapsed back into Texican. "Here's the boat's name and location. It'll be both our asses if you don't show on time." He handed me a sealed envelope, and I opened the cab door, walking away without a look back.

"Thanks for nuthin, and I hope your damn boat sinks!" he called after me.

I hoped that was sour grapes and not prophecy. Besides, that boat sunk five hundred years ago.

So, here I was, a lot of cash, a little time and a fake ID. I checked in, went to my room and opened the bag. Nothing special in apparel except that I looked much like a local blue collar worker bee. No white tennis shoes, baseball cap, yellow windbreaker or sunglasses to single me out as a flatlander tourist. Since I didn't sleep on the plane, my first mission was a good power nap. Hopefully without any more dreams.

I woke up to a dark room. It took a few seconds to remember where I was and what I was doing. The clock said 6:30. Was it a.m. or p.m.? Did I sleep four hours or sixteen? I looked out the window down at Shoreditch High Street, and the rush hour commute crowd clearly said evening. That was good. I hit the shower and dressed in local attire, then walked out of the hotel and left to the London Overground train at the Shoreditch station. Let's see. Off at the first stop, Whitechapel, then the Circle Line to Embankment, change to the Bakerloo Line to Piccadilly Circus.

Once you get the hang of the "tube" it's the best way to get around the old city. Fifteen minutes later, after three changes and a crush of commuters, I emerged at Piccadilly Circus. When I was a kid, I imagined this place had a Ferris wheel, merry go round and maybe a tilt-a-whirl. Long before my first visit to the UK, I learned that name came from Roman times and simply meant it was round. From the sixties to the late eighties, Piccadilly was anchored by a huge Tower Records store. That place has gone the way of all vinyl records, but the area still looks pretty similar. Regent Street curved off to the left, and just a little east of that, Carnaby Street and seedy Soho district. Carnaby was made famous when rock bands like the Beatles and Stones found fashion, and made a statement that changed the world for years, or maybe forever. From there, I made my way up a street, over two and found my favorite Indian restaurant, Punjab. I first ate here thirty years ago when I was young and foolish. If I do nothing else in London, I always have at least one meal here. I settled down to a feast of Cobra beer, *Naan*, and fiery red *Tandori*, surrounded by a multitude of sauces and sides. Far too good to pass up.

I never noticed the shadow approaching.

"You gonna eat all that?" I nearly jumped out of my chair at Tim's voice.

"What the fuck are you doing here? I left you in Miami yesterday."

"Ah, caught a ride on a G4 that happened to be headed this way. I was just going to hang around but I had a chat with Barnard who told me you were playing off the board. Bric this whole thing has to come off like clockwork or it's all a cluster fuck. People will die, including you, and some Iraqi terrorists will load a forty megaton dirty bomb onto a container ship and sail it into Miami Harbor. I don't think you, me or anyone else wants that."

"Sorry buddy, but I wanted to get a little air to clear my head, and I don't like flying too much before diving. I was going to keep the schedule and I don't see where my method of transportation should be an issue."

"Probably, not, and I'll give you this hall pass, but from here

112

on, let's stick to the game plan. And no side trips with Jackie what's-her-name in Liverpool."

"Jackie Litner, president of the Liverpool Beatles Fan Club. No, I would love to see her and do a backstreet tour, but she knows who I actually am, and no need to let that get out. I get the big picture friend. Sorry I ruffled your feathers."

Tim relaxed a bit and gave a little smile. "Ok Piasan, you got a waiver for this one. Take the train, enjoy your day tomorrow, find some dive in Liverpool, have a beer at the Cavern Club for me, and be at the boat by four on Thursday."

I was staring at my Naan, thinking about what I was into and came up with one more question.

"How do I know I'll get some decent gear and not be diving with Junior Swim Fins and a K-Mart mask and snorkel..." I looked up - and he was nowhere to be seen.

There you go.

The hotel alarm clock went off at 5:00AM. Thankfully and blissfully, no dreams again. I guess I needed outside sound effects to turn on the nightmare. The train departed London Euston station at 6:17 so I caught a cab from the Crowne Plaza. Train time to Manchester, two and a half hours – Manchester to Liverpool another forty minutes. I'll be there by ten thirty, find a room and be on the streets for lunch. The ride through England is beautiful. Green, canals with cargo boats, fields with cows and sheep and the occasionally medieval castle flying by. You want to stop and explore everything, and the distraction was good for me. I needed that for sure.

There was another Crowne Plaza in Liverpool in the middle of town and I had already made a reservation before I departed the Shoreditch hotel. I stopped to drop my luggage, knowing my room wouldn't be ready that early and decided to cruise this town I had visited so long ago. Liverpool has history and tragedy. It's the town that berthed Rock and Roll history. All four Beatles were born here, grew up here and were seasoned by the tough dockyards, and damp musty underground bars. The residents, many seamen or sons of seamen, like John Winston Lennon, brought home music in the fifties that much of England had not even heard of yet. Buddy Holly, Bill Hailey and the Comets, Gene Vincent and Eddie Cochran inspired the music, the attitude and the dress code of this rowdy town, and made a viable nursery for the Mersey Beat. There's a wonderful sculpture in a corner near the docks. I walked around for a while till I found it. It looks like no more than a pile of abandoned items – steamer trunks, suitcases, guitar cases. It makes no sense until you look closer and see the Titanic tags on the trunks, and names like Harrison, McCartney and Lennon on the guitar cases. The single snare drum was self-explanatory. From there I wandered down to the docks, now clean and bright, with upscale restaurants, and a Beatles museum. John's white grand piano is there, or at least one of them, and a few artifacts, more tacky than treasured.

I had fish and chips at a local eatery, passed on the beer and hydrated with bottled water. I didn't know exactly when I would be underwater tomorrow, but didn't want any issues. Looking out over the Mersey River, I reflected that this could very well be my last few days on earth. Well, I've had a few last days before.

Let's see if we can cheat that Grim Reaper one more time.

114

# A Good Day to Die

I guess my fear of bad dreams ensured I wouldn't sleep tonight at all. Sky news kept me awake with stories about suicide bombs in the middle east, gas prices at home and an effort to rescue a multi-million dollar unmanned sub in the North Sea that was lodged under a sixteenth century Spanish galleon. There wasn't much news on that, just about a recovery effort that was underway, but the location was secret so as to avoid looters. Anyone that wanted to dive down and steal artifacts at 660 feet was welcome to it. The night was a million years long.

I don't scare easily, but I was definitely a little uncomfortable right now. I didn't like the odds or the game plan. No part of this poker deck was stacked my way.

The sun rose on a typical Liverpool morning. Gloomy, drizzly, dark, cold. I still had all day to kill, but really wasn't in the mood to be a tourist. I ordered room service breakfast, and just hung out till mid-afternoon. I checked out and hailed a cab.

"Royal Seaforth Dock, berth 94, the vessel *Grande Southwind Explorer.*"

"Straightaway Gov'ner."

"Barnard? My we do get around don't we?"

"Jest makin sure me package is delivered safe and sound mate!"

"So you didn't need these instructions did you?"

"Honestly m'lord, I did. I handed you a sealed envelope with

115

no indication of the vessel. But I do know where I'm going now!"

"So tell me Barnard, if you had put me on a plane this morning in London, who would have picked me up just now?"

"Oh, it would still be yours truly gov'ner. Me friends have faster toys than that commercial puddle jumper you would have been on!"

Royal Seaforth Dock is one of the largest in Liverpool. It's at the mouth of the Mersey and a straight shot into the Atlantic. It's mostly commercial and container ships, and one of the largest such harbors in the UK. I don't know what I expected for a vessel, some rickety fishing trawler was my first guess, although the name *Southwind* didn't really fit. I was more than amazed when we pulled up to the ship. All of 260 feet long, she was sleek, new and looked very fast. There was a large winch at the back and a berth for a small sub, which was apparently currently resting on the bottom of the Atlantic. One advantage of this dock was the security. Barnard showed some sort of ID to get in, but it's likely the press, paparazzi and any subsequent bad guys would not have much of a chance of getting close.

"You can leave your luggage with me," Barnard said. "Just keep your passport and such. The rest will be safe and dry when you get back." He reached through the window with an outstretched hand. "No ard feelins mate?"

"No Barnard- I guess I owe you an apology too."

"Think nothing of it. We mighta surprised each other had it come to blows. Safe voyage! See you in two days." And with that he drove off.

The deck of the *Grande Southwind Explorer* was bustling with activity. Last minute supplies were coming on board, and the ship was getting ready to sail. I walked up the stairs and expected to be piped aboard like a welcomed admiral. As it was I had to wander around to find someone that, "A" spoke English and "B" knew I was expected. Finally, I was escorted to the bridge where a classic captain sat in a classic captain's chair. White uniform, shoulder boards with scrambled eggs, and a perfectly trimmed beard. Almost, but not quite, a Tim clone. I stuck out my hand.

116

"Gordon Shumway."

"You're early."

He didn't offer his hand, or his name. I felt as welcome as a leper. "I'm not sure why we're going thru this exercise Shumway. No human is worth six million dollars. My orders make no sense, but they appear to be non-negotiable so we will go through with this." He softened a degree and held out his hand. "Elliot Richardson, skipper of the *Southwind*, the world's fastest, most sophisticated deep sea exploration vessel in the world. We found this galleon, and some ham-fisted so called expert managed to jam my sub under it. Now they want to pay to recover it. Needless to say I'm not accustomed to taking orders."

"Well sir, I've been taking them all of my life, but I thought that was behind me. You can sort of say were both in the same boat. I'm not a big fan of this project too; somebody made me an offer that I can't refuse."

"Understand. And I also know you're not Shumway. I watch my Yank TV shows too. I'll have to assume you're qualified to do this. Would you like to examine your equipment?"

"For sure."

He took me below decks to a large prep room. I was pleased to see several items, including a large hyperbaric chamber, which I sincerely hoped I didn't need, an internal dive platform which meant I didn't have to bash my brains out going into the North Sea, and a very organized locker with dive gear. Dry suit, OTS Guardian full face mask with microphone and transceiver, back rack with four tanks. Also, one kick ass looking Diverbike, Marlin X2.

"It's specially modified. Good for nearly three-hundred meters and three hours of power, far more than you will need. Have you calculated the dive yet?"

"Just in my head. I was told you had the specs and the gear, so I didn't get too scientific. I'm guessing maybe ten minutes of bottom time, three hours on the way back at three hundred feet, and then another hour and a half at one-fifty, with a change to Nitrox at that station. Water is cold, and I'm concerned with hypothermia. What do you have for heat?"

"Thermalution heated undergarment for your dry suit. Keep you nice and toasty for the whole trip. I think we have it covered as best as possible."

Yeah, I thought, unless you were going a half mile each way and attaching a big ass box of uranium to the underside of a nuke sub.

Sheesh.

We pulled out of the harbor and into the Irish Sea, and passed the Isle of Man in the dark. Their galleon, and our uranium was located in the Atlantic, west of Donegal, off the shelf. It's a graveyard for more than wayward Spanish wrecks, as literally millions of tons of Allied convoy ships sunk here during World War Two, accompanied by a large honor guard of U-Boats that ran afoul of destroyers and sub-seeking aircraft. To say these were unsettled waters was an understatement. The North Atlantic is an angry ocean, with ten foot swells and gale-force winds being the norm rather than the exception. The *Southwind,* despite its apparent massive size sitting at the dock, was in heavy seas and rolling around like a cork not long after we made passage past the West lighthouse at Ratlin Island. As the skies turned from black to muddy grey, I realized it was my second night in a row with no sleep. Thankfully, the seas were relatively calm, if you could call it that, for this neck of the woods.

I knew the sound of the ships engines would bring back that dream.

"One hour!" The captain announced. "Perhaps time to go below decks and start your preparations Mister Shumway, or whoever you are."

I nodded and made my way to the dive room. There was already a crew there, and I could tell they were experienced with equipment and procedures. Now if only they were experienced with speaking English. I never could figure out what language, but I was guessing something Nordic or Scandinavian, and was surprised that they didn't speak, or didn't choose to speak much English. Before suiting up, I went over the dive scooter. It had

118

been modified to fit two Nitrox tanks, complete with regulators, one to get me down to one-fifty feet and one for the trip back. I would switch to the Tri-Gas Helium, Oxygen, and Hydrogen mixture below that. Controls all made sense – I had driven similar many times before. There was also some sort of box mounted between the grips.

"That's your direction finder," Captain Richardson startled me from behind. We will hover directly over the wreck and you need only point that thing toward the green light, head to the bottom and it will find the galleon. Five days ago we prepped the dive with a beacon that's attached to an anchor line that starts fifty feet below the surface. There are decom stations at fifty, one-fifty and three-hundred. I understand you can come from the bottom to three-hundred without a stop with that mixture. There's a computer on the scooter, a backup on your BC, and I see you have a chrono on your wrist. There's ample tanks at all stops plus a margin, along with the nitrox on the scooter for emergencies. You already know we have a hyperbaric chamber. Should you need to come up fast for any reason we will pop you in and bring you back up to pressure in seconds."

Whatever.

Time to suit up. First, strip down to nekkid, and put some baby powder on the tender places, to help with chaffing. Then the electric long johns. I could tell immediately that someone had provided my measurements. All fit well. I'm not shy but I really didn't want the crew, whatever nationality they were, to get a good look at my tattoo on my shoulder – An eagle perched on an anchor with a trident and flintlock pistol in his talons. Only one kind of person can wear that tattoo, and that tat can't be bought with just money. I almost got the warm suit on when one of the crew touched it with is index finger and said "*Sulje.*" That told me two things. Sulje was Finnish for Seal so I now knew what nationality the crew was, and also the cat, so to speak, was out of the bag. The sailor tried to ask me if I was a Seal and I just smiled and shook my head to indicate I didn't know what he was talking about. Too many other things on my mind, and too much explaining to do

119

through bad translations. Fortunately, the skipper, even though he could speak to the crew, didn't catch the conversation.

After the heater came the dry suit. If I needed to pee after this I would have to wet my diapers. Other matters had been well taken care of. The water pressure at six hundred sixty feet is two hundred ninety pounds per square foot. The organs in your body are under tremendous pressure and failure to do your morning healthy would likely result in a rather unpleasant experience inside a contained suit. The dry suit is, well, dry. The goal is to provide a cushion of air. This dive will be the bottom of what's called the Euphotic Zone, and not terribly cold, say forty or so degrees, but a wet suit, which is theoretically designed to leak water in so your body can heat it and create an insulating buffer, stops working when the water is this cold. Result; instant hypothermia. The dry suit, booties, gloves and hood will keep that water away. If I was going to be in the water for fifteen or so minutes I wouldn't worry about it, but in total it will be over six hours with the decompression stages. Heat and insulation are a must.

Now the BC vest. This one started as a Mares Hybrid Pro, but had been modified to hold a huge rack of exotic air tanks. Once cinched into that mess, it was wait time till we were ready to launch. Nothing to do but sit and think. I realized that I would probably establish a record that would never make the books- one of two records- the oldest person ever to dive this deep, or the oldest person ever to DIE trying to dive this deep. Funny, now that it's about to happen, and the fear and apprehension were starting to go away. It's a job – a mission. Get in, get it done, get the Hell out. If the equipment worked, and the direction finder equipment worked, it was really not that big of a deal. If any of it didn't, it wouldn't matter, and death would be almost instantaneous.

Then the PA binged and squawked; "Diver ready!", and the ship slowed. The *Southwind* was equipped with fore and aft stabilizers, but there was still a pretty good roll amidships. A crewman pushed a button and the floor opened a five by ten foot hole into pitch black water. One end had a bench and I crawled down the ladder to sit. Part of the crew came with me, and helped me with my fins- Scuba Pro fins like I used in the Seals. Then the pre-mounted rack of four bottles, mixed with nitrogen, hydrogen and oxygen. From above, the scooter came down on a winch and hovered just above the water. With over a hundred fifty pounds on my back I was as awkward as a walrus out of water, but as long as I sat still, they were supported behind me. With all that tank weight, I didn't need, or have, a weight belt. Last came my full face mask, communications hookup, headlight and regulator. Air for the start would come from the Nitrox tank on the scooter. I climbed on the scooter, sort of prone like on a café racer motorcycle, connected to the Nitrox and tested the com. "Test-test" was all I could think to say. "Loud and clear," answered the skipper. "Once you switch to the Hydreliox, we probably won't be able to understand your voice, but just check in occasionally. Ok?"

"Sure," I responded. He didn't know that I would shut the wireless off in a few minutes and wouldn't turn it back on until I was safely tethered to the first decompression zone at three hundred feet.

We went through equipment checks several times to make sure all was working. I was as ready as I was going to be. Just then my dive watch on the right arm, started to blink green. The Sub was in the area. Before anyone could notice it and start asking questions, I gave thumbs up and a nod.

Time to play in the water.

The drop was rather anticlimactic. The scooter was released and dropped a few feet; I pushed the dive plane down and thumbed the throttle. Despite a lot of extra weight, the scooter jumped forward – it was no doubt souped up nicely. I took it to an indicated fifty feet, and then referenced the watch again. The green light was on the outside of the dial and pointed at the Alaska. I did a few slow turns and the light moved appropriately. Zeroing in on the right direction, I eased the throttle to full speed, a snappy twelve knots. I guessed it would tell me when I passed over the location when the green light moved from "front" to "back" on the watch, and that's exactly what happened. I slowed, turned 180 degrees and pointed down into the dark.

Six hundred sixty feet.  A little more than two hundred yards –
half the distance across most Wal-Mart parking lots.  The height
of a seven-story building.  Two football fields.  It really doesn't
sound like much unless you are heading straight down into the
abyss.  The scooter would go a heck of a lot faster than I needed to
go.  As it was I had to breathe constantly to help equalize the
pressure in my body to the outside.  At depth you go through your
tanks like popcorn.  There's not a lot of oxygen in the mixture.
Hydrogen narcosis is as dangerous and potentially fatal as
nitrogen, and the symptoms can sneak up on you.  Another good
reason not to hang around too long.  It was dark as the darkest
darkroom.  The lights on the scooter and the lamp on my head cut
what seemed to be inches into the darkness.  Nothing but organic
"snow" to peer through.  The whir of the scooter motor filled the
air.  Had it been turned off, the silence would have been total,
complete.

At three hundred feet, I switched regulator mouthpieces to the
Hydreliox mixture.  It had to last me from here - time down, time
on the bottom and time back up to the first decom station.  Like all
canned air, it tasted metalicy and dry.  Below, I saw light.  Lots of
light – more than I expected for sure.  As I approached, the stern of
the big Ohio class nuclear sub started to become distinct.
Somebody smart had installed some huge underwater lights on the
deck, and the sub, barely resting on the bottom had the area lit like
New Year's Eve at Times Square.  I eased off the throttle and
motored down beside the ship.  The target, a big white box with
the words *"жизнь лодка"* in Cyrillic, (I assume, "lifeboat")
stenciled on it, was lying nicely on its side about forty feet from
the back of the boomer.  A fairly large compartment had been
apparently welded in haste near the stern of the sub.  I stepped off
the scooter, which had slightly negative buoyancy, and flipped up
the two key knobs on the box, turned them counter-clockwise, and
opened the compartment.  I glanced at my watch – forty five
seconds gone already.  The door dropped down and a long length
of high-tension cable fell out.  One end was attached to a ring and
the other had a large carabineer on it.  There was also a com set-

122

wired throat mic and speaker. I held the mic to my throat and the speaker to the side of my dive mask.

"Hello *Alaska!*" I sounded like Donald Duck trying to sound like Mickey Mouse, and speaking made me start coughing a dry cough, a by-product of having my lungs crushed to the width of a douche bag.

"Bric, you stud! You're almost done. Hook that sucker up and get the eff out of here!"

"Tim, just how many of you are there?"

"Just one, but I do get around. I'll meet you in London tomorrow and buy you a beer."

"Roger that. I'll let you know when I'm leaving. Thanks for the good gear."

With that, I dropped the com, grabbed the end of the line and dragged it over to the box. The cable didn't look strong enough to drag a ton of anything through the water, but that was not my problem. The carabineer slipped on nice, tightened up and I was done with this bitch. Watch check – four minutes. Quicker I got out of here, less time doing decompression. Good.

I grabbed the com one more time. "Hello *Alaska*. Done on this end – Give me a minute to clear and you're good to go."

I didn't even wait for a response. Seconds counted. Back on the scooter, clear the sub and head for three hundred feet. Not super-fast, but just a steady climb and slightly south. Surface too fast and you get the bends, not to mention the danger of blowing up like a puffer fish while your lungs expand. The goal was to find the decom station as quickly, but safely as possible. I shut the lights off the scooter so my vision wouldn't be compromised. Half mile south and up, look for the strobe beacon. No way to calculate distance, but let's guess, a very low angle, half mile, say three knots. That's a mile and a half in half hour, three quarters of a mile in fifteen minutes, so maybe ten-twelve minutes and if I'm going somewhat in the right direction I should be there. Watch check seven minutes- depth check - three thirty. Up a tad. Start looking. The "snow" – wasn't too dense here. I should be able to see a few hundred or more feet.

*THERE* – a faint blinking, almost dead ahead. The strobe got steadily brighter. I switched on the scooter headlights and the bundle of air tanks came into view. I checked the computer- twenty one minutes of exotic air left. Man you suck a bunch of this stuff up at depth. Nothing to do now but wait. Three hours at this spot while the body leeches exotic gas out. I could cut it at least fifteen minutes short from here because I wasn't on the bottom the max time. I resisted flipping the radio on. As much as I wanted to hear a human voice, it would have been too much explaining why the mission failed. Actually I could spend part of this time thinking up a good reason – maybe a sea monster got in the way – mermaid? I started to giggle with a mental list of excuses – wait – am I starting to narc? That's not good. First symptoms of narcosis, whether it be hydrogen or nitrogen, is euphoria, and some loss of judgment. It had happened to me before, and one way to combat it, is to be aware it's happening. I've seen divers take their mask and regulator off at a hundred feet. I've known people to drown because of it. I needed to concentrate. Concentrate. Concentrate.

Two more hours. A hundred twenty minutes. Heck, I've spent that much time on the bottom with a hookah looking for loose coins. Time to think about my late wife, Wendy, the kids, Karen. Thinking of Karen, that I never got to say goodbye made me sad. It was good – it was never great. We had things each other needed, but never really 'clicked'. We both knew it would never be as good as "till death do us part" but it was definitely better than "till something better came along." Somewhere in the middle – good sex and half the utilities, I think she once said. My respect for her grew huge when I cashed in the gold, and even more when I figured out where the mother lode was located. She didn't change a bit, either toward me or the money and it warmed me that she liked me just to like me. Then she flies the coop, shacks up with another woman, and cleans out my bank account. It didn't seem like her at all. What part of that am I not getting?

Time's up. Move up to one-fifty. Happily I exchanged BC's for the unit with just one Nitrox tank on it that was hanging on a hook. I dropped the five tank monstrosity and let it plummet out of sight into the darkness. The scooter was more nimble now, but I still had to take it slow. Following the line up, I could actually see a little light from above. The next station was now an hour and a half on nitrox. I stopped using the air on my back and took the mouthpiece of the unit tethered to the line. I was more than ready to get this over. The dangerous part was over, and in a few more hours, I would be warm, dry, and outside of a few scotch rocks. It was time to bid farewell to the scooter too. I dumped the ballast out of it and kissed it good bye. It would float to the surface, light a beacon and be picked up by the ship before I got there. Just less hassle that way. Guess it was time to check-in and catch Hell. I flipped on the com switch.

"Hello *Southwind!*"

"WHERE THE BLODDY HELL HAVE YOU BEEN? We've been calling you for three hours!"

"Don't know, skipper. Com was dead down deep. Just came to life when I came up to one-five-oh. Must have been a pressure thing."

"Status, please, diver," (I love people that, One, forgive quickly and Two, are short and to the point)

"No joy, *Southwind*. ROV is hopelessly jammed underneath the galleon. I couldn't even get close enough to find a hard-point to attach to. Gave it my allotted time and abandoned the wreck."

"Fair enough, diver. Wise choice to not push it. We have spotted your scooter and have launched a Zodiac to retrieve. Are you okay? Do you need assistance?"

"Good here. Just killing time so I can come back aboard."

"Very well, diver let........." and the audio stopped. The next sound was from above, and it wasn't the first time I had heard that in my life, the loud 'CRUMP' of an explosion, followed by the red glow of fire. The secondary concussion blew me completely off the tether line, and only experience and training taught me to spit out the regulator before I lost a mouthful of teeth. I reached for the regulator attached to the tank on my back, took a breath and looked up, only to see the front half of the *Southwind*, heading my way in a hurry. No choice but to turn and swim like Hell to avoid the wreckage that was already starting to rain down around me. I don't know how I avoided the pieces, but I did, and when I turned to watch, there was nothing to look at. No noise, no ship, no tether, and no more decom stations. I had maybe forty minutes of air and then I had to pop. That's a fraction of the time I needed to decompress, and I had the choice of dying down here or wishing I was dead on the surface, seventy miles from the shore in the middle of the North Atlantic, by myself and in excruciating pain from the bends.

Well, Bric old boy, looks like you just bought the farm. Game, set, match, and I didn't even get to fuck the prom queen.

I floated there at one-fifty, considering my options for a half hour. Ten minutes of air left. My only chance was to find that scooter which still had a tank and a half of Nitrox, and head back down. Thin but at least a chance. Up to the surface I went.

The sea was rough, it was cloudy and raining and the ocean was covered in fuel, debris and body parts. I had a few minutes to look for that scooter before the pain started. Then I saw commotion a hundred yards to my left and the ocean erupted as the conning tower of an Ohio Class boomer surfaced. The deck cleared the surface and crew members emerged from the con. I tried to wave, but my arms were quickly freezing in a fetal position as the gas bubbles in my joints were expanding causing unbelievable pain. Through the rain, I could see that the Alaska was equipped, likely for just such an occasion, with a Dry Deck shelter, a portable rescue module that has, thank heaven, a small hyperbaric chamber. Two divers from the sub dived in and swam to me, and with help from the crew on board, dragged me to the deck.

Five minutes later I was in the chamber, getting back under pressure, and feeling the pain in my joints subside. I drifted off to sleep as I heard the distant honk of the klaxon horn through the deck, signaling the Alaska was preparing to dive.

# There Are Places I Remember...

I woke to bright lights and motion outside the window of the hyperbaric chamber. There was just enough room inside to sit up, and when I did, the metallic squawk of a speaker came to life.

"Hey buddy, you doing okay in there?"

"Yeah, Tim, just duckin fucky. How long did I sleep?"

"Just a little over four hours. We were in a bit of a pickle. It looked like you were just sleeping, but we couldn't come in to check on you without decompressing you again. You're only at fifty feet right now so maybe two more hours and we can bring you back to the real world. You got a couple of docs out here that are breathing a sigh of relief. How do you feel?"

"Like I just went ten rounds with Tyson and then run over by the Conch Train. I answered, "sore as Hell. Also I'm thirsty as fuck and I gotta pee."

"Sorry friend. Wish we would have thought about putting some supplies in there, but it was a rush. We needed to get you in the chamber and the Alaska underwater in a hurry. If you gotta take a leak, you're just gonna have to let go."

I realized that, under the sheet, I was stark naked. "No big deal, I can hold it for a while," then I remembered why I was here.

"So, tell me what happened?"

"It appears the Southwind took a KH-55 Russian Cruise Missile amidships. We were hanging around after the exercise, partially because we can only do about three knots with this big box hanging underneath us, and the radio room reported the explosion and the sounds of a ship breaking up. The captain decided to risk blowing our cover and surfaced to start rescue operations. We came up amidst some floating wreckage, a few small fires and not much else. Then somebody saw you, and here you are?"

"Do you know who fired the cruise missile?" I asked.

"They didn't at first, but one of our satellites traced the heat signature back to a big mother ship Norwegian fishing trawler. At least it's flying a Norwegian flag. They are ready to splash that ship, but right now it's just us chickens that know what's going on. If we pretend we don't know the scorecard, we can work this back to the source. Biggest question is how did they know what the *Southwind*'s mission was when the *Southwind* didn't know."

"Lovely," I mused. "Thanks to you, I'm not only a target for the Greek mob, but now the Russians and the Iraqis are after my ass. Got any more good news?"

Tim answered slowly. "Actually I do have a few other items to go over, but it can wait. Let's get you back to one atmosphere so you can drink and pee."

I'm no fool. I can tell when someone wants to change the subject.

One day later, the *Alaska* surfaced long enough for a Royal Navy Lynx helicopter to touch down on the deck and transfer me aboard. I was outfitted in somebody else's dress whites, and was being taken off the ship under the ruse of a medical emergency due to unexpected decompression, which was fairly accurate. Forty minutes later we landed at the Royal Naval base in Liverpool, and I was transferred to a private car on the tarmac.

"Aft'noon Guv'ner! Have a pleasant voyage?"

"Barnard. I could have guessed! Yep, it was a regular walk in the daises."

He switched back to his Austin drawl. "Yeah, I heard about

the cluster fuck. Y'all okay?"

"Well, I'm one very sore puppy, but all things considered, it beats the alternative. Where we headed?" I asked.

"My instructions are to transport you to the US facility at RAF Mindenhall where you will be put in the hospital for a few weeks to recover, but for some reason, I suspect you will have a different plan."

I thought for a second. Spending two weeks in a hospital bed was the last thing I wanted to do. I was sore, but I've been worse off than this and had to jump out of a chopper into the ocean the following day. My R&R needed a little R&R.

"Do you still have my bag?" I asked.

Barnard switched right back to his Central London Cockney. "Right there in the bonnet, mate!"

"Okay. Take me to the Crowne Plaza in Liverpool. Pick me up in four days and get me home."

Barnard wasn't pleased. "Oh, mate, that's really not a good idea. What do you plan to do there? You know it's not a hundred percent safe for you right now."

"It sure isn't with this clown suit on," I answered. I'll change into civvies before we get there. I just plan to get a room, get some rest, and," I mused for a second. "Maybe get laid." There's nothing like almost dying that gets the juices flowing.

Barnard's voice this time wasn't Texan or British. "I suppose," he said, "that I could call in reinforcements and stop you from this foolishness, but you have risked life and limb for flag and country." He was silent for another minute and then appeared to make a decision. He turned off the A580 highway between Liverpool and Manchester, and headed toward town.

"Okay, change your clothes. A four day hall pass it is. Meet you in the lobby at oh-eight hundred sharp on Sunday. Do what you must, but let's be a tiny bit discrete, if possible."

"Look, Barnard, I gave twenty years of my life to flag and country. That little soirée was to get bad guys off my ass, nothing else. I did my part; you do your part, and were all square."

Without further comments, he pulled over to the side of the

road and fetched my bag out of the trunk. He drove while I changed clothes. The soreness in my joints would make this project tough in a bedroom. In the back of an English compact cracker box, it brought tears to my eyes. I think my hair hurt. We pulled up at the Crowne Plaza, and Barnard stepped inside to see if they have rooms available. "Happy to advise you're all set in a junior suite, compliments of Uncle Sam. Room, food and beverage. My Amex Black card has you covered."

I didn't even know there was such a thing as an Amex Black.

I settled into the room and took a screaming hot bath to try and get my body in some sort of mobility, then pulled the phone book out and looked for the number for Strawberry Fields Tours. Heck, it had been over ten years. She might not even be around now. Yep, it was there. I dialed the number.

"Strawberry Fields Beatles Tours!" the phone was answered. "Two to Two Hundred, no party too big or too small. My name is Jackie. Fancy a tour?"

"Only if it comes with the happy ending like the 1999 McCartney Concert," I answered.

"Excuse me? Who is this? Wait, BRIC! BLOODY HELL! Are you in town? Say yes!"

"Yep, just dropped by for a few days. On a business trip through London and thought a weekend in Liverpool would be a nice side trip. You free for... say the next three days or so?"

"Of course, for you! Days I work, but nights are yours! Come meet me at the Jacaranda Club right now! We'll go dancing, drinking, partying, and fuck our brains out all night long!"

"Hold your horses girl. I'm just a teensy bit subdued this weekend. Recovering from a wee bit of an accident. Can't dance, but some parts still work, at least I think they do. How about a quiet room service dinner and we can talk about old times?" I suggested.

Her response sounded concerned and guarded. "I've never seen you not up for a spot of merriment. Okay, let me drop by the flat, freshen up a bit throw on a little something, and I'll be right over." I gave her the room number, since it wasn't in my name and hung up.

I first met Jackie Litner nearly twenty years ago when I was briefly stationed in Northern England. Always a huge Beatles fan, I took a weekend leave and took the train to Liverpool. I saw a flyer at the train station for "Magical Mystery Tour", Beatles escorted tours and called the number. An hour later I boarded a bright yellow tour bus in front of the Liverpool Merseyside Dockyards along with a gaggle of British, American, Japanese and Canadian tourists for a two hour excursion to all the places famous to the Fab Four. The tour conductor was a diminutive lady with a classic Beatles porridge bowl hairdo, dressed in a day glow yellow vinyl Twiggy micro mini dress, black tights and white go-go boots. We hit all the spots, Strawberry Fields, Penny Lane (there actually is a shelter in the middle of a roundabout), Paul's birthplace, John Lennon's Auntie Mimm's house, the location where John and Paul first met, and walked through the cemetery next door, where you can find the headstone of one Eleanor Rigby, right next to the grave of Father McKenzie. (Paul wrote later that he had no idea those graves were there and made up those names). Later we disembarked for a short walk down Matthew Street past the site of the original Cavern Club. The tour was tacky but full of Beatle memories, and I could have listened to Jackie's Liverpudlian accent all week. At the end of the tour she stood at the bottom of the bus with a little tip bucket and thanked everyone. I made sure I was last off the bus. I dropped a twenty in the bucket and asked if she would like to join me for a drink at the Jacaranda Club later. She told me she doesn't date customers, but then smiled and said that there was nothing she could do if I happened to show up about seven and she happened to be there.

Drinks led to dinner, which ended up in a wild sleepover. I'd never met anyone with an appetite like Jackie, and over the years, I always spent a day or two in Liverpool anytime I was within three time zones. The last time I visited, over ten years ago, she invited me to a Paul McCartney classical concert. After the concert, she sneaked me back stage, warned me to not speak to, ask for autographs, or take photos of Sir Paul. I got within a few feet of him, and managed to snap off a clandestine photo. Needless to say, it made my night, at least up to then. We spent that night together too, and she surprised me by bringing along one of her other tour guides, an over nourished little blonde named Cindy. Wow.

Enough said about that.

Two hours later there was a soft knock at the door. I opened it and was rewarded with a gentle hug and a long, slow, wet kiss. She walked in and I closed the door. She pulled off her coat and threw it on the couch, and I stood back to admire the package.

"The years have been kind," I said. "You haven't changed a bit. Freshen up? Sheesh, I told you we couldn't go clubbing tonight. Sweats and tennies would have been just fine." Jackie wasn't actually my 'type'. Five foot two in three-inch heels, and soaking wet she couldn't have broken ninety pounds. Hair was a short, jet black bob (probably a little color in it at this age). Her smile was a little crooked and heaven knows why she even bothered to wear a bra. But she didn't wear one tonight. With the coat off, I could tell why she wore it to the hotel. A sheer, black spandex long sleeved top, with no back and the front plunging nearly to her navel. Small, dark and hard nipples pushed through on both sides of the opening. Crazy, spaghetti patterned nylons ended a full four inches below a leather skirt that would pass for a belt in many closets. The previously mentioned three inch-heels completed the ensemble. I gave an appreciated wolf whistle.

"Where were you planning on taking me dancing? A strip club or a bordello?" I asked.

"Oh, this little thing?" she asked. "Just something I threw on for the occasion. I'm absolutely famished and dying of thirst. Should I call out for Chinese and a six pack?"

"No baby, call room service. Order champagne, steak and lobster. I'm playing on someone else's nickel this weekend." She did just that, and two bottles of Charles Krug. I have to say she catches on to 'OPM" (other people's money) very quickly. Twenty minutes later, there was a knock at the door, and I expected her to either duck into the bedroom or throw her coat back on, but she answered the door in all her finery. The room service attendant was female, guessing Eastern European, and rather attractive. She took the outfit in good stride as I signed the check. Jackie slipped something in her pocket and whispered in her ear before she walked out. I don't know what the conversation was, but the attendant smiled and shook her head no, and left.

"Oh what the Hell, it was worth a shot," Jackie said.

"Not sure what you had in mind there, but I'm going to struggle to just keep up with you tonight," I pointed out.

She smiled and looked coy. "Wasn't exactly thinking about you right then," she answered. We cracked the first bottle of champagne, and dove into the steak. She could tell I was pretty sore, but didn't bring it up. All in good time. In the meantime, she talked nonstop about her adventures over the past dozen or so years, doing Beatlemania tours, going to concerts, raising her kids and sending them off to college, not to mention the occasional fling with errant old rock stars, both male and female, from the sixties and seventies.

"What does your husband think about all this, and come to think of it, how do you explain not being at home tonight, that is if you plan to stay?"

"Oh, I plan to stay," she smiled. "That old sod? He's more than happy to see me away for a few days. Less pressure on him to perform, not that he's got it up twice in the last fifteen years. Not enough man for me, that's sure, but he covers the mortgage and is paying for the kid's college. Heaven help him when the kids get out of school. He'll have to learn how to wash his own underwear, he will!"

We popped the second bottle of Krug and got to the bottom of it pretty quickly. Never one much to beat around the bush, she peeled off her top and slid out of the heels and skirt. She wasn't wearing underwear, and her pubic hair was shaved to leave only a little vertical 'landing strip'. She jumped on the bed and pulled the covers down. "I'll leave the nylons on," she said. "I seem to recall you like that." Jackie patted the side of the bed and I slid out of my clothes, gingerly climbing in beside her. She cuddled up next to me and softly said, "don't know what you've been up to, Mister Navy diver, but I suspect it's nothing you can share, or you would have already. I'm good for just a cuddle and a kiss, or if you're up to it, I'm just dying for a good shag. It's been far too long since I had a 'real' man in me arms, and under the sheets."

"Oh," I answered. "I think I can rise to the occasion. No swinging from the chandeliers, or bending you over the balcony, but we can probably manage to get where we both want to go." With that I kissed her on the lips for a while, then gently down to first one nipple, and then the other, before moving farther down to taste her. She scored the first orgasm, then rolled me on my back and took matters in her own hands, so to speak, and then her mouth. Score was one to one, but at this point, who's counting? The evening progressed slow and gentle, which was neither my style nor hers but I was running on about six and a half cylinders. She caught my pace, and it was wonderful.

Since neither of us smoked, the only after sex thing I could think of at the moment was to turn on the telly and watch some BBC. As normal, they were airing a four hour documentary on the making of cheese, followed by a two hour program in black and white about the Blitz. We relaxed and finally she turned and asked, "tell me, is there a missus Bric in your life these days? Can't honestly see you being alone all the time." I gave her the reader's digest version of losing my wife to cancer two years ago, finding a little treasure, re connecting with an old girlfriend, only to find out she was killed only a few weeks ago mysteriously. I could see she was shocked. Then she reflected. "Didn't take you long to get past your mourning period did it?"

"It's not about mourning her," I answered. I miss her like crazy, and when I get home, I plan to get to the bottom of what happened, but I just survived an extremely dangerous mission, one that nearly killed me. I guess I needed a release." I looked at her. "I don't mean to cheapen our time together. I think of fond things, and for that matter inappropriate things, about you often. I couldn't imagine being in Liverpool and not checking in on you."

"Good enough for me!" she answered. "Now shut up and fuck

me again. We got to make up for lost time." And she turned out the lights.

When I woke up the next morning, the sun was shining through the window, and she was gone. No note, no goodbye kiss. I was pretty sure she would come back tonight. Another hot bath to try and limber up, then I decided to take a walk and get the kinks out. (So maybe I could get a few kinks back in later on) I found a department store in the middle of town, and invested in some cross training shoes, shorts and a tee shirt. I went back to the hotel, changed and hit the fitness room. I felt like I needed oiling all over. Arms hurt, knees, hips, elbows, all the big joints were bruised from the inside out from the bends. And this was just a fairly mild case since the Navy guys fishcd me out and got me back to depth quickly. Recovery is slow, but at least some exercise made me feel like a human. I napped all afternoon, and early that evening, a soft knock on the door announced I wouldn't be alone tonight. I opened the door, and there she was again, this time in a floor length wool coat and a bright smile.

"Room service again?" she asked.

"Nope. I think we should go out for a walk and a bite. You choose. I'm good with a local pub or the best restaurant in town. Lead the way!"

"Brilliant!" she answered, grabbed my hand and spun around. "We're off then!"

We walked through old Liverpool, past the dockyards, back into city center, down Matthew Street where the Beatles cut their teeth at the Cavern Club, and landed a few blocks away at the Bellini Club. Not fancy, not sleazy, but dark and cozy with quiet corners to chat in.

"May I take your coat, miss?" the host asked.

"Oh, no," Jackie answered. "Feeling a bit of a chill, I am. I think I'll keep it with me."

He shrugged and led us to a table in the middle of the room. "That one," she pointed. "We'll sit over there." At this point I think the host was about ready to throw us out, but he shrugged again, and seated us. As I always do, I sat facing the door. Maybe too many Wild Bill Hickok movies, but that's always been me. Jackie plopped down and we ordered cocktails. After the waiter brought our drinks, she slowly unbuttoned her coat. I nearly coughed out my drink as I realized she didn't have a stitch above her high heels on. Sitting as she was, nobody could see the show I was getting. She peered over the top of her martini glass and slowly sipped while I leered. Then I felt a bare foot rubbing up and down my leg below the pant cuff, and the slowly up my leg, past my thigh, and started slowly massaging my crotch.

"Is it me, or is it hot in here?" I asked. "Can I take your coat?" and I smiled.

She reached up with both hands and pulled her coat down around her shoulders. "Don't dare me, or I'll do it," she said. I didn't tell her the waiter was approaching from behind. He caught a serious eye full before she pulled the coat up around her neck with a blush. She turned to him with a startled look as he stood there and stared....

"Sir, I can tell you are no gentleman!" she exclaimed.

"Yes," answered the waiter, "and it's very clear you are not one either!"

Nude under a coat didn't make me spit out my drink, but that did it for sure.

That night and the next were wonderful, and sorely needed medicine for this body and soul. My wakeup call Sunday morning was for six a.m., and I realized after answering the phone that she was already dressed and gone. No note, not a message.

Maybe it was best that way.

Barnard said he would meet me in the lobby for pickup. I was surprised, or maybe not, when both Barnard and Tim were sitting there. They were both dressed in suits and ties, but Tim still sported his chronic baseball cap.

"Ready to go?" I asked, walking past them toward the lobby door.

"Cop a squat," Tim said, looking a little worried. "We've got a few things to go over." I didn't like the sound of his voice.

"Ok, what's up?" I asked.

136

Tim started. "First, let me introduce you to my boss, Barnard 'Barney' Jacobs. He runs our program here in the European theater."

"Your boss? I just thought he was a unusually thorough cabbie," I said surprised.

"Bric, I have to apologize for the ss," Barney said, this time in a Midwestern accent. "This was a highly involved and top-secret mission, and I'm sure you understand we had to limit the number of people that were in the loop. As it was there was a security leak that cost the crew of the *Southwind* their lives. We're still looking for that source." He continued and reached out his hand. "On behalf of the United States and the free world, thank you for your service. I know how dangerous it was, and we owe you a debt of gratitude."

I didn't reach out to shake. "I did my part, you do yours and we're even," I answered. 'Get these guys off my ass, get me home and we are all square."

Silence. I had that eerie feeling that I wasn't going home, and we weren't all square.

"We've encountered a small snag," Tim started. "We were supposed to get some, ah, political backup to break the chain of violence. Our friends went limp on us. If we proceed now, it will just continue, or even escalate, and has the potential to become an international incident since these baddies are Greek citizens," he continued. "We can fix this, but it's just not going to be as quick, or as clean as we expected. Bric, I'm really sorry. We've already got the wheels rolling to get you a whole new identity, life and location. We don't think your kids are a target, and your Key West friends have done well to distance themselves from you. As you know, your girlfriend has already paid the price. Blowing up your van wasn't an attempt to kill you. It was just to get your attention and flush you out. They want to capture you alive, find out what you know, and then kill you after that."

I had a lot to mull over now, and I was counting slowly to ten before I said anything to make sure I didn't just stand up and go postal on them right there. I realized then why we were having this conversation in the middle of a public lobby. They might be real spooks, but they knew I could hurt them if I so chose and there wasn't a lot they could do about it. I was really pissed, but all the fight was out of me right now. If Tim's bottomless budget wasn't able to solve my problem, I guess my one man show would have to. I started thinking of a plan.

I told him; "I'll take you up on the "witless" protection program in a few weeks, but I need a little personal time."

He interrupted me there. "Bric, don't try anything cute. These dudes are bad business, and have already left a path of dead and dying. I know you're a big bad commando, but you are no match for the Greek Mafia."

"It's nothing like that," I responded. "I won't even go near Key West. Just have your jet jockeys drop me at Fort Lauderdale International, and leave me with a little cash. I'll call you when I'm ready to go to ground. I just want to do a little fishing with an old friend."

"Ah, well, that's just it," Tim replied slowly. "The baddies putting a missile through the middle of the *Southwind* have us concerned. We felt that we had a tight story and no trail, and yet someone knew our every move. There's concern in the bureau now that there might be a mole in the chain of communication." Tin continued, "there's a lot of internet traffic out there, both from Russians and the Middle East. We think they have people watching international terminals all over the UK, and on the East Coast of the US. They don't appear to know exactly what they are looking for, but you would stand out like a nun in a whorehouse if we just ship you home. You up to a little sightseeing on our nickel before you get back home?"

I got suspicious. "What kind of sightseeing?" I asked. "You want me to go fishing on a Norwegian trawler in November or something fun like that?"

I think Tim was expecting a more hostile response, and you could see him grasp for an opening. He looked at his boss and nodded.

"Ok, here's the deal," Barney said. "We'll put you in a C-20, that's a Gulfstream G-4 if you don't remember, from here to Zurich. Take the train from the airport to the main train station downtown, and then just play tourist for a few days. We don't care how you get there, but you have nine days to be in Paris. Then take commercial out of Paris back to the states. He handed me an envelope, "five grand in Euros, a Euro Rail pass for two and tickets on Delta from Paris to Atlanta and on to Fort Lauderdale. You have your G. Shumway passport with you. Sorry, no credit cards, but we didn't have much time to call an audible," he frowned. "I want to apologize that we couldn't meet our end of the bargain, at least not yet. I'll work on Plan B." In the meantime, we'll get you relocated. We do that part all the time, and it's almost never without a hitch."

"Yeah, it's that 'almost' part that worries me," I answered.

"Hey, wait a minute. 'Tickets' as in plural?"

Barney brightened a little and lapsed into his Texican drawl.

"Yep, we gotcha a sport wench for a travelling companion. If they're lookin for anyone, it's a single male. You'll blend in better as a twosome. You'll meet her in Zurich. Just kidding about the 'sport wench' part. Ilenia's a looker, but hands off. You will be sharing a room, but you will have to work out the sleeping arrangements. She is easy on the eyes though."

This was getting more and more complicated. "So, she's my bodyguard, your contact yada yada?" I asked.

"Ilenia's a fairly new, but qualified agent, combat trained with a few notches in her belt, but it's not like you can't take care of yourself," Tim broke in. "Actually, because of this possible leak, she's not wired, not packing and has no way of communication. Neither will you. We need to get you off the grid, and if there's someone on the inside, any communications through the bureau would light up like a Christmas tree. I will personally meet you guys in Ft Lauderdale and give more info."

"Well, I really want to go home but don't want to wind up dead in the process. I guess a few days on a train won't hurt me. Let's roll."

We left the hotel by a private car that took us to Manchester

Airport, where a US Air Force Gulfstream was parked on the private side of the terminal. Much to my surprise, Tim, zero baggage in hand, walked up the stairs with me. "You're coming along?" I asked.

"Yep. Mission is over on this side. Figured I'd freeload home while I had the chance. It would be complicated for me to 'leave' here on commercial when I actually never 'came' here. We'll drop you off in Zurich and then pop over to Tampa where the Ferrari is garaged. Good for all," he frowned again. "Wish you could just tag along, but we need you to drop off the radar for a while."

We were the only two people on the plane. The first officer doubled as a steward and offered us drinks and sandwiches out of Manchester. Seats were comfortable, and the exec jet was configured to seat about six when it would easily carry twice that many. No movie and the company wasn't that cordial – I was still really pissed at Tim, and he knew it. He pulled his SR-71 HABU baseball cap over his eyes and either fell asleep or pretended to. I stared out the window at the North Atlantic as we took off, banking over water I almost died in a few days ago, and dozed off to the monotonous sound of the twin Pratt & Whitneys. The recurring dream was gone, obviously a premonition of my dive disaster. Instead, I dreamed of Key West. There was Karen, hiding behind bushes, running, looking over her shoulder. People were chasing her, and she was looking for me. I could see her, but I couldn't call her name, I couldn't wave. Like so many bad dreams people have, I didn't have any clothes on. And neither did she.

It wasn't erotic – it was terrifying.

# Swiss Watching

The change in jet engine tone signaled our descent into Zurich. Big plane or little plane doesn't matter, and the fasten seat belt light came on overhead. I straightened up and looked out the window as the jet descended over dark green forests dotted with blue lakes, a forest so dark the locals call it black. Tim was either still asleep or still faking it. We banked left, and the Zurichsee came into view. Touchdown at the Zurich airport was just a little over an hour after takeoff.

Over the last few days, I had started to hatch a plan. I needed to get the goons that killed Karen to come to me, that part I knew. I also wanted to find some things out. I was tired, still sore and not in a good mood, nor really thinking that straight. As Shakespeare once wrote, "revenge is a dish best served cold." I shouldn't be doing this, but I really didn't care right now. I would keep working on the plan as I rode the rails across Europe.

The Grumman taxied up to the terminal in Zurich, and we all departed to clear customs. Switzerland has become very wealthy over the last half-century by being very careful but very discrete. Passport checks were cursory, and there were no questions as to my destination or reason for visit. Passport was stamped, and I strolled out of the regional terminal without a look back. I didn't need to be nice to Tim and understood my mission. I also figured my "escort" would know how to find me. The private terminal in Zurich is attached to the commercial building, unlike most airports, and it was only about a ten-minute walk to the entrance. The train to downtown Zurich lies directly underneath the airport terminal. (Why can't they do this in the states? Does the Mafia control the public transportation so strongly they won't let the cities connect transportation systems?) I bought a ticket to the Hauptbanhof (main train station), and walked into the middle of the terminal, and just stood there. And stood there.

After an hour I decided I had either been stood up or misinformed, and started looking at departing trains heading toward Germany or France. I really didn't care if I hooked up with this companion or not. I prefer to travel solo anyway, and likely the baddies didn't have a clue where I was or how I was going to get wherever the Hell I was supposed to be going.

It was really too late in the day to start out on a trip anyway, so I decided to overnight in Zurich. At the front of the Bahnhof (train station) was a little agency that booked hotels and excursions, and I stepped inside and waited my turn, looking at hotel rack cards on the display. I really didn't want a Hilton or Sheraton. When in Rome, be a Roman candle, they say. Maybe a little B&B.

"I hear the Kindli is a nice place," a voice said over my shoulder. I turned and was looking at a large pair of Christian Dior sunglasses, a mane of fiery red hair, with a fur parka collar surrounding it like a halo. "Did I surprise you darling?" she said and gave me a hug and gentle kiss on the cheek. "Sorry my train was late. Glad I found you." Holding my hand she stepped to the counter and chatted in fluent German. I caught a few words. "Dopel zimmer" (room with two beds), "ein nacht" (one night). The agent made a call and nodded approval. "One-twenty Euros, Gordon. Pay the lady," I forked over some cash, and "Ilenia" was handed a voucher. There was a taxi queue in front of the station, and we climbed into a black Mercedes cab.

"Haus Zum Kindli," Ilenia told the driver, and we drove off in silence. Only a few minutes from the train station,  The Kindli is in the oldest part of Zurich, perched on the side of a hill that marks the original fortifications put here by the Romans in about AD 400. When I say side of the hill, I'm serious. Like a thirty degree slope on a cobblestone street. I could envision what this might be like in a snowstorm. I only had my small grip and Ilenia had a little roller. From the street, you go up six of the steepest stairs I've ever had to climb. I'm guessing they don't get a lot of handicapped guests. We presented our voucher to the desk, showed our passports and were given an old-fashioned metal room key.  The elevator would make a phone booth look roomy, and we went up to the third floor one at a time. Typical old-world European guest room, beyond tiny, with two twin beds, a small dresser, 19 inch TV and the bathroom down the hallway. The view was beautiful, with an old renaissance era clock tower a block away and a glimpse of the river and the Zurichsee (lake) in the distance. Cramped, but it was only for one night, so no biggie. I flopped down on one bed, and turned on the TV, flipping through the channels till I found some F-1 racing practice and qualifying. She wasn't talking, so I wasn't talking. She finally took her sunglasses off, flashing a pair of eyes so green they had to be behind tinted contacts, and hung the parka in the closet. With her back to me I took a moment to check out the package. Maybe five–one, five-two, very curvy, and, as she turned, I could see ample boobalige in the front, apparently braless under a white turtle neck ski sweater. She smiled at me and then headed down the hall to the bathroom, bag in tow. Ten minutes later she was back.

"Hungry?" she asked. I could detect a distinct Eastern European, maybe Russian accent. After Barney, I didn't know if any of these people spoke in their real accent.

"Sure," I answered. "Do you know the area?"

"I do. Five minute walk across the bridge and there's a row of nice little cafés along the river. I'm sure we can find something there."

We put our coats back on and walked out into the crisp

November air, into a light mist. Navigating down that cobblestone street was scarier than that tech dive – almost. I survived the trip to the bottom. Ilenia took my hand, and we walked silently to the bridge that crosses the river. It was early evening, and there weren't too many people on the streets. I pulled her to a stop in the middle of the bridge. She reluctantly stopped. "Yes?" she asked.

"Ah, we haven't had the chance to formally meet. Thought we might get acquainted," I said.

"Mr. Shumway, or whatever your real name is, it's not my job to 'get acquainted'. I'm to travel with you to Paris and appear to be your companion, lover, whatever you call it, then fly to Florida together, at which point I can go back to my job, and you can go do whatever you do. I was happily in the middle of a tremendously interesting and properly dull job that permitted me to sleep in my own bed for a few months. Then I get jerked out of Moscow and planted in Switzerland with about four hours' notice." From a distance, it probably looked like a loving conversation, but her green eyes were flashing, and the Russian accent came out thick and dripping with anger. I held up my hands and replied. "Look, this wasn't my idea either, but I guess we're stuck with each other for a week. After failing to get me killed underwater, I guess your people want to keep the bad guys from dotting me out in revenge. I'll keep to myself, but let's be civil."

Her eyes softened a little. "Ok, Gordon, I guess I owe you an apology. You're doing your job, and I have to do mine. Let's make the best of it," she stuck out her hand. "Ilenia Teranarmov. By the way, what is your real name?"

I hesitated. I'm normally a pretty trusting person, and after all this person was some sort of CIA spook that Tim assigned to me, but it was a little surprising that she didn't know who I was. Maybe it was time to play a little closer to the vest.

"Who I 'was' doesn't matter anymore, Ilenia. That guy is history. When I get back to the states they are going to give me a whole new 'me'. Gordon is just fine." She looked a little perplexed, but seemed to adjust quickly. "Well, alright then Gordon. Let's go find that food." She turned and walked across the other half of the bridge without checking to see if I was following.

As promised, there was a row of little dining places along the walkway by the river. In the summertime, all the seating would be outside, but it was November and only a few degrees away from snowing, so the outdoor seating was vacant, but we found a place where the chairs and tables were under an awning and dry, so we plopped down to enjoy the fresh air. The waiter inside looked at us like we were aliens, and then reclassified us as "tourists." With a semi-disgusted Swiss-German scowl, he walked outside and threw a menu on the table. The menu was in German, which was a problem to me, but Ilenia translated. I had a ham and Swiss Panini and a coffee and topped it off with fresh hot apple strudel, with ice cream on the side. I almost had to threaten the waiter to add the ice cream. What Americans would consider the perfect dessert the Swiss apparently think ruins good strudel.

"So" Ilenia started. "I understand you participated in an exercise in the North Sea. Was it successful? Something went wrong, and your ship sank?"

I was more than a little surprised that she was asking these kinds of questions. I know the agency is departmentalized, but thought she would know more than she did, or perhaps she was asking questions to answers she already knew. I wasn't happy right now that I was completely cut off from Tim and anyone else. Generic answers were in order.

"Something like that. Some sort of accident. Fortunately I was rescued. Your boss was concerned that I was under surveillance, and in some danger, so they are sending me home by an out of the way route."

"You didn't tell me if you were able to recover what you were sent for." She was pressing. I thought I would see how much she really knew.

"I did" I answered. "But with the ship sinking, I don't actually know what happened after that. I was suffering from the bends and spent some time in a hyperbaric chamber. After a few days of R&R, they threw me on a plane to Zurich with loose

145

instructions as to where to go and when to get there. From here you, probably know as much as I do."

Her eyes narrowed as if she was trying to see if I was telling the truth or throwing her a line. Either way, she knew that digging much more would create suspicion. Our dessert finished, we walked back along the river to the hotel in silence. We got back to the room, and it seemed twice as small as it did when we left. I turned on the little portable TV to make some noise in the room, and sat on the edge of the bed. She sat in the one small chair and watched the program silently for a while. I was tired, and it was time to break the impasse.

"Forgive me", I started. "I didn't exactly come prepared for modest sleeping. Turn around if you don't want to see me undress." Ilenia smiled, leaned back in the chair and crossed her legs. "Go ahead," she answered. "We're both adults, and I doubt you would be successful trying to rape me in the dark."

"Suit yourself," I shucked down to my skin and climbed into bed. Thankfully I had been well satisfied by Jackie for the last few days and didn't have a brain full of sexual tension. I rolled over and fell into deep, dreamless sleep.

I woke in the middle of the night. Ilenia's bed was empty and hadn't been slept in. The TV was still on, volume low. Curious, I got up, slipped my pants on and walked down the hallway to the bathroom. The light was on, door closed and the shower running. I put my head against the door and through the sound of water, could hear a soft voice.

Speaking Russian.

# Sleeping With a Cobra

I quietly walked back to the bedroom, pulled my pants off and crawled back in bed. My mind was racing. Tim specifically said neither of us would have any communications equipment. Maybe he was lying – or maybe she was the mole they were looking for. My first thought was to grab my stuff and run like Hell, but it was very likely she wasn't alone in the area – after all she's the one that conveniently chose this hotel. I envisioned hypodermic needle being slipped in my neck, and waking up naked in a cold wet cell with a single light bulb while bad guys beat information out of me. But I was sound asleep for two or three hours, and that didn't happen. Maybe she was going to try to charm information (that I probably didn't know) out of me and let me go home. What did they want to know? What did they think I knew? Maybe the one part they hadn't figured out was how we got the nuke stuff off the bottom. Tim and Barney were hands-on with every step around that boomer, and the skipper of the Southwind was out of the loop. (*permanently now*) I bet that's the part the bad guys didn't know. I heard footsteps coming down the hallway and Ilenia quietly came in the room, closing the door carefully behind her. I listened carefully and was ready to react if she came close. I heard her rustling around her bed for a moment, then felt her hand on my shoulder. My reflexes made me sit up and spin, and she jumped back. "Oh. Sorry Gordon, I was just trying to wake you. I didn't mean to startle you."

I pulled the sheet back up to my waist. "That's okay. Military training. You have to be careful how you try to wake up a soldier. Just turn on a light next time," I answered, hoping that story held water.

"I'll remember that," she answered. "Anyway, it's almost

147

five. We can catch a cab and make the six o'clock express train to Munich."

"Wow, you have the train schedule memorized? That's a pretty slick trick." She stumbled a bit and then recovered.

"I checked yesterday before you arrived. I knew we were moving on this morning."

Gee, I thought she got there *after* me. Hmmm. Maybe I'm being a bit too much of a Sherlock at this point.

Then again, maybe not.

We dressed, checked out of the hotel and caught a cab to the train station, booked our seats at the ticket window and found our train. She wasn't talking, and I wasn't in the mood for banter, so it was a silent trip. I had traveled this way long ago, and it's a beautiful trip over the foothills of the Alps. I was happy to look out the window and take my mind off the cobra sitting across from me. The weather had taken a turn colder and wetter, and I had little doubt that we might see snow before we got to Germany. Sure enough, we were hardly out of the burbs when the raindrops began to turn to snowdrops. A few miles later the snow was sticking, and a half-hour later it was a winter wonderland outside, and beautiful. This train goes from Zurich to Munich to Prague and has a decidedly Czech atmosphere. The train staff was Czech, the food on the menu was Czech, and the wine was Czech. About halfway between Zurich and Munich the train stops in Lindau, a delightful little village on an island in Lake Bodenzee where it changes crews from Swiss to German. I have done this before without incident, but this time was a bit different. There was an additional stop on this train in Bregenz, and we watched the German train crew depart here instead of Lindau. Shortly after the train pulled out, a conductor came through checking tickets, which is also normal. We handed him our Euro Rail Pass, which permitted seven days of travel in six countries, including Switzerland and Germany. The conductor asked a question in German, and when I looked baffled, switched to English. Ilenia spoke fluent German, but for some reason kept silent. "Do you have a ticket to Austria?" he asked. "No," I answered, "I'm not

148

going to Austria, I'm going to Munich." "Well," he answered, "you are in Austria right now." Now this was a definite surprise to me. I had ridden these tracks before and was never aware that I was traveling through Austria. From there, the conversation turned into a scene from a 40's Bogart movie. He departed, and an official looking person walked up. "May I zee your papers please?" he asked. I handed him the ticket and my passport. "I zee you do not have a proper ticket!" he said. "You must have the ticket through Austria for passage!" At this point, I guessed that in a few moments, I would be asked to fork over some money, or else be handcuffed, have my forearm tattooed, thrown in a boxcar and sent to a gulag somewhere near the Russian front. As it turned out that they were in revenue mode that week and we dutifully forked over twenty four Euros for the privilege of traveling fifteen kilometers in Austria. Twenty minutes later we finally stopped again in Lindau, where the Austrians got off, and a German crew got on.

Boy I bet this was a hot little corner in the forties.

We arrived in Munich just a little before lunch. There was snow covering the ground just on the outskirts of the city, and the snow was just melting off the roofs in town. Like all European main train stations, there was a tourist office that offered excursions, dining and hotel rooms. Ilenia looked at the offerings and suggested the Platzl Hotel, a nice little place right next to the Hofbrauhaus in the middle of town. I wondered if this was something pre-planned too. I would have given anything to get my own room, but we were supposed to be flying under the radar as a couple, so the bad guys didn't kill me, even though I had a strong suspicion that I was *sleeping* with the bad guys. It wasn't time to let the cat out of the bag just yet. One thing for sure, sleep was going to be a problem for me for the next few days.

After checking in, we took a walk through the cold blustery streets, stopping for lunch at the Hofbrauhaus. The most famous beer hall in Munich, if not all of Germany, the Hofbrauhaus provides tankard-sized beer mugs filled with very good, icy cold pilsner beer, German sausage, fresh rye bread and spicy mustard for lunch. They have a much larger menu, but I can't ever get beyond this feast. We hadn't said ten words since leaving Zurich, but the beer loosened both of us up a little I guess.

"So, what do you do in real life Mister Shumway?" she started.

"Oh, this and that. I used to be in the Navy, and I still dive a lot."

"I assume you still work for the U.S. Government? Do you work for the Agency? Again, questions that I would think she would have known. Strange.

"Nope, this was a contract deal. Tim contacted me because I have some deep water experience. He didn't tell me much, just the mission and that it would be worth my while." I decided to probe a little myself. "I'm a little surprised you don't know much about the operation. Didn't they brief you?"

She chose her words carefully. "I'm a junior operative. I do low-level work in Russia as journalist, stringing for American fashion magazines. My parents are Russian-born American citizens, and I have dual citizenship, which makes travel between countries easy. This trip with you is far outside my normal duties. I think they had to act quickly, and I was unattached, convenient and nearby. Mr. Heminger just told me that people might be looking for an American traveling alone, so they added me. He also said you had conducted a covert operation in the North Sea which ended badly. I'm to escort you from Zurich to Paris by any route you choose, and we have a week to get there. You have my ticket to the US?"

"I think so," I answered. "Tim said there were two tickets to Fort Lauderdale from Paris on Delta. I didn't really look at them, just put them in my bag. We can check when we get back to the hotel."

We ordered another round of beers and drank in silence again. Normally, I would have been fat, dumb and happy, drinking cold beer with a plus-ten redhead in a foreign country, but my guard was up, and I was watching her every mood and mannerism. She seemed to be in thought again as if she was thinking over how to approach a subject. I wasn't disappointed.

"Do you believe the container you recovered was lost when the *Southwind* was attacked?"

The hair on the back of my head stood up again, but I answered as casually as possible. "I guess so. There wasn't much left but kindling wood and body parts. Anything that could sink would be lying in six hundred feet of water. I was lucky that I wasn't on the ship yet, or I would have gone down too. I was also lucky that the British Navy sent a chopper out to investigate the explosion quickly, and I was rescued." And I stopped talking.

I never told her the name of the ship I was on, and never said it was attacked. Why would Tim share that info with her, and not tell her what my mission was?

We rode the rails for the next two days. Munich to Brussels, ending in Paris. She said the same thing that Tim told me; get to Paris by rail any direction I chose, but *she* was making all the choices; when the train left, which way we were going, and chose the hotel when we arrived. I wasn't being followed, I was being led. I wasn't sure where this journey would take me, but I was pretty confident that "they" whoever "they" were, had no intention of letting me leave Europe. I hadn't slept since Zurich and was seriously fighting sleep deprivation. I dozed on the trains and pretended to sleep all night in the hotels, but stayed wide awake with my radar up. Ilenia was cordial but distant, and hadn't tried to probe any more since Munich. I felt she was waiting for something, or someone. I always looked around me when I was on the train and saw the normal mix of businessmen, tourists and college kids. Nobody looked out of place, but it's likely I wouldn't be able to spot another spy.

In the meantime, the trip provided a great diversion. The trip from Munich to Stuttgart runs through more of the Black Forest and offers never-ending vistas. Stuttgart to Mainz is flat farmland and a good spot for a little nap. When you pass Mainz, the birthplace of printing and the Guttenberg Bible, you pick up the legendary Rhine River, focus point of boundary wars and battles from the times of Julius Cesar through World War Two. Medieval fortresses clutter hillsides like so many sandcastles on a

Sunday afternoon beach. Some are crumbled ruins while others are still inhabited. There's a winery in one, and a hotel in another. For nearly two hours, you are never out of sight of a castle. Dusseldorf, Cologne with its massive church, Koblenz, at the confluence of the Rhine and Mosel rivers, and other cities that read like a list of 1944 Allied targets came and went. Finally, you come out of the gorge and into less scenic farmland. The train came to a stop in Duisberg where we changed trains to Brussels. There was about an hour between trains, so we strolled across the street to find some lunch. Nearby we walked past an Italian restaurant that was emitting delicious smells. The menu looked interesting, and we walked in. Here, in the middle of Der Fatherland, was a true Italian restaurant. The waiter greeted me in German but with an Italian accent. I speak Italian every bit as good as I speak German (zero equals zero), so I felt right at home. Ilenia speaks fluent everything it appears, so she translated the menu. Actually I know a few words and can read a dago menu perfectly. The menu was in German and Italian, and I ordered in Italian, which delighted the waiter. Wine was poured, bread was served, and a very nice cannelloni with a four-cheese sauce that would have been perfect in Milan. I would rate it among the better meals on the trip.

The weather continued to be nasty, cold and blustery, and, as we pulled into Brussels, it actually spit a little sleet and snow. So much for a walk about town and a visit to the Leonidas Chocolate store. Again Ilenia suggested a hotel, and I didn't feel like fighting. As I stood in line at reception, I had this strange feeling of deja-vu as if I had stood in this place before. THAT'S IT! This was the same hotel I stayed in during my very first visit to Belgium ten years ago, on my way to Budapest. Suddenly everything jumped into focus. Train station to the left, shopping to the right and across the street. The Sheraton Brussels is a nice, but rather uninspiring place, not much different than the Sheraton in Frankfurt, or for that matter, Detroit. Another silent dinner and another sleepless night. I had to hang on for two more days, one way or the other.

Tomorrow, Paris.

# Don't Forget Paris

The TGV high-speed bullet train pulled out of *Brussels Midi* train station, gently rocking to and fro on the "common" rail tracks, a space-age marvel rolling past renaissance era buildings. The atomic structure of the 1962 Brussels World's Fair theme building loomed in the middle distance, a giant silver cluster of orbs floating eerily in the fog and rain. As the train cleared the city, it began to gain speed, first slowly, then with noted acceleration, until the fences were a blur, and telephone poles indeed began to look like a picket fence. From the overhead speakers, a voice in French made unintelligible sounds, followed by unintelligible Flemish, and finally the English translation. *"Ladeess and gentlemen, thee train 'as reached eets maximum speed of three hundret kilometres per hauer."* That's about one eighty five to us Americans, the fastest train in all of Europe, run by the French. Estimated time between Brussels and Paris; one hour twenty minutes. Smooth as glass on seamless tracks, the TGV train banked through the corners like an airliner. The first class section is actually laid out much like an airliner, except that the seats on this particular day happened to all be facing backwards, which made the mind wonder if there were such a thing as a "Frequent Rail" program, would they take away miles if you were going backwards?

Shortly after we were up to speed, lunch was served, al-la airline style, on trays, but with real china, glass and flatware. The meal was French, but rather uninspiring, with beef, potatoes, green salad with no dressing, and a rather uninspiring Bordeaux wine.

153

Superior French technology and inferior French cuisine.

Boy, there's a switch.

My previous experience in Paris was a total of one hour, changing trains from Frankfurt to London, and I would have normally been looking forward to taking in the cuisine and culture, but at this point was just hoping to leave town in an airplane seat and not floating face down on the Seine.

Arriving at the train station, Ilenia again barged in front of me at the little travel agency and selected a little bed and breakfast on Isle St. Louis. Time for a change-up. While she was selecting her "random choice", I looked over her shoulder and scanned the rack brochures on the wall, memorizing a few names. We caught a cab, and she gave the address and directions to the B&B on Isle St. Louis in perfect French. A few blocks from the train station, I sat up as if a light came on. "Driver! Parlez Vous Englais?"

"Oui, Oui, *un tout petit peu*," he responded.

"I remember a hotel that a friend stayed at recently. Do you know of the Best Western Hotel, just a block from the Seine, directly across from the Eiffel Tower?"

"Oui, yes, I know that hotel. Do you wish to go there?"

Illenia looked flustered. "We already have a reservation at the Bed and Breakfast. I paid a deposit."

"Not to worry," I answered. "I'll give you your money back. I still have lots of Euros. I was told this place is perfect and close to the Paris Metro. Driver, let's go there." Ilenia was totally frustrated, but knew she couldn't make too much of a fuss. After all, I was supposed to be calling the shots. It would be amusing to see how she alerted the hit squad.

We arrived and verified a room was indeed available. Two double beds, with bath. *Merci.* After checking in, I wanted to play tourist. Ilenia was torn. She likely wanted to be alone so she could make a call with that non-existent cell phone in her bag, but didn't want the big fish to get away. Reluctantly we took off for the Eiffel tower, about a ten-minute walk from the hotel. For those of you that have never been to Paris, let me tell you about the Eiffel Tower – it's *BIG*. I'm used to attractions and landmarks that

154

somehow seem smaller than the posters and pictures show – well you won't be disappointed by the Eiffel Tower. It's over a thousand feet tall, and literally looms over everything in the city. We bought tickets for the elevator and headed to the top. Wow! What a view! You could see Notre Dame, The Louvre, Arc du Triumph, and the Champs Elysees, Champs Elissess, Champs Elissess, oh Hell, that big wide street. For lunch we dined at a nearby local's restaurant. French food (go figure), French wine (duh) and again, very nice French people, both the staff and other customers. The people were just plain nice. In fact, I did not meet a single rude person, waiter, cab driver, ticket taker, or salesperson during my entire stay. My entire opinion of France has changed, and I will undoubtedly return. I then realized - like, ohmygawd – I've become xenophobic. Me, world traveler that will eat fish tacos off a handcart in Tijuana, ride a Tuk-Tuk in Bangkok and a subway in Manhattan. I had taken traditional images portrayed by American movies, and a couple of personal experiences with a half dozen tourists and created my own bigoted opinion of all the people in France.

After a big lunch something less spectacular for dinner was in order. As I so often do on trips, I elected to do an in-room dining experience. We walked through a little market area, buying bread in the bread store, wine in the wine store, fruit from the fruit stand, and cheese from the cheese store. I picked a nice hard cheese and a musty Camembert. Dinner was delightful and peaceful. I wrapped up the remains in put them in the mini-fridge and went to bed.

The next morning. It was the best of cheese, it was the worst of cheese. We got up, took turns showering, then made our way downstairs for breakfast about eight o'clock. Upon return to the room, I went to the refrigerator for a drink of water. Opening the fridge door, I was slammed by a reek that was nearly visible, and almost audible. The tasty Camembert, such a delightful addition to last night's dinner, had turned extremely angry during the night. What makes fresh French food so tasty is that they have no preservatives, which means they don't last real long once tampered

155

with. This one needed to leave the building, and right now. I wrapped it in two plastic bags, and shoved it, the bread, the fruit, and the water (everything reeked) into a third bag, and made my way out of the hotel, killing flowers and curling up wallpaper en route. Holding the bag at arm's length like a dead skunk, I went searching for the first possible receptacle to dump the evidence. Next to the local grocery store was a large green container, and, as I walked by, I lifted the lid and gratefully dropped the package inside. As I walked away, I heard a loud shout. Across the street, some guy in green coveralls was yelling and pointing at the trashcan. I did not need to understand French to know that I had been busted. Dodging down the alley, I rounded the corner out of sight, hoping he wasn't so passionate about his trash can he would follow.

I realized that, during my cheese excursion, Ilenia had likely taken the chance to alert her cohorts. She was probably looking out the window at the street to watch for my return. In the back alley behind the hotel, I entered through the kitchen, earning wrath and anger from chef to dishwasher in the process. Ignoring them, I stepped through the kitchen door into the dining room, and, instead of taking the noisy tiny elevator, walked quietly up the stairs. Hoping there weren't too many loose boards, I padded up to the door. I could hear Ilenia, speaking in French this time, very softly. Slipping the old-time key in the door, I turned it and stepped into the room in one motion. Ilenia, facing the window overlooking the street, spun around and dropped the phone on the floor behind the chair, hoping I didn't see it.

"Looking for me?" I asked.

"Yes, I was starting to get concerned." She froze but glanced toward her bag. I'm sure there was something in the bag I didn't want her to get her hands on.

"Stay right there," I ordered. "I don't know what else you have in there besides that phone on the floor, but no need to take chances. How many people and how soon will they be here?"

Her body sagged a little. I couldn't tell if it was resignation or a ploy.

"Gordon, I work for your side and the other side. We are, as they say, 'on the hook' for the item you helped recover. We just need some help relocating it. The person I was on the phone with is in another country. Nobody else in Paris but me."

"So, I spill my guts, everyone's happy and I stay healthy, we fly home tomorrow and go our separate ways, and I don't tell Tim any of this happened?"

"Something like that," she said with a smile, and she took a step toward me. Before I could speak again, she dropped her shoulder and spun into a full turn spin-kick aimed right at my left temple.

But my head wasn't there. With her in that stance, I reacted automatically. Crotch punches are as painful to a woman as they are to a man, and I landed this one solidly with my right hand, hard enough to take her off her feet. She landed with an "oof" on her back, in pain, and the wind knocked out of her. I dropped a knee on her chest, put a thumb on her carotid and covered her mouth with my other hand. Her eyes were wide as she gasped for breath.

"Hold still and relax. I won't hurt you. Get your breath back." Ilenia nodded, and after a minute she was breathing normal again.

"Please take your knee off my chest. It hurts!" she gasped.

I leaned harder on her tits and tightened my grip on her neck. "Wrong answer. You were talking on the phone in French. I'll ask one more time before you take a nap. How many and how soon?"

She gasped again. "I can't breathe! Please! I'll talk to you but let me up." Stupid me, I did. She sat up, and pulled her sweater up to her neck, looking at her chest. She was braless. "I think you cracked my sternum." Of course, the pig in me was staring at her boobs when she took one more shot at me. I didn't expect a throat punch, and I barely deflected it, caught her hand, jerked her body toward me and clipped her in the jaw, a right uppercut, Joe Louis style. She went down in a heap.

Now it was survival time. I had maybe ten minutes before company came. I rummaged in her overnight bag, found and

157

pocketed a little .25 caliber Beretta boot pistol, and found two bras I used one to tie her hands and one to bind her feet, then stuffed a pair of black thong underwear in her mouth to keep her quiet, using a pair of panty hose tied behind her head to hold them in place. Checking to make sure she was still breathing I picked up the limp body and put her in bed, covering her head to toe. Then I called the front desk. "Hi, it's Mister Shumway in number nine. Listen, we're celebrating our honeymoon, and we don't need housekeeping today. Yes, in fact I would ask that under no circumstances are we to be disturbed until tomorrow, especially by her family that may be coming to play a prank. Yes. Fine and thank you." I hung up and took my money, passport and airline tickets from my little grip. This hotel had a central atrium a ledge and a fire escape ladder. I opened the window, walked the ledge to the ladder and climbed up to the roof. Buildings in Paris are jammed together. I crab-walked on slanted roofs over three buildings before I saw a flat roof with a doorway. The hinge was rusty, and I managed to knock it down after a few solid kicks. Four flights of stairs in some apartment residence, a doorway to a back alley and a quick sprint to the street behind the Best Western. Once in the street, I turned into a regular pedestrian, walking casually away in a drizzle up ahead a long stairway led to the Metro. I got a ticket, stepped inside and sat, catching my breath. I rode three stops, got out and hailed a cab. I smiled a thin smile because I half-expected Barney to be driving. *"Aéroport du Charles De'Gaulle"* was all I said in my best French accent. The driver nodded, happy with a hefty fare and took me to the terminal.

*"Compagnie aérienne?"* he asked.

"Delta"

# Land of the Free, Home of the Braves

I presented my Delta ticket to Miami to the agent. "This is for tomorrow Monsieur"

"Yes, I know. My friend is still going home tomorrow, but I have a business appointment that I have to meet. Yes, I know it's for Miami, but Fort Lauderdale will be fine." They were happy to split the itinerary for a cool eleven hundred Euros. The flight left in two hours, and I knew it was more than possible they would come hunting at the airport. I took some more of my Euros and did a little shopping at one of the airport men's boutiques, changing my wardrobe to look a little more French. After ditching the Beretta in a men's room trashcan, I went through security and boarded the flight without incident. (Hard for bad guys to get past security with an ΛK) I could relax a little when we were wheels up on the way to Atlanta. One more gauntlet, U.S. Immigration in Atlanta. If the Paris authorities report a murder in a room I'm registered in, I'm dead meat. At the same time, the bad guys will not be too quick to blow the horn, and the front desk had instructions to not disturb. I might just squeak by. Sometime after I get home I'll be changing names anyway (if I don't go to prison for killing Tim).

No drinking on this flight, and not the slightest chance for some sleep even though I had napped about forty minutes in the last four days. I was running on pure adrenalin at this point. Arriving in Atlanta, we shuffled of the plane, down long sanitary hallways to US Immigration. Foreigners to the left, US Citizens to the right. My turn came, and I approached the counter. The agent took my passport and slid it into the bar code reader.

"Good morning," I sounded as cheerful as possible. The agent just nodded.

"Where are you coming from?" he asked.

"Out of Paris this morning."

"What countries did you visit?"

I had to think for a second. "Ah, let's see. England, Switzerland, Germany, Holland, Belgium and France. I had a Euro rail Pass." He appeared to be carefully looking at his screen. I know for sure the US Immigration people don't have immediate access to international records, but I was starting to sweat a little. Then my heart sunk when I saw two other uniformed agents approach the counter. The agent handed my passport to one of them, and they spoke quietly for a moment.

"Mister Shumway, will you come with us please?" I knew better than act surprised or belligerent. I just nodded and followed. One walked in front of me and one behind. They escorted me into a small, windowless room with a table and two chairs and closed the door behind me. I could hear the click of the lock. I cooled my heels for about twenty minutes when I heard the click of the lock again and stood up. One of the Immigrations people let a guy in a black suit in. He nodded thanks, and then waited for the door to close and lock again. He reached in his inside jacket pocket and pulled out his wallet, and flashed some kind of Government I.D. The accent was Georgia all the way "Agent Bill Foster. Tim Heminger sends his regards, Mr. Wahl," he extended his hand, and I didn't take it. He shrugged, sat in one chair across the desk and motioned for me to do the same.

"As country folk say, Mr. Wahl, you're a hard dog to keep under the porch. You were supposed to be flying through here tomorrow afternoon with some pretty Ruskie redhead in tow. We had your passport flagged to alert us if you were off schedule. Tim told me you played off the board a lot."

"Yeah, well where is my old buddy Tim?" I asked. "He just seems committed to making me dead. I was thinking about

160

repaying the favor. Probably best he sent one of his flunkies," that was meant to get a rise, and it did.

"Mr. Wahl, I'm the one asking questions right now. Unless you want to sit in this room till Hell freezes over, I suggest you start yakking. For the moment, I'll ignore the 'flunky' line, but let's stop the games."

I gave a heavy sigh. "Look, I just spent five days with someone that was supposed to be an escort and quasi-bodyguard, because you people were concerned there was a mole in your agency that was tipping off your 'Ruskies' about the covert operation. Well, here's a revelation. I found your mole. My escort. I left her unconscious and tied up in room number nine at the Best Western Tour du Eiffel at thirty-five Boulevard de la Tour-Maubourg, but I seriously doubt she's still there." You could have knocked him over with a feather.

"How? Why?" he asked.

"She was asking a lot of questions from the get-go. Things I thought she should have already known. I overheard her speaking in Russian one night on a cell phone that she supposedly wasn't supposed to have, and then caught her doing it again in Paris, this time in French. When I confronted her, she told me more or less that she was a double agent, and wanted info on the item I helped you guys recover. Then she attacked me. I don't like to hit women, but I had to defend myself." And I stopped talking. Foster was speechless for about twenty seconds, and then excused himself, knocking on the door so the Immigration agent would let him out. I sat another hour. So much for my connecting flight. Foster finally returned.

"Okay Mr. Wahl, your story sort of checks out. No tied up woman at the Best Western, but they found the hotel manager and a maid dead in a closet a few hours ago. We've had Delta sequester the manifest on the flight you were on, so it's likely they don't know where you have gone even if they know people who can check. I spoke to Heminger, and you are instructed to fly commercial to Miami, where you will be picked up by the agency and put in protective custody. I'll put you on the plane here personally." He reached in his pocket. "Here's a company cell phone with Tim's number in it. Call him when you get off the plane and he will arrange to pick you up."

"Got it," I answered. "Can I make one teensy request?"

"I've been briefed on your 'requests' Mr. Wahl. We need to get you under protection immediately. I'm afraid there will be no further requests."

I stood up. He stepped back. "Foster, I have had almost two weeks of your so-called 'protection' and have nearly died two, no make it three times. The only reason I'm alive right now is because of me, not you. I can take care of myself, and I have a commitment to take a friend fishing in Fort Lauderdale. Give me two days and a phone number, and I'll be a good boy and turn myself in. I'll wait here while you call Tim and clear it."

"Mr. Wahl...."

"JUST DO IT, FOSTER" and I slammed my fist on the table. He scurried out of the room and came back ten minutes later. "It's against our recommendation, but he said 'go'. Give me your ticket and I'll get your flight booked."

"Thank you," I said. "One more thing. Tell Tim he really doesn't want to be the person that I meet when I'm done with my fishing trip. I owe him at least a trip to the tooth fairy, if not more."

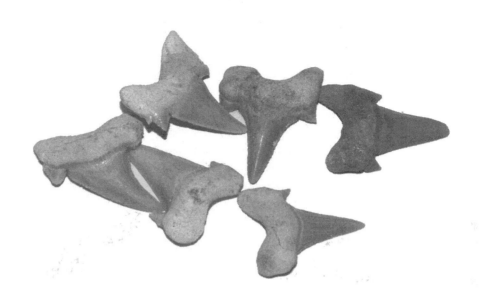

# Revenge - A Dish Best Served Cold

Four hours later I was in Fort Lauderdale. I hailed a cab outside baggage claim. "Marriott Hollywood Beach," I instructed. The cabbie grunted acknowledgement and drove off. The ride was only fifteen minutes, but it gave me time to call information for Marriott's toll free number, and call in a reservation. The reservation was for two people, Bricklin Wahl and Gordon Shumway. No, I didn't have a local phone number. Yes, I would be checking in shortly. When I got to the Marriott, I checked in both of us (me and me) and paid a largish cash deposit in lieu of a credit card. No, I didn't plan to have any incidental charges. Yes, two keys. Mr. Wahl would be checking in shortly.

Now for part two of Operation Goontrap.

I sat in the business center, and started pulling up bars and nightspots in Key West. All my local haunts. First The Fishwagon "Hi Annie, it's Bric. Yeah, been out of town. All is good. Hey, favor to ask. I've got some friends on the rock that I'm supposed to hook up with up in Lauderdale. I don't have their number, and I don't know where they are staying. Two or three guys with foreign accents. They have already? Okay, good. If they come back, please give them a message that I'm staying at the Marriott Hollywood Beach, and I'm looking forward to getting together. Yeah baby, me too. Miss you. Let's have a beverage next time I'm back in town. Ok, cool. Bye."

Then I repeated the story with servers and managers at Schooner Wharf, Sloppy Joes, Hogs Breath, Sunset Pier, Turtle Kraals, and, oh yeah, almost forgot Hogfish. Over half the places told me that my "friends" were indeed asking about me.

The best way to hide from someone is to let them know how to find you, then don't be there. Then I remembered something else. I dug around in my bag, and found a business card lying at the bottom, flipped it over and dialed the number. After a few rings, there was an answer.

"Yes?" It was skinny.

In my Cuban spanglish accent I answered, "Señor, this is Juan. You gave me a ride a couple weeks ago to Beeg Coppitt Circle K."

"Yes, I remember. What do you call me for?"

"That person, Meester Brickwall, my friend he says he talk to him two days ago."

Skinny sounded interested now. "Yes Yes. Thank you! Can you tell me where he is right now?"

"My friend says he go to Hollywood to go feeshing, and that he was going to be staying at the Marriott in Hollywood, the one on the beach. He axed my friend where was a good place to feesh there."

"Yes, Marriott Hollywood Beach. Thank you. Your name is Juan? I promised you a reward. How can I reach you?"

I had to think how to get around this.

"Señor, I live in Opa Locka. Ees not very far from Hollywood. This is not my phone. Can I call ju tomorrow and I'll tell ju where to meet me? Weel that be hogay Señor?"

"That will be fine. Yes. Call me tomorrow afternoon. By then we will have taken care of Mister Brickwall, and we can give you what's coming to you also."

Yeah, I bet.

I figured they would leave immediately and could get here in no more than four hours if they hit the traffic perfect. I had a little prep work to do. I caught another cab and directed the driver to Bass Pro Shops, located right off the end of the Fort Lauderdale Airport runway. They should have what I needed. I gave the cabbie a fifty and told him to wait. I needed protection, but knew there was no way to get a gun in short notice. I seriously missed not having that Springfield that had been blown to smithereens in my van a few weeks ago. I had to settle for a couple of KA-Bar US Marine full size knives. I'd had KA-Bar knives all my life, and, other than some smaller version dive knives, were my favorite. I also knew that I was going to be bringing my knife to a gunfight, two or three guns likely, and the odds weren't promising. My best option would be to divide and conquer. I didn't want to kill people; I just needed some info, at least that's what I kept telling myself.

Back to the hotel, and then to plant some more clues. I went to the concierge and the front desk and told them I was supposed to be having dinner with some friends with foreign accents. If they came looking for me, let them know I had a table at the Greek restaurant down the block, Taverna Opa, and I would meet them there later. Then I walked out of the hotel, wearing a bomber jacket and one of the KA-Bar's belted behind me. The walk to Opa was only about ten minutes, but it started to rain as I walked. I found a doorway in front of a closed T-shirt shop across the street, pulled my hat down to keep the rain out, and waited. I had no idea if I could spring the trap, but these guys were both relentless and predictable. I had an advantage that I knew what they were driving and what they looked like.

Three hours later, maybe nine o'clock, I saw the black Ford Expedition pull into the restaurant parking lot. The SUV backed into a space quite a ways from the restaurant entrance with the intracoastal waterway just a few feet behind them. It couldn't be more perfect for my plan. The three guys got out and walked inside. The first guy that out of the car was the driver, short and bow legged, wearing a jacket, so I guessed he was packing. I called him Shorty. The second guy was the big galoot that had sat in the back with me, had just a tee shirt on, and looked like the muscles in the operation. I labeled him Ugly. Number three was tall and slender and dressed a little better. Might have a gun, might not. I decided he was the brains, and I named him Skinny. I guessed they would probably sit at the bar while one of them cruised the restaurant looking for me. I'm sure they were cautious, but maybe curious that I might be interested in making some sort of deal since I had made myself so easy to find. I had no doubt they would kill me either way, but the off-chance that I might offer a bribe is what makes this a fairly easy trap to spring. Time for the next step. I walked across the street and then through the parking lot and up to the valet. Acting a little drunk, I was a little too loud, and my voice slurred. "Hey man, I got a big problem. I just tagged that big Escalade in the parking lot. I need to let the owner know." The attendant looked down the parking lot and pointed, "that's not an Escalade, it's an Expedition – you mean that one?"

"Ya, whatever, that big futhermucker black SUV, whatever it is," I answered.

He looked a little disgusted and motioned me to go inside. "No, man, I don't want to cause a problem," I reached in my pocket and pulled out a couple of twenties. "Here can you go in and find them? Just ask around or make an announcement or something. I'll wait by their car." The forty bucks worked, and he pocketed the money, walking into the restaurant. I walked back to where the Ford was parked, and waited in the dark. I smiled as Shorty, the wheel man, came walking out through the parking lot. He had a jacket on, just a nylon windbreaker, and it was getting soaked in the rain that was starting to really come down. These guys didn't know what I looked like, and hopefully he would be more pissed than suspicious.

"What is this?" He asked loudly as he approached, in a thick accent.

166

"Wow, sorry man, I jus miss judged how friggin big that barge of yours is. Caught it right in the door when I pulled in." I reached in my jacket pocket, sort of quick, partially to see if he reached for his piece. His eyes narrowed, and I saw him pat the inside of his left arm, indicating the gun was in a shoulder holster. Good. That gave me time.

"Over here man, on this side," I slurred. He walked around to the far side of the Ford and looked at what I was pointing. Lighting in that part of the Opa parking lot is dim, and he couldn't make out what I was trying to show him. He walked closer and leaned over to investigate. A second later, I put my hand on one shoulder and put the tip of the KA-Bar on the side of his neck. I leaned close and whispered.

"Keep your hands in sight and stand up straight. Move fast and you might have an accident."

With that, he suddenly moved away and spun around, reaching under the jacket for his gun. My Navy combat reflexes took control as I moved forward with him, shoved him up against the side of the Expedition, and shoved the KA-Bar knife through the windbreaker, under his sternum and into his chest up to the hilt. The surprised expression on his face was frozen in a scream that wouldn't come out. My face was inches from him, and I whispered again.

"Sorry buddy, that wasn't the plan. But while I'm here..." and I twisted the knife up, and backward, likely cutting his heart completely in two. "This is for what you did to Karen." I knew he was dead, but his eyes, his ears and his brain were still functioning. He heard what I said, but it didn't matter. I held him till his body slumped, and slowly let him settle to the parking lot. I removed the knife, cleaned it on the bushes, and put it back in the scabbard on my belt. I wanted his gun, but didn't want to unzip his jacket and risk getting a lot of blood on me, but I did dig into his pocket and got the keys to the Expedition. I looked around to see if I had drawn attention, then pulled him by the arms over to the breakwater, and shoved him over the hedge, tipping him over the side and gently into the water, watching him drift away with the tide, and slowly sinking in the darkness. He would be found fairly soon, maybe as soon as tomorrow morning. It didn't matter.

I figured I had maybe ten more minutes before the other two came hunting for their buddy. I clicked the lock and started looking through the Ford. One gun in the right side passenger door, a cheap little .32 stainless revolver, and a very nice Sig Sauer P226 .40 Caliber, loaded and ready in the glove box. Nothing much else until I got to the back cargo area. Some rope, duct tape, blankets. Oh! My travel bag! I unzipped it, and there was my beautiful Springfield .45, loaded, literally, for bear, and Julie's Glock, rescued from the yard. I still didn't know if she was part of the posse, or one of the victims.

Now what? Hell, I'm making this up as I go. I had accomplished part of the plan, cutting one person out of the pack, but he got frisky and made himself dead. It felt like a first date with a pretty girl. The "can't we just talk?" line didn't appear to be working well. I mulled over just waiting till another walked out looking for his buddy, and figured the chances of doing something like that again successfully were pretty slim and would eventually get spectator attention. What the Hell. I put the two guns in my travel bag, locked the SUV back up and headed to the restaurant. I walked past the attendant who raised his eyes. "He's waiting at the car for a cop to make a police report," I said. "He sent me in to get his buddies. Where did you find them?"

"Sitting at the bar," pointing indoors.

I walked to the bar where Skinny, and Ugly were sitting where they could survey the crowd. There was an open seat between them, and a half full bottle of Hillas Greek beer on the bar top. Why not? I thought. I strolled up to the bar, squeezed between them, sat down and finished the beer.

"This stool taken," Skinny said.

"Yeah, by me." I answered, and then switched to Spanglish "Remember me, señor?" Skinny's mouth dropped to the countertop. I went back to my normal voice. "Your buddy decided to go for a moonlight swim. If you don't want to join him, you will sit here pleasantly, finish your drinks, and then we will

168

take a drive," I smiled innocently. "I'm sure you don't want to make a public scene, so let's take this to a more secluded place. Okay?"

"You are Mister Brickwall?" Skinny asked. His accent was the least noticeable of any of them. I was right to label him the brains.

"Bric Wahl, not Brickwall, dickwad. Yes, I'm your murder target. I have an offer to make you. Can we take that drive?" He nodded yes, paid the tab. I finished off the dead guys beer, and followed them out the door to the Ford, unlocking it with the key fob. I assumed Ugly didn't drive, at least not in America. So far he hadn't spoken at all, and I wasn't sure he could speak much English. Skinny got behind the wheel, and I opened the door on the passenger side for the big guy, then got in the back seat. Ugly had already opened the glove box for the Sig and was surprised when it wasn't there.

I pulled the .45 out of the bag and brought it into sight. The end of that barrel is big enough to put your pinkie into, and could intimidate Chuck Norris on a good day. "I'm not that stupid, boys. Look, I said to play nice. Any further quick moves and you will be sleeping with the fishes like your driver. I assure you that I'm armed and capable, and more than willing to punch your ticket with very little remorse. Drive out of here, turn left and follow the speed limit. I'll tell you where to go from here." And I tossed the keys to Skinny.

This was a gamble, but I guessed they would go along until they either heard the deal, or got the drop on me. I didn't think he would crash the car into a phone pole or anything. It was likely neither of them was in the US legally, and probably didn't want to draw attention.

We drove south on A1A until it ended at Dania Pier and the entrance to John Lloyd Park. The pier was open all night, and the parking lot by the pier was well lit. A hundred yards farther north, it was dark, secluded and quiet. "Stop here. Back into that spot," I directed. He backed the Expedition into a parking space at the far end of the lot.

"So, here's how it works. I ask questions. You answer to my satisfaction, and I let you drive off into the sunset. How simple is that?" I said.

"What is deal?" Ah, Ugly had a voice.

"The 'deal' is that you both get to live to see the sun rise. If you don't play along, you don't. *Katalavaíneis?"* (do you understand?)

That got no response for a moment, then they started to quietly talk to each other, in Greek.

"English, please. Not polite to speak in foreign languages in front of strangers," I said.

Suddenly, Ugly spun around the seat, and I saw a glint of a small barrel. Probably a boot pistol or something little. He got off a shot, which just missed my head and went through the rear window. Before he could take a second one, I chopped the little gun out of his hand and grabbed him by the wrist. With the butt of the my .45, I broke his nose and yanked his right arm out of the socket with my left hand. He screamed in pain. Another pop to the side of his head with the pistol butt and he went limp, falling toward the door. I turned to skinny, and he put both hands up. He was definitely not a combatant. I pointed the .45 about an inch from his nose.

"Get out of the car, hands in sight. One little twitch and you won't have a head." He stepped out and stood there. "Ok, I'm done playing," I said. I took him by the arm and walked to the back of the Ford, opening the lift gate. Taking the rope, I cut off one piece and tied his hands, then sat him on the tailgate and tied his feet. With the knife, I cut a strip of blanket and gagged him, then shoved him in the back, hogtieing the hands to the feet. Then I got behind the wheel and checked on ugly. He was sound asleep and as hard as I hit him, I wasn't positive he would wake up by morning.

I drove back to the Marriott and parked on the street. The windows on Harry's Expedition were super dark, and it was late, so I trusted I could leave my prisoners there for a while. I went to my room, got my bag and walked out the front door without checking out.

That's the last time anyone named Russell Bricklin Wahl would exist.

From the Marriott I drove to an open parking lot at an abandoned Publix grocery store on Federal. I just needed to wait a few hours until morning. Fatty was still sleeping – I checked, and he was breathing, and skinny was in the back making "muff, muff" noises. I figured I'd let him cook a while. I didn't know if he wanted to sing or just go potty, and I didn't give a damn.

At seven thirty I dialed a number from memory.

"Good morning, Doctor Roddy's office."

"Hi there, tell Doctor Roddy that Russell Wahl is on the phone."

Doctor Jon Roddy was one of the top foot doctors in the state. On a number of occasions he's helped me with some jungle grunge that the VA never managed to clear up. He's also got one sweet fishing boat.

"Bric! A pleasant surprise! Are you in the neighborhood? Want to go fishing this weekend?"

"Hi Doc," I answered. "Yes, and no. I want to go fishing but can't wait. I've got a rich European that's got the hots to get a bull shark on the line. Any chance I can rent the *'Fun-Guy'* from you this morning for the day?"

"Sure," he answered. "The normal three-hundred bucks and a full tank. That's what we always used to do. Oh, and give it a bath. I know how messy shark fishing can get. Sure it can't wait till Saturday? I'd love to tag along."

"Nope," I answered. He's only here for today and heading back up to Disney tonight and back with his fraulein and the kinder." I hesitated and took the chance. "You're welcome to play hooky and join us today," I crossed my fingers.

"Nah, I've got a full docket of bad feet to smell, but thanks for the offer. Okay, side gate is open, and the spare key is in the magnetic key holder under the steering column. Have fun!"

I hung up and thanked my luck. Roddy's boat is berthed on a canal behind his house. All I had to do was get in the boat without drawing too much attention, and we were all set. I still didn't quite know what to do with Ugly, but hopefully he would wake up before we got there.

I had two more stops to make on the way. First Outdoor World and the scuba shop next door. I tied fatty's hands to the bottom of the seat just to make sure he didn't wake up and cause trouble, locked the car and went inside. More nylon rope, some five gallon plastic buckets, a couple of ski jackets (didn't want bright colors) and two weight belts and some dive weights. Oh, sunblock and a couple of hats. Sunglasses for me. From there a quick stop at the bait shop for some chum, a chum bag and frozen ballyhoo. Doc had good tackle.

Next stop the doc's house. The gods were watching over me as fatty started to come alive about ten minutes before we got there. He figured out where he was, and then realized who was driving. He was breathing through his mouth since his nose was clogged with blood. I told him to sit quiet and nice, and I promised not to put him back to sleep. I think he got the message, and besides, his dislocated shoulder pretty well had the fight out of him.

Roddy's place was on a canal in a very nice neighborhood in Fort Lauderdale. I backed the Expedition into the driveway, so the license plate was not easily visible, shut off the motor, and turned to fatty. I spoke loud enough so skinny could hear me. He was still making grunting noises.

"Okay boys, here's the deal. I've got three guns, two knives, two hands and two feet, any and all which are capable of sending you to *Ouranos* (heaven) in five seconds. Or maybe in your case *Hades*. I promise you here, and now, if you cooperate, I will not kill you. We're going to take a little boat ride, have a conversation, and if you answer my questions, I'll let you go. I'm telling you the truth, but I don't care if you believe me or not. I do promise that if you give me one second of crap, I'll start breaking bones. I'm going to untie both of you and then we will walk quietly out of the driveway and get in the boat. Do you understand? Fatty nodded. I really wasn't worried about skinny.

I got out of the truck and opened the back. Skinny was still tied up nice and tidy, and his eyes were big as saucers. I untied his feet and removed the gag so he could set up. Then I got one of the weight belts, estimated his weight and added three eight pound weight bags to the belt before buckling it on him, with the buckle at the back. Then I untied him. "Wait here," I instructed. Then I opened the passenger door and untied fatty. He was in a lot of pain, but I wanted to keep him that way for a while. I fitted him with a weight belt too, this time with six bags of shot. "Be a good boy and I'll fix that shoulder for you in a little bit," I said. He nodded that he understood. I pointed toward the side gate and walked them through it, pointing at a bench for them to sit on.

"Why these?" skinny asked, indicating the weight belts.

"Let's just say nobody will decide to accidentally fall over. You can swim with them, but not for very long," I answered.

The back garage door was open, and I ducked inside to grab a couple of rods and reels, heavy stuff, along with Roddy's tackle box, keeping half an eye on the backyard to make sure my goons stayed put. I also raided the garage fridge for several bottles of water, and a couple of cans of beer. There was an ice chest on the floor, and I loaded it, plus ice from the freezer. A little food would have been appreciated, but that wasn't in the plan right now. I loaded the gear and chest, and then motioned for the boys to join. I had to help fatty on the boat. He was pretty tough, but that dislocated arm was really painful. I could fix it in two seconds but didn't want to draw attention with the automatic scream.

The *Fun-Guy* was a sweet boat, thirty one foot Sea Ray with twin Mercruiser 350's. Easily a hundred grand worth of boat and perfect for the ocean. The deep hull would do well in rough seas, and the cabin slept four, had a nice head, fridge and even a decent stereo. The GPS was Garmin state of the art, but it would stay off today. I didn't want to leave tracks. She fired on the first try, and I cast off, motoring down the canal, into the intracoastal and out into the Atlantic. My boys were sitting in back like gentlemen, but as soon as I cleared the breakwater, I backed down to idle, got the rope and tied their feet. I also told fatty to brace himself, and I popped his shoulder back in its socket. He let out the obligatory

173

scream, and then completely relaxed as the pain almost instantly stopped.

"See, I keep my promises. You guys have behaved. Again, I will not kill you, and after we talk, I will let you go."

I gave them each a bottle of water and a hat, and sunblock, then headed out a few miles. "I'm going to fish, you're going to watch," I explained. Watching the fish finder, I motored out till I started marking fish. I idled down, baited two lines with ballyhoo and started trolling slowly. I wasn't going for quality, but quantity and I was happy when the line snapped tight and a few minutes later, boated a nice bonito. I dropped it in the well, re-baited and caught another a few minutes later. My third was a little kingfish, and the forth a little blackfin tuna. Before dropping the tuna in the well, I sliced a nice loin off and enjoyed some fresh sushi. It tasted like candy. I had all I needed after only about an hour. Throttling up to thirty knots, I headed east, toward the gulfstream. A half hour later, we were well off shore, far away from other boats. For this time of the year, the water was pretty calm, and when I cut the motors, we just bobbed a bit. The fish finder indicated six hundred feet. Without talking I put the life jackets on both men and then tied both men's hands behind their back. Fatty started to give me lip, and I asked if he would like his right arm returned to its uncomfortable location. He shut up. Then I looped the rope through skinny and with about twelve feet of space, tied it onto fatty, then, without much warning, pushed both of them out of the boat. The weight belts kept them low in the water, and the ski vests kept them afloat.

"What are you doing?" skinny yelled, "you said that we would not be harmed!"

"I said," I reminded them, "that I would not kill you. You need to learn to listen." With that, I pulled the first bonito out of the well, leaned over the side and started slashing his belly open. I cut him several times and let him drift off. Then I reached for the next one and did the same. I calmly started to explain. "You see, in close to shore, it's just black tipped reef sharks. They aren't too large and won't take on things as large as a man. Oh, they might nip off a finger or a toe, or maybe your dick, but nothing to get too worried about." I reached for the king. They are always nice and bloody. I continued, "Now, out here, it's different. In the Gulfstream, that's where the pelagics hang out. bull sharks, tiger sharks, hammerheads, even an occasional great white. You never know what you might chum up. These guys can smell blood from nearly ten miles away. I figure you got maybe twenty minutes before company starts showing up for dinner."

With this, they were both yelling, all in Greek, both at the same time. "Mister Brickwall, please. You promised you would not kill us. Please let us back in the boat. We will tell you anything we know."

"I said that *I* wouldn't kill you," I answered. "I didn't say anything about what a tiger shark might do." I reached in the well for another bonito. "I promised to let you go, but we have some unfinished business first." I started asking questions, and skinny started singing like a songbird. Ten minutes later, I had as much information as I thought they knew. "Okay," I said. "My end of the bargain", and I untied the other end of the tether, tied the last bonito on it and threw it in the water.

"Wait, wait!" They both yelled. "You said…."

I cut them off. "I said I would let you go, and I just did. Heck, who knows, we're actually a long ways from shark territory. They might not find you at all. The gulfstream moves at about three knots, so you will wind up off North Carolina in a week or so. Maybe a passing ship will see you, although with those dark ski vests, that might be tough. Hey, I'm giving you a fighting chance. That's a helluva lot more than you gave my girlfriend."

And with that I turned my back, fired up the *Fun-Guy*, and throttled up.

I couldn't help but notice the grey fin slicing the water off to my right. I'm sure the engine noise drowned out the screams.

It didn't take too long to get back to the Doc's house. I looked in the garage and found the soap and scrub brush in a bucket, grabbed the water hose and gave the boat a good scrubbing to get the fish blood cleaned off, then left three crisp hundred dollar bills under the matt at the back door. I called the Doc's office and told the receptionist to thank the doc for me and where to find the cash. "Hold please for the doctor." After a moment, he came on the line. "Bric, why don't you hang around till Saturday and we'll hunt blackfin."

"Sorry, Jon," I answered. "Places to go, things to do."

"Okay, another time then. So how was the fishing today."

"We killed 'em Doc. It was truly a day to die for," I answered, with a thin smile.

# One Last Time

I fired up the Expedition and headed south. I hadn't driven anything bigger than a Jeep over the last ten years. Last time I was behind the wheel of something this big it made a wake. I noticed Skinny's cell phone was still sitting on the seat, and it showed eleven missed calls, all with a familiar 813 area code.

Harry Sykas. I always knew he was behind this, but there was the real proof.

I drove west to I-595, then south on the turnpike to Florida City. I wasn't in a huge hurry, and truly didn't know what I was going to do when I got back down to Key West. Tim had warned me not to go there because the bad guys might kill me. There might be other bad guys, but at least three were off the list. Well, I had four hours to figure out what to do, but first, I decided on taking Card Sound Road and having dinner at Alabama Jack's. It had been too many times driving by that place without stopping. I figured that, at least for a little while, nobody was looking for me. I pulled in and opted for the bar instead of sitting on the water and watching the fish. It was just about dark now anyway, but I did squeeze in before Happy Hour was over.

"Beer, a backup and a basket of dolphin fingers and fries," I ordered. The first beer lasted five seconds and the first time in a month that I actually didn't have some grandiose plan looming in front of me. Life was far from calm, and I figured when I stopped moving long enough, I would probably break down for a good cry. I had a third beer and was ordering a fourth when one of my two cell phones started buzzing. I dug in my pocket and looked. It was the CIA phone that Bill Foster had given me. Oh, what the Hell.

"Hullo Tim. What's up?"

"Naughty, naughty, Bric. We told you not to go to the Keys," he started.

"Here you go with this 'we' shit again. Ah, for one thing, old ex-buddy, you *ASKED* me not to go, not told me. You also said don't go to Key West. I assume by calling me that you know darned well I'm not anywhere close to Key West."

"We have a fairly decent idea where you are. Do me a favor and stay put for a while so we can pick you up and get your relocation plan underway."

"Not," I replied, "just quite yet. I've still got a few days of fishing ahead of me in Fort Lauderdale. I just drove a little south to breathe fresh air, clear my brain and eat some real food. I'll give you a call sometime next week."

"You know Bric, you're a really crappy liar," Tim replied.

"Yeah, well, you don't tell the truth for shit either." And I hung up.

I stood up and started to heave the phone into the canal and then stopped. Hard to break old habits, I thought, smiling to myself. I chose a bright orange Alabama Jack's cap to replace my "Old Guys Rule" hat that went down with the *Southwind*, paid my tab and walked out to the parking lot. There was a couple, mature but not old I would guess, walking out in front of me. They walked up to an orange Jeep Wrangler with the top down and a spare tire cover that said 'Go Topless'.

"Nice Jeep! I had one myself last year," I called out. She turned and smiled. "Thanks, we love it," she said. She was pretty, wearing a Tiger Woods visor over a mass of spiky hair, white Ray-Bans, tattered cutoffs and a thin black spaghetti-string tank top. There was a large hibiscus tattoo peeking through on her right shoulder. Her husband was wearing a scowl because he noticed I was aware she was braless under a thin black tank top with a hibiscus tattoo. He checked me out to make sure that I wasn't either going to rob them or hit on his girl too seriously. I gave my best all-shucks smile and turned to him.

"Hey, I'm heading down to Key West. Did you guys just come back? Any traffic problems?"

He relaxed a little with the question. "Yea, we just drove up from Hawks Cay. Smooth sailing all the way." I nodded, smiled, and walked to the back of the jeep admiring the tire cover, then waved at both of them. "Safe travels!" I called, and waited till they drove off before I walked to the Expedition, hopped in and drove south toward Card Sound Bridge. I figured the only way Tim would have known my approximate location was to either have a locator on the SUV or in the cell phone he gave me. Since he would have never had a chance to put a bug in the Ford, I figured his boys conveniently put a GPS locator inside the cell phone Foster gave me in Atlanta. Now, with that phone, ringer turned to silent, and safely tucked inside of that "Drive Topless" tire cover, they would chase me up the turnpike all evening and put twenty-four hour surveillance on this poor couple's house all night before they figured out my trick. I smiled, and searched the Sirius radio on the Expedition until I found the Margaritaville Channel. Windows down and radio at full blast, I sang along with Jimmy again at the top of my lung.

"Wasting away in Margaritaville, searching for my, lost shaker of salt......"

For a few moments, my world was at peace. But not for long,

not for long.

I had skinny's credit cards, but decided that cash was untraceable and a better option. I filled up in Tavernier, bought an Amp Energy drink and a box of Dots and continued south. I knew there was one last piece of unfinished dirty work before I cashed in on Tim's deal. I suspected Harry was in Key West, and either way, I was pretty sure I could get him to show up. The "when" part took care of itself when Skinny's phone chirped. I answered but didn't speak. The speaker erupted in a thirty second burst of screaming. I still kept quiet until he realized nobody was talking on the other end. "Dimitri?" Harry finally said.

I broke the silence. "Dimitri? I'm guessing that's the skinny one. Sorry Harry, I never caught his name. He's a little tied up now and can't come to the phone. I'm not sure if he's going to shower this afternoon, or just wash up on shore tomorrow."

"Wahl! Where are you? YOU ARE A DEAD FUCKING PERSON."

"Perhaps, but I am assembling a nice honor guard. I only need one more escort to complete the set. I have something I think you want. Would you like to settle up?"

"You're telling me you have my gold?" He asked. "I don't think so. In fact, I'm almost positive you don't, but I'll meet you. Where and when?"

Key West, tomorrow night at midnight, in front of the Fishwagon. Come alone, come unarmed." And I hung up. The phone immediately started ringing again. I was tempted to throw it off the Seven Mile Bridge, but decided I might need it again, so I just shut it off. Bait planted, trap set, but why? Nothing to be accomplished for killing more people, but I didn't have all the answers I needed. One little chat with Harry and I guess I'll change my name to Joe Smith and run a chrome plated dildo store in Dirt, South Dakota.

For joy.

There was no reason to hang around the island all night. I didn't want Harry or any of his other family members to accidentally run across me. As I came through Summerland Key,

I turned off onto Mako Drive and followed the road until it turned into a pothole filled goat path. I parked at the place the locals call "The Swimming Hole", a dug-out channel a hundred feet or so long, the victim of some long forgotten failed housing project. I looked around to make sure there were no teenage couples coupling, stripped off and took a refreshing dip in the clear ocean water, then flipped the seats down on the SUV and took a nap.

I woke to the sounds of a dog barking and sat up. A half dozen women were strolling down the path, all with dogs on or off their leashes. Apparently a Summerland social group on a morning outing. Realizing I was laying there with the tailgate open, naked on a towel, I quickly gathered the towel around me, hopped out of the back and opened the front door to get my clothes. I tried to dress as modestly as possible, using both open doors as cover, but still gave them a bit more of a show than I wanted. "Morning, ladies, sure is nice out."

"It sure was!" came an answer from across the canal. Sheesh. I beat a hasty retreat up the road. Thankfully there was nobody I knew in that crowd. More thankfully, I would never see any of them again.

Cruising into town, Stock Island, Roosevelt Boulevard past Sears Town, by Hilton Haven Drive and Bo's place, over Garrison Bight and into Old Town, I realized that might be the last time I ever saw these places. It was bitter sweet. I do love this strange old rock, but the shine was clearly off the penny, so to speak. Maybe time to be moving on. If this was the Last Supper, maybe it should start with a Last Breakfast. Blue Heaven or Pepe's? Both good, both public, and today, both possibly dangerous. Oh, that's right. Pepe's is closed for renovation since the blast. Blue Heaven it is. I headed into Bahama Village and found a meter on a side street. I was done hiding, but didn't need to be stupid. I walked back around the corner and into Blue Heaven, took a seat in the outdoor patio section, back to the wall. I found out that they have exceptionally low staff turnover. . Blue Heaven is in Bahama Village and has a claim to fame that the upstairs area was supposedly one of the places Hemingway engaged in his

181

impromptu boxing matches. Whether or not that's true, it's a neat outdoor place for breakfast, and you can share bread crumbs with the local chicken population that are comfortable running under your feet for table scraps.

"Morning Bric," the server said. "Coffee and the usual?" Crap, I hadn't eaten there in well over a year. This gal had the memory of an elephant. Hell, I didn't remember what my "usual" was.

"Sure, thanks," I answered. I'm sure it would be edible. She brought me coffee, ice water and fresh orange juice and later a mushroom Swiss omelet, home fries and white toast. She also brought a bottle of ketchup and Tobasco sauce. Yeah, she knew me well, and I didn't even know her name.

Breakfast done, and I had nothing to do all day long but kill time. I would have loved to cruise Duval street, drop by the Hogs Breath and watch Barry Cuda, maybe catch Pete and Wayne at Sloppy Joes this afternoon, sit in for a song on two with the band at Buzzards, but these people have probably forgotten my name. I didn't see any advantage to showing back up for one day, and then vanishing forever. There's no better way to kill time, other than a fishing trip, than to sit on a beach and watch the world go by. I stopped by a news rack, picked up a copy of the Key West Citizen, and headed for South Beach. I thought about going back to Higgs Beach to see if Rio was there, but that chapter was closed, it would reopen too many thoughts, too many memories. I found a parking meter at South Beach, fed it a few dollars and walked out on the sand, keeping distance from the tourists and street bums, and started reading the Key West Citizen. I hadn't actually read the paper since I got back to town – just too busy part of the time, and the rest of the time any papers I found I used for a blanket and a pillow. Ah, page one. "White Street Sewer System Upgrade Delays." Hell that was a headline twenty years ago. Then the Crime Report had a story about two women arrested in a domestic violence dispute, hauled away after a knock-down, drag-out fight over the ownership of a large vibrator. More stories about politics, local events, high school sports, and lots of national stories gleaned from the newswires. No wonder the locals call it the Mackerel Wrapper. It has little other value than wrapping up fish and shrimp. Then, on page four, there was a photo of a boat and caption. The ships design caught my eye. The huge curved "mailboxes", devices designed to divert propeller wash downwards to clear sea bottom away- were hung on the stern, and a large crane mounted at the back identified the boat as a salvage vessel. I read the caption. "*Mary McDonald* back in port for a week." There were a few more lines about the ship being back in port for supplies and repairs after working a wreck off the coast of South America for over a year… then it came to me. Brody! My son is on that boat! I read farther that the boat was docked at Safe Harbor Marina. Safe Harbor. That's Stock Island, next to the Hogfish. I dropped the paper and almost ran to the Expedition. The drive to Stock Island took ten minutes but felt like hours. I parked across from the Hogfish and walked down the dock. I saw the *McDonald* across the marina, tied up not far from two Mel Fisher's treasure boats. I walked around to the other side of the marina and up to the *McDonald*. I stood around for a few minutes, and then Brody emerged from below decks, carrying dive tanks. Suddenly I couldn't see clearly, eyes a little blurry with a tear. I honestly thought I may never see him again, or at best, many years, and there he was, thirty feet away. I gave one, low "tweet" whistle, a sound he had heard all his life from me. Brody spun around in his tracks and saw me. I froze the yell he was about to give by putting my finger to my lips. His eyes narrowed, but he caught right on. I gave him a little salute and pointed at the Hogfish. He nodded understanding, and I strolled off.

Aside from selling the second coldest beer in Key West and its namesake, hogfish sandwiches good enough to be the only reason to drive to this island, the Hogfish has some bittersweet memories for me. Lots of delectable food and drink, and an encounter with an old nemesis, Itchy Roberts, rest his soul that nearly got me convicted of murder. I had a lot of old friends, and for that matter enemies, that hang around here. I was hoping neither was here today, or they didn't recognize me with a goatee. I took an outside table with my back to the bar and ordered a Bud. Brody walked up behind me a few minutes later and sat down across from me with a huge grin.

"Dad, I didn't think you were here. I got in two days ago and asked around. I stopped by Buzzards, called Bo and ran into Scarlett. Everyone said you or Karen hadn't been around for over a year."

I interrupted. "Scarlet?" Kevin's in town? I thought he had moved away." Kevin Montclaire, AKA Scarlet, was my ex tenant when I was briefly a slumlord houseboat owner before turning it into a ship and sailing it to Tarpon Springs. Scarlet is a six foot, five inch tall, three hundred pound cross dressing drag queen that worked for years at Aqua on Duval Street before turning undercover cop and helping bust up a drug ring. "I would love to say hi. He/She's been a good friend."

"Heck dad, after work, I'll borrow a car and go pick him up. We can do dinner."

"Well," I answered. "It's not that easy. That's why I shushed you on the boat a few minutes ago." I took a deep breath. This shaggy dog tale was getting longer and longer. I gave him the Reader's Digest version of what had been going on over the last few months, leaving out some bad stuff, embellish on the parts I knew he would like.

"Wow, six hundred sixty feet, dad. That must have been amazing." His eyes were big as saucers.

"It was scary as all fuck," I recalled. "I nearly died three times that day, and when I finally survived, I wanted to die before they got me in that hyperbaric chamber. I don't recommend that party for anyone."

"So, you're going to see Harry tonight?" he asked. "What then? You gonna kill him?"

"I agree, he deserves killing if anyone does, but there's been too much killing already. I've lost someone – he's lost family. In my book we're even. I got some answers from the bad guys before I, ah, let them go, but I need to hear Harry's story, why he had Karen kidnapped, why he killed her. I guess, then, I'll just go

184

away." I heaved a heavy sigh. "I'm tired son. I need the world to slow down."

Brody took it all in. For only being twenty one, he was wise beyond his years. He could have asked a million questions but only had one. "Want me there tonight?"

"Thanks, but no. I told him to come solo, and I should respect that. Told him to meet me on Caroline tonight, in public, so I'm not expecting funny stuff. I've got an arsenal in that Ford over there, but I don't think he's got the balls to shoot me." I smiled grimly, "he's probably running short of hoodlum family members too. No, I should be okay."

"Ok dad. Come by on your way out of town tomorrow. We pull out at three and won't be back for more than six months. How will I know how to find you?"

I thought for a few moments, reluctant to use the word 'friend'. "Ah, some people that I know, the ones I helped in England, are going to relocate me. I'll make sure you and Gracie know where I am. I don't have much more info than that." With that, I stood up and reached out my hand. "You have no idea how much I want to give you a big bear hug," I said, "But it's not safe for people that know me well. I don't know if anyone's watching, but I don't want you in danger."

"Got it, dad, but I can take care of me." He returned the handshake, "you watch your back pop. I love you."

"Shut up son, you're going to make me a blubbering idiot. You take care too. See you tomorrow morning." And I turned and walked away, then stopped and turned. "Brody! How do I reach Scarlett? I'd love to pay a visit."

"The unit over the print shop, across the street from the Chinese restaurant on Simonton. There's a gate to the left. Know where I'm talking about?"

"Yeah, I know where," I answered. "I actually looked at renting that place before I moved into Bo's houseboat. Thanks buddy."

I drove off, emotions mixed and mind in a whirl. Scarlet worked undercover for the DEA, and helped break up a large drug

185

ring before hitching a ride on our houseboat to Tarpon Springs. I owed Scarlet a lot when she came back to Key West and provided an iron-proof alibi for me when I was arrested for suspicion of murder. I might never see this gentle giant again, and welcomed the chance to visit one more time. I drove to Scarlett's place and walked through the gate to the side yard. The steps were as rickety as I remembered. I was afraid to walk up them and couldn't imagine a three hundred pound man in eight inch pumps would even try. No need for a watch dog; the creaking steps announced my arrival half way up the steps. The door opened a crack, and then flung wide open when he saw who it was. A second later I found myself wrapped in a huge set of black arms. I was more than surprised that "Scarlet" was "Kevin" today. Normal attire means a huge blonde wig, size fifty-two fake boobs, spandex skin-tight pants and black fuck-me-please pumps. I wasn't actually sure what Scarlet's sexual preference was. I know she didn't like being called queer, and more than once just announced that he was just a big black man in a dress. Oh, well, today it was Kevin, and aside from the bulk, was almost unrecognizable to me. Bermuda shorts, a tank top and flip flops were more strange to me than seeing him in drag.

"Bric! How have you been? WHERE have you been? I got back a month ago, and everyone said you and Karen were still on the road. Tell me!"

I was weary of the story and just plain weary. "Just in town for a day. Ran into Brody and he told me where you were at. Couldn't leave without saying hi." I stopped talking and hoped there were no more questions. Kevin's not much of a gossiper, and I guessed right he wouldn't probe. I got filled in on the last year – trip home to New Orleans, suntans on some beach, somewhere, shopping on Aruba, dancing in Hawaii.

"Sounds like a good time. Glad you got some 'you' time," I said. "What brought you back to the island?"

"Well, 'normal' in other places doesn't replace 'normal' here. I can be who I am on this rock – and no place else. It's that simple."

I was running out of questions, and didn't want the conversation to get around to my life. I jumped up, gave one last good man hug, and left. It was sad to say goodbye to people I cared for so much, and hard to walk down those damn stairs looking through blurry eyes.

# Showdown

The wait till two a.m. was agonizing. The Fishwagon closes early, but you honestly can't lock up that open air bar. A little after one I stepped over the rope that serves for a door and took a seat in the shadows. I didn't want to underestimate Harry and end up on the bad end of a sniper scope. Other than a few cars going by, and servers on bikes and scooters getting off early from swing shift, all was quiet. Then there was some movement to the left on the dark street. That was the advantage of sitting in this dark place. My cat eyes were wide open. Then I caught second movement in a doorway to the right. Aw, I thought to myself, Harry didn't keep his end of the bargain. A few minutes later a cell phone lit up on the guy to the right. It went dark and a few moments later the unmistakable fat slob persona of Harry Sykas waddled into view from the left down Caroline Street. Showtime, but did I want to show myself. I wasn't worried with two or three opponents, as long as they weren't shooting. As an afterthought, I regretted not tucking the gun in my belt. Oh Hell, Bric, wanna live forever? I stood up and stepped over the rope and walked off the curb. Harry stopped about fifty feet away and looked left. I saw motion in the darkness, and my combat radar made the hair on the back of my neck stand up. I relaxed when I saw it was Brody and Scarlett coming into view. My son never did take directions very well, bless his heart. I gave Brody a heads up with my little tweetie-bird whistle, but he was already checking out the talent. Looked like four guys total, plus Harry, who was guaranteed he would only be a spectator until after they had 'taken care' of me. All of them had some sort of implement which was encouraging because that meant they were likely not carrying things that shoot.

188

We squared off in the middle of the side street, OK Corral style. I decided to make the first move…

"Gentlemen, what austere moment gives us the pleasure of a visit?" I ventured.

Harry shouted from behind and the left, well out of any hint of danger. "We're done fucking around Bric. I don't know why you wanted to see me. I know you don't have any gold. You're not in a place to bargain. Oh, I'm not going to hurt you. I'm going to make you watch your son get beat to death, and then I'll mark up the face of your faggot girlfriend so he will never be able to prance on a stage again."

"I ain't no 'faggot' you fat assed dickwad," said Scarlet. "And you need more than four friends to put a mark on my face. Bring it on."

Brody was being Brody. Looking gentle and helpless, but I could see that he and Scarlet had slowly spread out a little and were getting ready for a fight.

I gave a weary sigh. "Harry, I'm an idiot. I thought I could reason with you. I have suffered a loss – you have suffered a loss. Can't we just go our separate ways? I don't know where the gold is, people have told me you killed my girlfriend and I've got about three hundred bucks in my pocket. Tell you what, same deal as before. I'll split it with you sixty forty. You want it in tens or twenties?"

I was just killing some time while our eyes got more accustomed to the dark. We had just walked off Caroline that was pretty well lit, and I didn't see any way out of this cluster-fuck, regardless of how badly planned it was.

"Bric, I'm on the hook to my family for this money. I won't just go away you know. I think you're lying, and it's time to get some truth."

Two of Harry's new bad guys paired up to take care of me. One had a sap and the other a billy club. They were beefy, but looked like they had the combined IQ of slime mold, and I don't think they were near as talented the so called 'pros' that I just finished dealing with in Hollywood a few days ago. The other two

189

moved at Brody, assuming that Scarlet wouldn't be a player and just stand there and look frail while Brody got beat up. Two on one wasn't even fair. Brody was a second degree black belt in Tai-Kwan-Do, and Scarlet's a cop. He never even saw the side kick, which landed a number twelve Nike flip-flop squarely on the jaw. The sound of teeth breaking, and loud crack of a broken jawbone meant that goon was done for the night. Brody turned to jerk number four, but he had just been introduced to a candy-apple red eight-inch fuck-me-please stiletto toe pump directly into the crotch. I would guess that half the shoe disappeared into never land. He screamed like a six year old and hit the ground in a fetal position. My escorts had watched the four-second show with slack-jawed awe. They weren't looking at me so I took the liberty of grabbing the nightstick from number two and gave his left knee a good solid thwack. I felt the kneecap go with a satisfying crunch and he joined his buddies on the asphalt. So far nobody was dead, but I really wasn't that concerned with knocking one of these guys off. I turned to the last standing dickhead and brought the billy club up to ready.

"A crushed Adams-apple is a terrible way to suffocate to death," I said casually. He caught the hint, dropped his sap and ran down the street. I picked it up and flipped it to Scarlet, who caught it behind her back with one hand. I walked down the sidewalk and came around the van where Harry was cowering. This plan hadn't gone exactly the way he wanted it to.

"Okay Harry, checkmate. Again. Like I said, I ain't got your gold, and I don't know where it is. I think you know that too for some reason. Maybe it's time for some answers from you."
Harry never saw Scarlet come up behind him. One little love tap with the sap on the side of his head and Harry went down like the sack of shit he was.

We woke Harry up a half hour later with a bottle of water being poured on the back of his head. He no doubt had a screaming headache, but that was the least of his issues. It took all three of us, but we had managed to drag his fat ass into a little garage a few houses down from the scene of the crime on

William. It belonged to my great aunt, who had been in an assisted care facility in Altamonte Springs for the past year. The house was closed up, and the garage was unlocked and unattended. It had been an old carriage barn back when there were carriages, and it had been there for a terribly long time – more than a hundred fifty years and was just barely standing. I found an old nail keg with one end busted out, and Brody, Scarlet and I managed to drape Harry over it, then tie him spread-eagled hand and foot on a couple of loose boards. He woke up in this rather undignified position, and immediately noticed that his pants were down around his ankles.

"You must have a death wish Bric," said Harry. I wasn't going to kill anyone but that deal is off. You won't live through the week."

"Harry, if you don't shut the fuck up, you won't live through the night. At least you will want to be dead. Scarlet, give Harry a preview of his next two hours of entertainment. Scarlet, walked around in front of Harry, pulled down the Capri pants and un-tucked about a foot or so of black fire hose. "Harry, look a little scared so's I can get this thing hard. This is gonna be fun! I ain't normally into little tight pink assholes, but I'll make a 'section tonight." It always made me chuckle a little to myself to hear Scarlett lapse into slang. With a degree at Tulane, Scarlet could speak white boy English better than I.

"NO! Why are you doing this? I don't have anything to say to you!"

"Really?" I asked. "I think you do. Anyway, I thought you Greek types were into this kind of thing."

"Not Me!" Harry cried.

"I'm surprised at you," Scarlet answered. Somewhat philosophically. "I mean what guy wouldn't want love-making that always starts with a blowjob and always ends in anal sex? Ain't nothing wrong with being gay. Not that *I* am, but like I said, just as a favor to Bric, I'm gonna join the other team, just for tonight. Yep, gonna dry-fuck your little shithole. Yep, right up the poop-chute, up the old Hersey Highway until I reach your tonsils.

191

What do you think Bric? Use a little grease or just see how far I can get it up there dry?"

At this point, Harry was covered in sweat, and he'd already wet himself. He might have also lost control of other body functions, but he had his ass cheeks clinched so hard it would have taken the Jaws of Life to get anything in or out.

I sat down, cross-legged on the ground in front of the jerk. "Okay Harry, I would say that we are in, let's say, a position of advantage. I think you have a story to tell, but let me start it for you. First, the three family members from across the pond that you loaned your Expedition to are dead. I lured them up to Fort Lauderdale, caught them, got enough info to make sure you were behind all of this, and then sent them to rot in Hell. Those four guys tonight you were just willing to sacrifice weren't hired bad guys, but family from Tarpon Springs. I recognized one of them, and the rest had a clear family resemblance, dim witted, unibrow, and calloused on their knuckles from dragging them on the ground. Your family sent them to find the gold, and you told them I knew where it was, so I made sure you knew how to find me. But you already have it, or know where it is, and want to keep it all for yourself. You killed Karen, something for which I will personally deal with you later, and you figure by making it look like I wouldn't talk, so you kill me too so all the witnesses and persons of interest are off the scoreboard. How am I doing?"

"That's preposterous!" squeaked Harry. "I...."

"Okay Scarlet, he says he's good with dry. Think we need to gag him?"

"Nah, I'm gonna fuck his throat from the bottom up. He won't be able to scream."

I picked one of Harry's dirty socks off the garage floor and shoved in his mouth. "Screams are like gunshots. They draw too much attention and Harry, I do believe you are about to scream a whole bunch." To which Harry responded with "mrfffff! mrffff!."

Scarlet walked out of Harry's eyesight. "This is sure gonna hurt you more that it's gonna hurt me!"

Harry's "mrfffs!" got a little more animated. "Care to chat

192

Harry?" I asked. He nodded vigorously, and I pulled the dirty sock out of his mouth. I sat down back on the dirt floor, brushing aside the loose square nails that littered the dirt. Reminder to me. Old nails like these, probably from the Civil War era, can be sold for a few bucks a piece. Probably several thousand bucks laying around this old barn. Aunt Emma won't mind if I suggest to Brody that he does a little floor cleanup for root beer money later.

"Spill it!" I instructed.

Harry was hyperventilating to the point of blacking out. I motioned Brody to give him a sip of bottled water, and he caught his breath. He began, "where do I start?" he was panting. "Bric, believe me or not, but a lot of what's happened isn't me. I made the mistake of talking about our 'agreement' one night at a family gathering. I told my family that I wasn't happy, but I did think I could trust you, I just didn't know when you were coming back." He struggled against the ropes. "Wahl, this is undignified. Can you please release me from this ridiculous position?"

"All in good time, Harry. You aren't out of the woods yet. Keep talking."

He closed his eyes in rage, then took a breath and continued talking. I think I knew he was digging a hole for himself and his story. Maybe his grave.

"So my hot-headed brother told me I was being played for a patsy, that you guys had already taken the treasure, and just used the story to make the trail cold. My response to that was that you could have just never told me anything if you wanted to do that, and your plan was to use my salvage license to legitimize the treasure find. More water please." Brody gave him another sip. Harry nodded thanks and continued.

"Next thing I know they are on the phone to Greece, and have three distant relatives on their way to the US. I don't know how they got in because they all have criminal records a mile long."

"Toronto," I answered. "They came across the border in Toronto." Harry looked surprised that I knew that. "Keep yakking, Harry. So far so good," I said. He started talking a little faster.

193

"So, they come to Tarpon Springs and spend a few days. I chatted mostly with Dimitri. He spoke the best English, and my Greek isn't that hot. He doesn't look like a crook, but I've been told he's the most dangerous. We pinched a van and put cold plates on it, and they drove it to Key West." I chuckled to myself, having done the exact same thing at about the same time in Opa Locka. "They got in touch with a family member that lived there, and started looking for information. After a few weeks, someone, I don't know who, told them that a person matching Karen's appearance was living with Julia. They went to her house, and convinced her to tell them where she was."

"Yeah, 'convinced'," I interrupted. "They made her talk, then sold her into slavery in South America. She's dead now."

Harry pinched his eyes tight, as if to block out what I said. "I said they were bad people, Bric. I'm not that surprised they would do this." He opened his eyes again and looked at me.

"That's most of what I know. They picked Karen up, she said she wouldn't give any information, so they decided to get rid of all the evidence at the same time by killing her, putting her in that stolen van and setting it on fire. Please believe me when I tell you that was never my plan. I wasn't even here when all that happened." Then he tried to throw me his best liver lips smile. Looked all in the world like Jabba the Hut about to eat one of those salamander looking things in Star Wars.

"But, you see, it didn't," he looked smug that he knew something that I didn't know.

"What do you mean?" I questioned.

"For one thing, they didn't kill Karen. I don't know how, but she survived that bomb. I talked to her on the phone two hours ago."

"STOP! Give me her number right now! Forget it, Brody, check his pants for his phone!"

"You won't find a number. She always calls me and the numbers blocked. You can check if you want. Will you please untie me?"

"Not just yet. I haven't called Scarlet off yet. She's jones'n for a tail right about now. Talk quicker."

Harry looked genuinely scared at this point. He started to babble and the story was close to what I suspected, with a twist. "Karen called and said I could have my forty percent if I called off the family, let you alone and left town." He was hyperventilating his confession. "My family wouldn't let me settle for that deal so I was told to hold you hostage and make her give it all. Then we were supposed to kill you both." That last part was almost a whisper.

"That's a lot of killing Harry."

"It's a lot of gold," he replied.

"How much?" I asked. I had never actually seen it.

"She said there are forty nine bars." I couldn't help but emit a low whistle.

"So where do we go from here?" Harry finally asked.

"Oh, I'll cut you loose, you can put your pants on and walk away. Scarlet don't do white boy butts anyway. I'm going to keep your phone and wait for Karen to call." I dropped the one in my pocket on the ground in front of him. This phone belonged to your skinny friend Dimitri. He didn't need it where he was going. You know the number. If you're telling the truth and she's alive, I will call you and tell you how we will get your share to you. At that point, it's done, it's over. Complete. If you, or anyone in your family every try to as much as mention my name you will consider two hours of anal sex with a big black cock as a pleasurable interlude. Cancel the contract. *Katalavéno?*"

He nodded. I motioned to my son. "Brody, let him go. On second thoughts, we'll keep your pants to slow you down just a bit. Let's go guys."

Outside on Caroline Street, I thanked and hugged Brody and Scarlet. "I thought I told you to stay away. You ever going to listen to me?" Brody made me smile when he adopted his dad's "aw shucks," look. I taught him well. "Gee, dad, just thought we would hang on the sidelines to make sure everyone played nice. When we saw the odds were bad, we decided to get on the scoreboard. Besides, it was fun."

"Yeah, fun. Well, glad nobody was packing. It could have got ugly," I observed.

Scarlet reached behind her waist and pulled a Sig Sauer out of the Capri pants with a smile. "I never come to a gunfight with just my dick in my hands. Just didn't see a need to show my hole card."

The conversation was interrupted when Harry's phone chirped. I looked at the display, and it said "Unknown." I took a deep breath, hit answer and put it to my ear.

"Hello." There was a pause on the other end. "Harry?" It was Karen's voice.

I answered, voice cracking. "Karen, it's me."

Another very long silence – ten seconds – she was almost in a whisper.

"I'm so, so sorry."

"For what?" I answered. "Whatever, forgiven, forgotten, all behind us. Where are you? I'm across from the Fishwagon."

Another silence, then, again very softly. "Meet me in Mallory Square in ten minutes." And she hung up.

# First Kiss

The first kiss was salty with tears, as was the second, third and fourth. I think her hug cracked two ribs. We just held on to each other without speaking for what seemed like an eternity. I was holding someone that I truly felt I would never see again. Think of all the people in your life that you didn't get to say goodbye to, and what you would give to have that chance – just one last word, one last kiss, one last hug – and now she was back – forever I hoped.

We sat down on a bench in Mallory Square, dried our tears and composed. I had a million questions, and really didn't care what the answers were. She would talk about it now or later.

"I know you need to know some things," she started.

"All in good time," was all I could answer.

"No, I need to tell, explain. Some might make sense and some might not. I was trying to save your life, and almost lost mine in the process. It's been a surreal month for sure." Karen took a big breath, looked at me and smiled. "Here goes."

"When I got to Key West, I went to Bo's like we planned, and he gave me the cash. I found a store front that I thought would work, and tried to lease it. You won't believe it, but cash doesn't work here very well. People wouldn't have anything to do with me without a checking account, business name, etcetera, so I opened an account at TIB bank, using our Key West Camouflage name that we own. I deposited nine thousand, nine hundred and ninety nine bucks at a time, a dollar under the ten grand that sometimes gets the government interested, and waited for thecheckbook to come in the mail. I used your old address on the houseboat, and let Bo know to keep an eye on the mail. I was just hanging out, staying at Casa 325 Guesthouse on Duval and working on my tan. One Friday night I went to the Fishwagon for some beers and Barry Cuda music and ran into a couple of old friends. Remember Dorothy and Meg?" she asked.

"Yeah, lesbian couple. One works at the Shipwreck Museum," I answered.

"Yep. That's them. They were surprised to see me, and motioned me outside by the street. They asked if I was aware there were people looking for me and you – bad people. I asked how they knew about it, and they told me that Julie, a server at Fat Tuesdays had been asking around, and said there might be a reward if anyone had reliable info. It didn't make any sense till they told me that Julie was Greek, and I started putting two and two together." She looked up again and smiled, weakly.

"So I decided to play superhero. I hatched a plan to solve your problem. I dyed my hair black, cut it short and butched it back in a little mullet. Bought some Birkenstocks, black rimmed glasses, cut off a pair of blue jeans, threw away my bra and put on a tank top. Nobody in town recognized me, even close friends so I knew the disguise was good. Then I started dropping by Fat Tuesdays late in the evening for drinks. It didn't take too long for me to catch Julie's eye, and only a few days longer to get an invite for after-dinner drinks. I used my middle name – Alicia – but later that night I let her know who I was. I couldn't keep up the ruse. I know it was a risk because all she had to do was make one phone call and I would be toast, but she said she wouldn't tell them. It was only a few days later that I moved in."

"So," I interrupted. "I know part of this story." And I told her about breaking into Julie's place and what she told me. "I guess that opens up a few obvious questions."

She took a long time to answer. "Yeah, I guess that does. Yes, we made love. Won't say I liked it, won't say I didn't. Julie is a sweet, wonderful, soft and kind person. I had to gain her confidence, but it grew beyond that I guess. I hope you can forgive me."

"Nothing to forgive," I answered. "I understand why, and I also know what you mean, but you probably don't know that she's dead."

Tears instantly welled up in Karen's eyes. She buried her face in my shirt. "It's my fault!" she said. "She tried to help me, and those bastards made her pay for it. How did it happen?" I didn't think it was something I should share – I would take that story to my grave.

"It doesn't matter," I said. "And remember she had a mission to find you and turn you over to the bad guys. It was you or her, a no win situation, and you were the survivor. There's some more to that story too."

"I should have just run away, back to Puerto Rico, and none of this would have happened."

"Not true." I replied, "they were looking there just a few days after I left for Vegas. They had a sizeable budget – no limits, and had an assignment to find you, me and the gold, no matter what. They would have never given up, and no limit on the people they would have killed to find it."

I wanted to get back to her story, and get her mind off Julie. "I would DIE for a Mojito," she said, with a little bit of a smile.

"Baby, it's barely sunrise. I don't know where to get a drink at this time of day, but maybe we can find a place where we can get a Mimosa. Would that be okay for a starter?" She nodded yes.

Without saying more I got up off the bench and took her hand. El Meson De Pepe was just a few feet away, and they were just setting up for breakfast on the outdoor patio. "Dos Mimosas, por favor," I said to Manuel, who has been a bartender as long as El Meson has been open. *"Si, Señor. Grande?"*

*"Si, dos Grande,"* I answered. I would judge this place to make the best Mojitos in Key West. Just the right amount of sweet, mint and rum, and I was sure the Mimosas would be as good. I handed one to Karen, and we found an empty table, a convenient distance from other customers. Neither drink lasted long.

*"Otros!"* I motioned to Manuel and he nodded. This bar is normally cash and carry, but he knew me. I don't drink Mimosas often – I prefer beer but I could manage a few of these this morning. Manny brought the second set over and sat them on the black metal table. *"Gracias,"* I acknowledged and dropped a twenty on the tray.

After one and a half champagne and orange juice drinks, the stress on Karen's face began to relax. She looked at me with

199

serious eyes. "Sorry I'm getting teary. I ain't a candy-ass you know."

"I know that," I answered. "Don't worry about it." Time to get to the rest of the story.

I continued, "so, according to the papers, someone was in that van that blew up, and they found your octopus necklace in the debris. I'm almost surprised that nobody came forward because lots of people saw you wear it around town, but then you haven't been around for a while. But how did it get there, and who was in the van?" I could tell this was something uncomfortable to talk about. It took a while before she started to talk again.

"They caught me walking down Simonton Street late at night. I don't know how they knew it was me, but I was definitely the target. The van pulled up, two guys got out, grabbed me and threw me in the back and got in with me. I started to fight and scream but a few well-placed punches in the gut quieted me down and took the fight out of me. While I was busy barfing on the floor, they tied my hands and feet and left me there to retch. About ten minutes later, they stopped again and grabbed another woman, a pretty chubby girl in tourist garb. They weren't quite as 'gentle' as they were with me, and she was unconscious when they threw her in on top of me. I got my breath back and started to ask questions and one of the men, in a very thick accent, told me to shut the fuck up or they would kick my teeth down my throat. So I shut up."

She sat in silence for more than a minute, looking at the ground.

"We drove for maybe twenty, twenty five minutes. The last part was at highway speed without any stops, so I knew we were going up US-1. The van slowed and turned, from what I could tell, right, south. Another ten minutes and it slowed, and then stopped. I would guess it was maybe two a.m. The back of the van doors opened, and they pulled the unconscious girl out and dropped her on the ground. She was still out cold. Then my turn, drug me out by my feet and dumped me next to her. It was dark but moonlit, and I instantly recognized the end of Geiger Key Road, where the concrete barriers are. One of the goons unzipped and peed on the girls face, apparently trying to wake her up, but she didn't move. He shrugged, and him and another guy picked her up and draped her over one of the concrete barriers, and jerked her dress up over her head. Then for the next half hour, they took turns on her. Raped, sodomized, bottles, other things. One guy put his cigar out in her vagina. Thankfully she never regained consciousness. She might have died from the blow to her head, or, as chubby as she was, she might have asphyxiated by being leaned over that barrier. The whole time they talked and joked, I think in Greek. That would have made sense anyway."

Karen started crying again.

"One of them turned to me and said "It's your turn *kólpos*" which means vagina in Greek I think. Then he said they just warmed up on fatty and were going to do a good number on me unless I wanted to share some information. I told them I didn't know what they might want, even though I was pretty sure I did. One of the other guys said that I had knowledge of the location of certain items that belonged to them. If I wanted to tell them where the gold was, they would let me go the moment they had it in possession. If I didn't, they would make me suffer beyond belief, and then I would die."

She wiped back tears and looked at me. "I knew they were lying. I was a dead person either way. I told them I had never been told where the gold was, that I had not seen or heard from you for weeks and that I was getting on with my life. I knew that wouldn't be an acceptable answer, but if I was going to die anyway, I didn't want them to have the pleasure of getting the treasure."

She cried, softly now. I knew how hard this was. Her voice was low, almost a whisper.

"One of them took out a big knife. Another one untied my legs, and then jerked me to my feet by the rope around my hands. I felt the knife at my back, and then he started cutting my clothes off me. When I was naked, they pulled me over to the concrete barrier next to the other girl, and bent me over it. The tall skinny guy asked me one more time if I had anything to tell them and I shook my head. One of them jammed my underwear into my mouth and tied it around my face with my bra," she shuddered. "Then they started. What they say about Greeks is true. I don't have to tell you what the target was. They took turns, one holding my hands, and the others penetrating me. I felt other things too. Beer bottle, maybe a gun barrel. The pain got so bad I just zoned out. But I did keep struggling. I guess one of them finally got weary of me fighting and clocked me with the back of a gun or something. I blacked out."

She brightened a little. I guessed the worst part of her ordeal was over.

"Next thing I knew, I woke up, naked with a splitting headache and a bleeding asshole, tied to the other girl on the floor of the van. I couldn't believe I was alive. The van was dark, but lights from the outside dimly lit the interior. I could smell gasoline, and then realized my skin was burning. I was swimming in gas and the floor of the van was covered in it. There were several containers, plastic gas cans on the floor, and something in a clear plastic container sitting on the seat. I knew this couldn't be good. There was a lot of rope around us, but with the gas, I was slippery. Her body was cold, so I knew I didn't need to be delicate. I started working the ropes off of me, and broke both of her arms trying to twist out of it. It took maybe twenty minutes to get free."

I ordered another round and the waiter brought us some chips and salsa to soak up the alcohol. Chips and salsa weren't normal breakfast food, but I think Manny picked up this was a serious conversation and was trying to be attentive. Three mimosas will get me pretty buzzed, but I think it was helping Karen relax a little. Maybe it was the champagne, or maybe she was moving past the most traumatic part, but she started talking a little faster and a little more animated.

"I knew I couldn't help the other girl, and also needed to get away from that van in a hurry, plus I needed to wash off that gas. I pulled the handle up on the door and it opened. It was still dark, but maybe a little hint of dawn in the east. I looked around and recognized the top floor of the city parking lot on Caroline. I didn't know if they were watching, but I couldn't see or hear a soul. I didn't have a choice and ran down the ramp to the third floor, and then for the stairwell, stark naked. Just as I reached the door, maybe a hundred feet from the van, it exploded. Not a huge boom but enough to light off those gas cans. It erupted in a huge ball of flame. I headed down the stairs and never looked back."

She finished her third drink. I motioned off Manny with my eyes. I wanted relaxed, not shitfaced. "So, there you are, no clothes in the middle of town? What did you do?"

Karen looked embarrassed. "Didn't have a choice. I knew the place would be overrun with cops and fire trucks in a few seconds. I bolted out the door at street level, turned right and ran toward Finncgan's Wake, turned right again and down the street. There's a row of conch houses there, and I ran into the first backyard that was available, and sat down on a bench to catch my breath. The fire trucks and cops started coming, and it was a helluva noise, woulda woke up the dead. I got ready to bolt as soon as the house lights came on, but nothing. Nobody was home. So I looked around the back yard, found a water hose and washed off the gasoline burn, then sat down on the back porch to think. I figured I had nothing to lose, so I decided to knock on the back door. I figured if somebody answered I'd cook up a tale about getting drunk and waking up naked. I knocked several times and nobody was home, and no dog barking. Any chance for another Mimosa? They're going down real easy."

"One more, but we better slow down a bit," I answered.

"Good idea," she answered. Her voice was a tiny bit slurred. "Okay, where was I?"

"You were about to break into a house, I think," I responded.

"Yeah, okay. That's what I did. I was going to break the window on the back door, but I decided to check around, under the matt, over the door sill. I found the key in a flowerpot with a fake flower in it, and let myself in. I did a couple of loud 'hello's' but still nobody around. Nobody home. I was still burning from the gasoline, so I took a long, hot shower, lots of soap. I needed that for more reasons than one."

That last sentence was so quiet she whispered again. Then she brightened up.

"I was starving and thirsty. There was a six-pack of Bud long-necks in the fridge, and I started with that, found bread and peanut butter and made a sandwich, just wrapped in a towel. After the sandwich, I went in the bedroom to see what I could wear. It was a guy house, but not a big guy, or maybe guys. Found a fishing shirt that was only three sizes too large and a pair of boxers that would pass for shorts and a floppy hat that covered my face. Everyone wears Crocs that are too big, so I figured I could pass on the streets as just a sloppy dresser. I wrote a note and left it on the counter that apologized for breaking in and promised to pay for what I took when I had the chance. Went back out the back door, and to the left, away from the action in the parking lot."

"Where did you go from there? That's almost a month ago," I asked.

"I walked out of there without a clue of where to go," she reflected. "I figured the bad guys would have left the area and wouldn't be looking for me, but I didn't dare go back to Julie's house, but needed a place to hide. Then I remembered Lollie's house. You remember that shotgun conch house on Pecon Lane? That was like two blocks from where I was standing. She was on an extended vacation in Mexico with some dude and I know the place was empty. I already knew where the key was hidden, and it was a three minute walk. I was safe, out of sight and under a roof. That was all I really needed at that point. Power was off, but the water was still on. Lots of canned food in the cupboard. Cold food and cold showers, but I was safe. She had girl clothes too, a few sizes too big as you can see, but more presentable." She stood and pirouetted. We were walking a fine line between buzzed and drunk.

"And you have been there till now?" I asked.

"Yep. It took a while to heal, both physically and mentally. I will tell you some bodily functions were not pleasant for the first week. I found some mad money stashed in a cookie jar, went to

Dion's and bought one of those pay as you go cell phones, and loaded some minutes. I tried to call you, but your phone was disconnected."

"Yeah, it's sleeping with the fishes off the Irish coast," I answered. Her eyebrows rose. "Sounds like you have a little catching up to do too," she said.

"Yeah, lots, but your story first," I responded. I was mulling over what parts of my story I wanted to share.

"So, I thought it over and decided the only solution was to make a deal with Harry. His number was always stuck in my head, and anyway I'm good at remembering numbers. I called and hit his voicemail. Those throwaway phones don't show a number on caller ID, so I knew it was safe. I told him who it was, that I wanted to make a deal and would call him later. When I called back he answered. I offered him your original deal, twenty five percent if he would call off the wolves. That's when he told me that his wolves were dead, you were killing everyone in sight, and that the only deal he would make would be to take all the gold. He said if I did that he would leave us alone."

"Wait a minute," I stopped her. "You have the gold? Where is it?"

She giggled. The alcohol was obviously getting the upper hand. "Yeah, I got the gold. I'll tell you about that in a second." And she giggled again.

"So I asked him how would I know that he would keep his end of the deal. I told him I didn't even know where you were, or even if you were alive. He told me you were alive, in Key West and he was going to see you tonight. He then said the only way you would survive the night would be to agree to his bargain. I didn't know what else to do so I said I would have to talk to you before I made a deal. He said to call me back later, and when I did, you answered. And now you are telling me that Harry is no longer a threat. Did you kill him? Please tell me that you killed him."

"No, he's still alive and scared to death. I also convinced him that, as far as the rest of the world knew, both of us were dead and gone, so we were about to vanish into the sunset and he would never find us. We can deal with him later. I have a plan," I sighed, "yes, I killed some people, bad people that hurt you, and, until a few hours ago, people that I thought – they thought – had killed you. There's been enough violence in this town, and in our lives. I could have punched Harry's ticket, but instead I rendered him harmless."

She slid her chair around to my side of the table and kissed me, and put her head on my shoulder. She looked up again. "So I guess you have a story too."

I told Karen my story, Baja, not being able to find her, coming to town in disguise, finding Julie and hearing you were dead. Then the "deal" that Tim made that turned out to be a bust, the trip to England, the dive, rail trip through Europe, coming back to Key West and luring the bad guys off the rock, dispatching the bastards, and coming back, capturing Harry, and finding her. I didn't tell her about Jackie or Ilenia. I know the Jackie story wouldn't be a big deal to her, after all I thought she was gone, but she didn't need any more discomfort or uncertainty. As for Ilenia, the less remembered about that, the better for all of us. I would tell her that story eventually. Maybe.

"Wow. I thought my story was pretty crazy. I'm an amateur," she said.

"No," I answered. "That was an incredible adventure, and decidedly scary. You're beyond lucky to even be alive." Then I remembered. "You said you had the gold. It's not important anymore, but, well, if you have it….where and how?"

She giggled again. I love her laugh. "Where's the best place to hide something?" she asked. "Did you read your Edgar Allen Poe?"

"The Purloined Letter?" I asked. "Hide in plain sight?"

"Yep," she smiled. "That's where I hid the gold. Have you seen the new diorama at the Shipwreck Museum?" she asked.

"Haven't seen it, but I saw a picture in the paper. Tacky, cheesy, dust covered Paper-mâché faced dummies in pirate costumes and Paper-mâché wenches with huge cleavage, a big

206

wooden treasure chest full of fake jewels, fake pieces of eight and fake gold bars… oh shit, don't tell me?"

"You got it!" She grinned, and slapped me on the knee. "Dorothy swapped out the fake gold painted plaster bars for the stash. Thousands of people walk by every day within arms-reach of five hundred pounds of Spanish gold," she grinned. "Dorothy and Meg were so pleased that I jumped the fence, and turned lez, they fell over each other to help me out. I eventually told them that I was still a switch hitter and they were cool with that too. The gold is safe there as long as we want to 'hide' it. So, where do we go from here?"

"Wait a minute!" I stopped dead in my tracks. "Five hundred pounds? The manifest of the Capitan only lists fifty gold bars, and we found one of them on the wreck. Harry said you offered him forty percent of forty nine bars. You mean to tell me you dug up five hundred pounds?"

"Yep, you heard right. Not like we officially weighed them, but the three of us had to make a couple dozen trips from the hole on Boca Grande down to the boat in the middle of the night, then hung around till sunrise to make sure we didn't miss any. Looked like there were three chests there, just with gold bars."

"Yeah, I was there too, just a few weeks ago," I told her. "Likely as not that the manifest had one official chest of gold bars and there were two others on the *Capitan* that were 'unofficial'. When I saw the empty hole, I didn't know what to think. I was starting to believe that Harry got you to tell him where it was, then killed you and wanted to kill me, so there would be no one to cause a fuss. Now it all makes sense."

"His hired men tried really hard to get me to talk, but I didn't see any reason to give them the pleasure, other than the pleasure they had with me." She blinked back more tears and took my face in her hands. "Bric, let me call Harry and tell him he can have it all, just to leave us alone. I don't care about the gold. I've got a hundred grand of your money in the bank. Let's give it all to him, send him on his way and have a normal life," she pleaded.

"Karen, it's a wonderful idea, but I think we're past that. I've got a few ideas that I want to share, but first we have some getting acquainted to do. Let's blow this popsicle stand, and find some beach, somewhere." She leaned over and kissed me again. "Deal, but I have to tell you one thing. Get any part of your anatomy anywhere NEAR my posterior, and I promise I'll yank it and associated body parts out by the roots."

"Sheesh, one more fantasy down the drain. Based on your recent lifestyle, I suppose a three-way *IS* a possibility now?"

Glad I can still duck a punch.

The afternoon and the night were awkward. It really hadn't been that long, but both of us had gone through a lot of personal experiences, traumatic, stressful, and I guess in a macabre way, exciting, and after sharing stories, we were almost retreating to our individual corners to re-group. There was almost a feeling, and I think looking back, mutually, that there had been too much water under the bridge. They say, time will heal all wounds. We shall see.

The first item on the docket was to see if we could get Harry off our asses and out of our lives. That concept kept me up all night, and I think I had a plan within a plan, within a plan.

"You have any bright ideas on how to safely square up with Harry and dispose of our share of the gold?" I asked Karen. It was a somewhat rhetorical question, but she needed to be in the loop and part of the decision process. After all, she paid dearly.

"My first thoughts," Karen said, "Is to give him all of it, open our little clothing store and pretend this chapter never happened. But it chaps my ass to give him a fucking dime." She seemed deep in thought for a moment. "But I know we should give him his share to make him go away. I think by now that will satisfy him. As far as the rest. Not a clue."

I smiled. "I may have a fairly simple solution for that too. If that simple solution doesn't work, then as far as I'm concerned, it can sit in the Shipwreck Museum and gather dust for the next hundred years. First off, let's call Harry and give him the schedule. You up to a little road trip?"

"I would die to get off this rock for a while."

With that acknowledgement, I called information for the number of Coastal Angler News in Orlando, and left a message for a fishing buddy I met a few years ago, Phil Wolf. Phil and Giselle own a condo on Pine Island, near Fort Myers. They rent it out, and it comes with a boat. Couldn't think of a better place to be close and yet very far away. Then we caught a cab to Blue Heaven for breakfast. I ordered a ham and cheese omelet, Karen had steak and eggs, and we both ate like Vikings. Just as the waitress cleared the table, the phone chirped. "Hey Phil! How have you been? Yep, all good down here, just looking for a little getaway. How much for a week in the condo with boat privileges? No boat? Ok, we can rent one from the marina. No biggie. Okay, cool. I'll leave the cash with your neighbor in 214. Perfect. He has the keys too? Okay. Good to go. Thanks friend," and hung up. Karen was just staring at me drinking her coffee. I could tell she was interested, but was saving questions till she knew the rest of the story. I dug in my shirt pocket for Dmitri's phone number, and called it. Harry answered on the first ring.

"Yeah." All the manners of a fart in church.

"Hi Harry. Okay, were going to keep our end of the deal. Twenty gold bars. I will call you one week from today and meet you someplace within an hour or two of Tarpon Springs. Not that you're good at taking instructions, but if anyone else is around but you, I won't show. This chicken dance is over, we want to settle up with you and go on our way, and you have to cancel the contract or whatever you call it, on me."

Harry's squeaky, nasally, wheezy voice started ramping up. "Why a week? Why can't we just meet here in town in ten minutes and get this done, and I'll be on my way? Why all these games?"

I counted to ten Mississippi's, "because the gold is off the island for one thing," I lied. "It will take me a few days to get access, and I would rather meet on neutral ground. Look Harry, as I've reminded you a dozen different times, I could just vanish into the sunset at any time, and I can pretty well promise you would never find either of us. I made this offer over a year ago, and I'm sticking to the deal. I have all the rights in the world to tell you to go fuck yourself after everything that's happened, but I honor my deals. Suggest you do the same or all bets are off."

You could hear the resignation in his voice. "Okay Wahl, one week from today. What time?'

"Not sure, but probably evening. Just be ready to drive an hour or more when I call." And I hung up. "Okay," I turned to Karen. "let's go pay a visit to your friends at the museum."

The Shipwreck Museum was open from ten to five, and we got there at quarter till. Karen banged on the front door, and a lumberjack voice inside said in a sweet voice. "Can't you fucking read the fucking sign?" Karen yelled through the door. "Dorothy, it's Karen. Open up!" The door lock clicked, and Dorothy opened the door. Brushing past me like I was an inanimate object, she enveloped Karen in three hundred and thirty pounds of lion-headed lesbian love hug. Karen returned the hug, even though she could only reach about a third the way around Dorothy's waist. "You okay girl?" she asked, with sincere concern. "Yeah, I'm good now. Dorothy, you remember Bric?" Having no neck, Dorothy swung her whole upper torso around and actually acknowledged that I did exist. "Hi Bric, howya been?" I just nodded, and she turned back to Karen, ignoring the inferior male half of the species. Karen explained that we were ready to swap the gold out. Dorothy asked her, in front of me like I didn't exist, if I was coercing her, and she assured her it was a partnership 'business arrangement' deal and she was cool. Dorothy relaxed a bit. I think if she told her it was pure love that I might not have lived to see the sunrise again. We made arrangements to come by after closing time tonight and make the swap. Dorothy had the fake gold bars in a storage closet and guests would never know the difference.

That day we stopped by the Sears store and picked up a half dozen heavy sports bags, each enough to hold eighty or so pounds comfortably, and that night, just after dark, we backed Harry's Expedition up to the back door of the museum, bagged the gold bars and loaded them in the back. It was in a rush, but the sheer volume of the gold, probably the most ever discovered in one single place, had me blown away. Before leaving, Dorothy gave Karen one more bone-crushing hug, and told her that *she* was always welcome back if she was ever in need. She then turned to me and gave me a curt nod of dismissal. I scurried to the driver's seat, and we drove off.

That woman scares me, and I don't scare easily.

# Getaway

We went back to Lollie's place and waited till it was late in the evening. Karen gathered up her meager belongings and left a note with some cash for Lollie. We couldn't 'check in' to the condo till about nine in the morning, so no need to rush out of town. Anyway, this was probably the most dangerous part of the trip, even though I was pretty sure Harry didn't know I was driving his SUV. Déjà vu all over again, leaving Key West for the last time. Stock Island, Big Coppit, past Rumpy's house, Cujoe, past Boondocks, Looe Key Bar, Summerland, Big Pine, Bahia Honda and over the Seven Mile Bridge. Marathon, Tavernier, Islamorada, Key Largo. I opted this time for the Seventeen Mile Stretch, avoiding my favorite drive over Card Sound Road past Alabama Jacks. Off the Keys and onto the turnpike. I suddenly got nervous wondering if Harry's Ford had been reported stolen, or if there were any wants and warrants. Well, too late at this point to worry about the little things in life. Drive the speed limit and keep on truckin.

We took the turnpike north to I-75, known as Alligator Alley and headed west. A full moon was setting in front of us as the dawn slowly backlit the highway. Alligator Alley is straight as an arrow for over seventy five miles. You feel like you could put a brick on the gas pedal and bungee cord your steering wheel straight, crawl in the back seat and take an hour nap. As the sun rose, you could frequently see the unmistakable shape of gators, ranging from two feet to eight feet, cruising in the canal on the side of the road. Thank God for chain link or you would be dodging love struck gators crossing the highway every mile. We hit a Perkins for breakfast, gassed up and drove into Fort Myers on Colonial Drive, crossing over to Cape Coral and then stopped at a Publix to get supplies, food, snacks, beer, sunblock, soap and shampoo. Still on the road, I fished in my pocket again, and called one more number. It rang twice before it answered.

"Don't recognize the number," was the answer.

"Do you recognize the voice?" I responded.

"Ah, there you are! Bric my old sport, you are indeed a hard dog to keep under the porch. Where might you be?"

"Not quite ready to divulge that my friend. In fact, this call will only be about a minute as I'm sure you guys are hard at work trying to trace the cell tower this phone is bouncing off of. So let me talk fast. Two things. One week from now, someplace near Tampa we will want to be picked up and start our witness protection gig. Two. Would Uncle Sam have use of about four hundred plus pounds of nearly pure Spanish gold bars?"

Long silence. "Don't drag your feet Tim. I'll hang up and put this project out to a higher bidder. I just want face value. It's too hot to be sold as treasure."

"Okay. Deal and deal. Let me get some more info….."

I cut him off. "Signing off now. I'll call you in a few days. Start the process and figure out how you can give me about twelve million bucks in clear hard cash, or a reasonable facsimile." And I hung up.

Karen hadn't said much since we left Key West. She slept a lot, and the rest of the time rode looking out the passenger window. Now that she heard the whole story, she had questions.

"So we can't be Bric and Karen anymore? When were you going to fill me in on the details?"

"Well," I slowly said. "You said to take lead. Yes, I don't think we can be us, at least for now. Details might change in the future, but right now we should let the trail get cold and vanish for a year or two, then see what goes from there." I could sense her hesitation, and decided to take the plunge. "Karen, if you want to get off this ride, I totally understand. Whatever we get from this pile in the cargo compartment is half yours. I love you, I care for you, and I want to spend my life with you, but if you feel it better to go a different direction, at least for a while, I can deal with that."

There, I said it. Karen didn't answer. She just continued to look out the window as we drove on.

We crossed over the bridge into the Key West styled town of Matlache on Pine Island, then a right turn to the end of the road to Bokeelia, past the Lazy Flamingo and found the condo. Home away from home for a week.

Unless you knew exactly where to look, we were in a very safe place. The condo was way at the back of the complex, upstairs with a carport underneath. The crunch of gravel would announce any car a hundred yards away. We set up house, and I drove around the inlet to the Marina where I negotiated for a nice little flats boat for a few days. Since I didn't have credit cards I had to plop down a ton of cash and It wasn't till I gave them Phil's name and number so they could give a verifying call that I was a safe risk before I could get the keys to the boat. I thought about getting some fishing gear, but decided a boat ride was more in order than a fishing trip. Back to the condo to pick up Karen, and we cruised out of the inlet into the Gulf. Outside of Boquellia are hundreds of small islands – I guess you would call them all keys if you were a little further south – some uninhabited, and some, like Cabbage Key were developed with zillion dollar homes. It was too cold to swim, but I motored around the end of Cabbage Key out past Charlie's Pass, and eased the boat up on the beach. I brought a cooler with some beers and a couple of beach towels.

"I don't have a swim suit," Karen observed. "Just us chickens and I don't see any other chickens around." I answered, and demonstrated by dropping my shorts. Karen shrugged and lay down on the towel dressed. The day was glorious, and a few minutes later she slid out of her top, but left her shorts on. She's normally not shy at all as long as other people aren't around, but it wasn't a time to point that out. We sat on the beach through the afternoon, drinking beers and getting sun. I waited for her to start another conversation, but she stayed quiet. I know when to give someone distance. Late in the day, I got up, dressed and moved toward the boat. She followed, rolling her top into the towel and helped me push the boat into the water. We headed back to the marina as the sunset painted the western sky in a million colors.

Karen put her top back on as we approached civilization, stepped off the boat as we docked and started walking toward the condo while I tied up. When I got there, she was sitting on the screened patio. Feet on the chair, arms wrapped around her knees. I opened two beers and handed her one. She nodded thanks and took a sip.

I couldn't stand the silence any longer. "Penny for your thoughts?"

More silence. She took another drink and looked up at the sky, apparently searching for words written in the cotton candy clouds..

"Bric, not sure this is what I want. I know at least some of this is my fault, but just a lot of wrong place – wrong time stuff too. Please don't be upset, but I think I need to head back home to Oklahoma for a while. I'm not saying forever, but I am saying not right now. I honestly care for you, and you have become such a better friend than before. This probably sounds like something out of high school, but this is more me than you."

I expected this. "Got it and I understand. Let's give it a break. I do think you need to be invisible for a while so when you go home, will you just stay with family and keep a low profile? If there are any repercussions from this, I don't think you will be the target, but just want to keep all the ducks in a row. And, tell you what, I'll drive you there. I'm going to hit Tim up for a little RV so we can camp our way to Oklahoma. Good with that?"

"Yeah, as long as there's two beds. Not much in the cuddle mood right now."

The next morning, I called Tim with my directions. "Meet me in Punta Gorda in five days with my new ID, and a Class C mini motorhome. What about the gold?"

"Uncle Sugar has agreed to purchase your gold at current 'buy' price. We will pick it up when we give you your RV and ID, and after it's weighed and assayed, we will create an offshore account in yours and Karen's new name, and provide you debit cards to draw from. Work for you?"

I explained to Tim that Karen was probably going her own

215

way, but I would be okay with his plan and work on getting her share to her as needed. I then told Tim I would call him in two days to confirm the location and hung up. Next call to Harry. I told to be in Port Charlotte on the agreed day and wait for my call at nine. He didn't fuss much, and that was done.

The next few days were quiet and dragged slowly. I turned the boat back since Karen didn't seem that interested in boating. We ate meals at the Lazy Flamingo and Reds, and didn't talk much. She was cordial but kept to herself, and slept on the couch in the living room. At the end of the week, we packed, left the key and cash with the neighbor and left Bokeelia. The late November weather had turned cold and blustery, with off and on rain through the drive. An hour later we were in Punta Gorda. I scouted a good location for my meeting with Tim and decided on a big muscle car museum and showroom with a huge parking lot on highway 41. After dark, it's vacant, quiet and unlit. I called Tim and gave him the location. "Ten minutes away," he answered. Shortly a lovely Four-Winds mini motorhome rolled into the parking lot, followed by three black Chevy Suburbans with heavily tinted windows. They stopped at the back of the Expedition, and I helped transfer the gold, less a smaller bag with twenty bars. We stepped into the RV and Tim and I conducted business, getting my new identity, passport, and an Amex Platinum card. "That will be your income source. You can do up to ten grand cash advance daily. I won't say it's unlimited, but if your math is right, it will be worth a lot more in a few weeks."

Tim stood up and was smart enough to not reach for a handshake. "I know this didn't go like we planned, Bric. I have pretty good information that you took matters into your own hands and that wasn't very smart, but it is what it is. So, you're going to give your ex-boss part of this gold? I don't recommend that either."

"Well, call me stupid, but I made a deal, and I think his family will honor it. Regardless, after tonight, we'll be gone gone gone. After you made a cluster fuck of the whole mess, I had to work this out on my own."

"Got that. Game, set, match yada yada. Alright, friend. You're in charge from here. Stay in touch. Oh, one other thing. We're going to find your 'bodies' off Boca Grande in a week or so. We'll let your kids in on it, and they will hold services, and then know how to stay in touch with you. That should clean up the loose ends. We can talk about trust funds and such later on."

"How about Bo? He deserves to be let in on the deal," I pointed out.

That smile again. "Bric, he knows the whole deal. Bo Morgan has worked for us since the sixties."

Well I'll be dipped in shit.

With that, Tim dipped his hat, walked out of the motorhome and the motorcade sped away into the dark.

One more step and this deal was over. We sat in the motor home till midnight. I dialed Harry's number and he answered. "Yeah."

"Muscle Car Museum on 41, just south of town. Look for a black Expedition – yeah, your black Expedition. Keys will be on the top of the left front tire. The people that left it there are already gone. Be there in twenty minutes."

"If it's already there, why can't I come now?" he whined.

"Because I want to make sure everyone is out of range. Just do it." And I hit the off button on the phone.

"You wait here," I told Karen. "I'll go park the car and walk back across the parking lot."

"No," she shuddered, "I'll go with you."

"Suit yourself," I said.

The parking lot was huge, and totally dark and vacant. The traffic on Highway 41 was sparse at that time of the day, and nobody paid attention as we drove the Expedition over to the other side of the lot. We got out and locked the doors. I started to put the keys on the tire and saw a car pulling into the lot. The headlights were on bright as they drove directly to the front of the Expedition. Both doors opened, and a heavily accented voice said, "don't move."

I couldn't believe it, but I recognized that voice. "Dimitri?"

217

"Correct. The person you left in the ocean to be eaten by sharks. Alexis was eaten right in front of me. His screams will forever be in my ears. I was spared, and a fishing vessel came across me a few hours later. I acquired a vehicle and followed you back to Key West." Then the voice from the other side of the car spoke. "Mister Brickwall, do you still want to crush my windpipe?" It was the guy I let go in the street a last week. I could see a dull glint of a gun in his hand.

Dimitri continued, "I lost you for a few days, and then found my cousin Euclides, who I believe you met in the street the other night, and he told me Harry was supposed to meet you somewhere near Tampa. We waited on a side street in Marathon till you passed by and followed you, then lost you again near Fort Myers. I drove up and down Highway 41 for a week, and then saw you pull in to here this evening. Then all the black vehicles showed up, and then left. I suspect you have gold in this vehicle for Harry, yes?"

"Harry's on his way," I answered. "He doesn't know either of you are here?"

"No, if you have his gold, we will take it. Either way, you will have to answer for the deaths of my family." He turned to Karen. "It is you? How many lives do you have? This is convenient. I can eliminate a witness at the same time." He stepped in front of his headlights and I saw he was also holding a gun. My arsenal was two hundred yards away in the motorhome. I thought about making a move, if for no other reason than to create a diversion so Karen could run, but he was smart and had the gun pointed at me. Shoot the dangerous one first. Kill the girl second.

And here I had thought of him as the brains and not the killer, but he looked plenty comfortable with a piece in his hands. At ten feet, I knew he wouldn't miss, and the other guy was there for backup. Then I heard a soft 'pop' sound behind me. Dimitri looked down, and a flower of blood bloomed on his white shirt. Then a second sound and the other guy went down in a heap. Small caliber stuff. Dimitri looked up again and raised the pistol toward me. The third 'pop' came just an instant after a small hole showed on his forehead. His head snapped back, he dropped the gun, and fell first to his knees and then face down on the asphalt, dead.

I spun around to see where the shots came from. Across the highway was one of the Suburbans with a window cracked. It started up, crossed the street and pulled into the lot. Tim got out of the passenger seat. "Get out of here Bric. We'll clean up the mess, and be clear before Harry shows." Tim smiled his little Cheshire cat smile. "Go! We're even now." We didn't need to be told twice. I grabbed Karen's hand, and we sprinted to the motorhome, jumped inside, and headed north on Highway 41. An hour later I saw a sign for a campground and we pulled in for the night. The dining area made up into two twin beds. "You take the cab over sleeper. I'm happy here," I said.

"No. You go up, I'd rather sleep down here." She hadn't spoken since Dimitri pointed the gun at us, but she sounded a little more upbeat. Well, nothing like a near-death experience to make you appreciate what you have. I jumped up on the bunk, peeled off my clothes and went face down asleep in about four seconds.

Sometime during the night, I felt a body close to mine. I rolled over and was greeted with a kiss. I slid my arms around her and found a bare back. Her kiss became a little more intense as she pulled close. I touched her neck, cupped her breasts and touched her nipples, all feeling so familiar and yet so strange. My hand wandered to her navel, and I reached down only to be surprised she was smoothly shaved. I felt, rather than saw her smile in the dark. "She liked it, so I did it, and now I like it too. That's why I didn't take my shorts off on the beach." Her kisses and touch also worked their way down my body. "Take it slow and easy Bric, but please, take it," she said softly.

I had a million questions, but decided not to ruin the moment. Either she was sleepwalking, or I was dreaming. Either way I didn't want to fuck up the moment.

This was sure better than most of my dreams.....

# Every Syrupy Story Needs a Happy Ending

The next morning I woke first, made a pot of coffee and poured two cups, climbed back up and handed one to her. "So," I started, "a change of heart?" Karen took a long sip of coffee and composed her words. "Started out being one thing, and then became another. That night when that terrible man was pointing a gun at you, I could sense you were thinking of a way to take the bullet so I could get away. If that's not true love, I don't know what is. At the same time, I realized that this may not be over. Running to Oklahoma and moving in with any one of twenty families, all named Murphy, would keep me in danger, and also endanger all of my family. I'm as safe with you and 'your people' as I can be anywhere."

She finished her coffee and handed the cup back to me for a refill.

"And?" I offered.

"And, I don't think this adventure is done either. We don't have to worry about work or money. All we have to do is live our lives, and I want that to be with you." She closed her eyes for a moment, deep in thought, then smiled and looked up. "One more thing. Other than the gold you couldn't find, was there anything else on the manifest that you had expected to recover?"

I thought for a minute, and it came to me. "Emeralds. The manifest said there were a hundred and fifty gem-quality emeralds. We never found a single one," My eyes narrowed as I looked into her baby blues. "You're not telling me......"

220

Karen reached into her purse and pulled out a violet Crown Royal bag. Pulling open the top she turned it over onto the dining table. Small, medium and large green stones rained out on the countertop. "I was going to just throw these in the ocean when we were in Boquellia. The gold has caused so much pain and suffering, I didn't want it to start back up again with emeralds," she scooped them back in the bag and held them out. "Here, they're yours."

I took the bag and poured the stones back on the tabletop. Looking through them, I selected one and held it to the light. It was maybe five carats and appeared nearly crystal clear with no occlusions. "This one I have a plan for. The rest let's throw off the Sunshine Skyway Bridge, or better yet drop them in a collection plate at some small mission on the road. Maybe all the bad mojo will follow."

Suddenly a light came on in my head. I got up and started a systematic search of the RV. Light fixtures, vents, fans, cupboards. Karen curiously watched me from the cab over, wrapped in a bed sheet. "Ah, there it is at least one of them." Under one of the twelve-volt lights was a tiny black dot of a microphone with a wire running through the ceiling. I talked into it. "Hey Tim, just to let you know I found one of your wires. I'm tempted to rip it out, but you probably have five backups, and anyway, you saved our bacon last night. Thank you, I guess. At least be a gentleman and don't share the sex scenes." I turned to Karen with my eyebrows raised. That was a trick we always had, the ability to almost read each other's minds. She smiled and nodded. "One more thing. Karen needs her new ID also. Since you know where we are, where we will be and where we're going, I'll trust you to figure out how to rendezvous. Signing off," and I thwacked the mic with my middle finger before closing the light cover. If anyone was actually listening they probably just got a nasty earache.

I got misty eyed, and made a decision. Looking in the cupboard, I rummaged through the cans until I found what I was looking for; Dinty Moore beef stew. Grabbing the can, I pulled the

221

ring to open the top, and bent the tab back and forth till it came off in my hands. Reaching for her hand, I pulled her down from the bed, still sort of wrapped in the sheet, and stood her up. She looked at me like I was an idiot, which at that point, I probably was. When I dropped to one knee, her hands flew up to her face, the sheet dropped around her ankles, and she started to cry.

"Karen Murphy, the second I have the chance, I'll get that emerald cut, polished and placed in the finest setting that money can buy, but for now, I hope this will do," and I slipped the pop top on her finger.

"Will you marry me?"

# Epilogue

Brody here.

Well, I thought at first it was just another disappearing act. After all, dad and Karen had managed to vanish a couple of times over the last few years. Then this CIA spook arranged for them to genuinely go away, whole new name, identity, past and passports. Dad married Karen after that and drifted off into the sunset in a neat little 85 foot two-masted schooner, fully stocked and cash in the bank, courtesy of Uncle Sugar. I guess that boat was a drug ring confiscation prize, so it wasn't like it was a huge out of pocket expense for the feds. I really don't know what favor he did for Tim, but it must have been a big one. In the meantime, we had a cool fake funeral for dad and Karen in Key West several months before that. Only Gracie and I knew the truth that the ashes in the two urns were from my last roasted pig barbecue. I dumped it out and washed them thoroughly, and now they hold Oreos in the kitchen at my apartment.

I might have never known what happened after that except that there was a little blurb in the local news that the schooner "More Miles to the Galleon" out of Mobile, Alabama had sunk in a tropical storm off the coast of Columbia. No survivors found, and only some wreckage recovered. My first thought was that pop had done it again. Then the news reported a few days later that they had recovered two bodies, reported to be Julius Cecil, and Karly Morris, American ex-pats. Those were the new fake names for dad and Karen. I wanted to figure out a way to positively ID the bodies, but there are still some bad guys out there, and it would not be wise to associate *me* with anything near them at this point. It would have been easy. The Vietnamese dragon and viper tattoo he had done to cover the Navy Seal tat would be unmistakable. He hated to erase his Seal emblem. It's a tattoo that was hard earned and written in blood. It doesn't make it any easier to say they died doing what they loved. They are still gone, and I'm just lost. Dad was my best friend. Grace and I spent so much of our lives away from him, and it's only been the last few years that we all got back together. We lost mom, then we found dad, now we have nothing. The trust fund they set up for Grace and I mean we will never starve. I would throw it all in the ocean today just for one more fist pump and slap on the back. I really miss him, and I still haven't got up the nerve to tell Gracie. Guess I need to fly to Washington.

Dad said that if something actually happened to him, I should go see Bo Morgan. I went over to the compound, greeted the rots on the dock and knocked on his houseboat door. Bo looked a little older, a little slower, a little smaller and a little more tired than I remembered. He motioned me in without a word and gestured to the couch, then reached in the cupboard for his Appleton's and two glasses and pulled a Coke out of the fridge.

"I don't drink, Bo," I reminded him.

"I know," he answered. "But you'll have a little one with me today."

"So you know," he said. It wasn't a question but a statement.

"Yes. But the question is, Bo, how do you know? I thought nobody knew the new names but me and Grace."

"I figured it out when they 'died' the first time. I knew his old Navy buddy that had gone CIA was in town, and rumor had it he needed a mercenary, and then suddenly Bric and Karen are dead. I just kept my eyes open and figured out they got a government protection deal. I called a few friends and filled in the blanks. Answers are easy when you know the questions. His friend Tim nearly had a heart attack when he found out I've been an underground spook for Central Intelligence for over forty years."

"So this appears to be the real deal?" I asked.

"I would be more comfortable if I saw the bodies for a

positive ID, but yes, I think they actually bought it this time. Are you okay?"

"No, I'm not. I Feel like I've been kicked in the belly. I don't know what to do."

Bo handed me the rum drink, and I took an obligatory sip. It smelled like dad's breath when he came home late from playing with the band. It just made me sadder.

"Dad said I should come to you if something happened. Do you have a message, words of wisdom, the secret to the meaning of life?"

Bo smiled, but just his little thin smile. He wasn't in a humor mood.

"You already know your dad left you a trust fund. Enough to help you find your way, but not enough to make you forget the zest of life," Bo said. "Do you know anything about the rest of the gold?"

"Not really," I answered. "I know they managed to keep their share of it, and the Greeks finally tore up the contract. I don't know where they went, but a few weeks after that I got a package, with a general delivery address in Sundance Wyoming with a stuffed Jackalope head so I'm guessing they were in Wyoming. From there they apparently ended up on a sailboat in the Caribbean. The rest of it, you and I know about the same."

Bo took another small sip from his red Solo cup. He waited so long to answer, I almost thought he zoned out. Then he spoke.

"Oh, there's more, a lot more. But that's all I can tell you now. The rest will show in time, In time." Bo seemed to come to a decision, finished his drink and turned to me. "Forget your trust fund for a few years. Life is better when you don't know where the next meal will come from, or if you will have a dry roof over your head tonight. Money is like marriage. It's a young man's folly and an old man's comfort. There's more story to learn, and a lot more to tell. All I will say is the story's not over just yet. Time for you to add a few chapters to your own book. Go see the Southern Cross and the northern lights. Kiss an island girl and wake up with a tattoo that you don't remember getting. Listen to the wild geese calling, and follow them. If you came here for advice, well, that's the best I can offer."

With that Bo stood up and opened the door to his houseboat. His eyes were closed to tiny slits, and I saw both a tiny tear in his eye, and a hint of a smile in the corner of his mouth. I walked out without saying good bye – I think that's what he wanted. I stopped to give Scooter one last scratch behind his dusty ears, walked out of the compound and up Hilton Haven drive.

It wasn't a time to look back.

Also Available on Amazon
The first novel in the series

**Treasure Key**
Too Close to Key West –
Too Far From Reality

By Wayne Gales
www.waynegales.com

Made in the USA
San Bernardino, CA
26 March 2014